"*The Drowning House* is deliciously eerie, atmospheric, and impossible to forget. The setting, the friends, and the washed-up house itself combine together to create one of this year's best horror stories."

—Darcy Coates, *USA Today* bestselling author of *Dead of Winter*

"*The Drowning House* has taken up permanent residence in my subconscious alongside the briniest haunted houses around. Be forewarned: there's an undertow to this novel. Once you start reading, it'll suck you right in."

—Clay McLeod Chapman, author of *What Kind of Mother* and *Ghost Eaters*

"Propulsive, exciting, often terrifying, *The Drowning House* effortlessly threads compelling mysteries and horrors into a supernatural thriller, drawing readers in from the first heart-stopping pages and not letting go until the end. Priest once again proves she is a masterful storyteller promising secrets and revelations. She delivers on all counts."

—John Hornor Jacobs, author of *A Lush and Seething Hell*

"Cherie Priest has made something truly special with *The Drowning House*, a haunting story of ghosts, family, friendships, and horror. This is one of her best."

—Stephen Blackmoore, author of *Dead Things*

"Cherie's Priest's *The Drowning House* is a haunted house tale of a totally unique order. I consider myself a hard reader to surprise. Priest's thrilling and heartfelt novel will keep surprising you."

—Nick Cutter, author of *The Handyman Method*

"Fiercely original and bone-deep chilling, *The Drowning House* is as satisfying as it is unsettling."

—Carter Wilson, *USA Today* bestselling author of *The Father She Went to Find*

"Cherie Priest can be counted on to tell a bang-up tale with engaging characters and exciting twists. She is one of our most underrated horror authors."

—Poppy Z. Brite, author of *Lost Souls*

"Cherie Priest is our new queen of darkness, folks. Time to kneel before her, lest she take our heads."

—Chuck Wendig, author of *The Book of Accidents*

"Cherie Priest is one of our very best authors of the fantastic. Brava!"

—Jonathan Maberry, *New York Times* bestselling author of *Ghostwalkers*

"There are few writers I'd rather have keep me up half the night than Cherie Priest."

—John Scalzi, author of *Starter Villain*

IT WAS HER HOUSE FIRST

CHERIE PRIEST

Copyright © 2025 by Cherie Priest
Cover and internal design © 2025 by Sourcebooks
Cover art and design © Will Staehle

Sourcebooks, Poisoned Pen Press, and the colophon are registered trademarks of Sourcebooks.

All rights reserved. No part of this book may be reproduced in any form or by any electronic or mechanical means including information storage and retrieval systems—except in the case of brief quotations embodied in critical articles or reviews—without permission in writing from its publisher, Sourcebooks.

No part of this book may be used or reproduced in any manner for the purpose of training artificial intelligence technologies or systems.

The characters and events portrayed in this book are fictitious or are used fictitiously. Any similarity to real persons, living or dead, is purely coincidental and not intended by the author.

All brand names and product names used in this book are trademarks, registered trademarks, or trade names of their respective holders. Sourcebooks is not associated with any product or vendor in this book.

Published by Poisoned Pen Press, an imprint of Sourcebooks
P.O. Box 4410, Naperville, Illinois 60567-4410
(630) 961-3900
sourcebooks.com

Cataloging-in-Publication Data is on file with the Library of Congress.

Printed and bound in the United States of America.
VP 10 9 8 7 6 5 4 3 2 1

Bartholomew Sloan

1932

My dearest friend's execution was largely a private affair, despite public interest in the condemned man and the mystery of his motives. It took place in less than twenty minutes on the lawn behind the courthouse—with a perfunctory prayer and a very small audience gathered before the gallows. Mostly the spectators were friends of the doomed man's late wife, wearing hard expressions of righteous vindication, but a handful of others were in attendance as well: a court secretary in a crisp gray dress observed the proceedings; a reporter with a press badge tucked into his hatband took notes; and a tired-looking photographer snapped pictures with the too-bright, sizzling pop of a flashbulb.

The inevitable write-up in the newspaper was a real doozy, even though the judge had closed the scene to prevent the curious crowds from getting a morbid eyeful.

In the end, Oscar Amundson's death was witnessed by fewer

than a dozen people, and at the request of the man in the noose himself, I was one of them.

Oscar had begged me to attend. Obviously, I couldn't say no to the man's last wish, and I couldn't look away when the trapdoor dropped and my friend dangled, feet bound together and swaying, heavy and limp, like a fortune teller's pendulum.

At least it was quick. The hangman had tied the knot correctly, and the snap of Oscar's neck had come a split second after the click of the floor's release. A loud crack, a sharp twitch, and a brilliant, innocent man was lost to this world—leaving everything behind to me, for all that I didn't deserve so much as a penny.

In the wake of that fresh, excruciatingly specific horror, I found myself at loose ends, with no idea at all what to do with myself.

I didn't know what to do with Oscar's estate or his money. I didn't know what to do with Seattle. I didn't know what to do with my hands as I stood in Oscar's parlor. My fingers fluttered at my sides as if they were searching for something, and I suppose they were. I'm not sure what.

Everyone was dead except for me.

It was a cold comfort, indeed, knowing my reputation could survive the damage if I could survive my sorrow—and what choice did I have? Heaven only knew what greeted Oscar on the other side, but I had a horrible, if vague, idea of what would await *me*. It would be a fate far worse than mere grief or regret.

I was no longer a young man, but neither had I wandered too deeply into middle age. The silver in my hair was fresh and sparse, and the spread of my waistline had only cost a single notch on my favorite leather belt. With luck and clean living, I might have lasted another forty years. Another fifty, even. Why not? My grandfather lived to see a full century, plus a year and a half past that.

This was both a true story and a comforting fairy tale, one I repeated to myself at length, at night, when the gaslights were turned down to a hiss that was almost as soft as silence, and the curtains scarcely fluttered from a breeze that whispered through the night's wee hours.

But fairy tales were of no use to me.

I'd made my bed, and in time I'd surely sleep in it.

But then, there, in the aftermath of Oscar's death, I stood alone in the otherwise empty Amundson home. At the time, I believed this meant that I was officially the house's sole survivor, since everyone else who'd ever lived or loved within it was gone—all three of them, taken in the span of a year.

Oscar, Venita, and Priscilla Amundson.

Oscar, lost to the gallows for the murder of his wife—the silent film star Venita Rost, who met her own tragic end at a rocky overlook...or perhaps at the bottom of the Sound, considering the coroner said she'd drowned after hitting her head on the boulders. She was likely unconscious when the final darkness took her.

Small mercies, perhaps. For all that I would've liked to strangle her myself for what she did—and for what happened in the wake of it—I couldn't begrudge her that solace at the end.

After all, we were dear friends once, and everything that became of her and her family was my fault—though for reasons vastly beyond my control, I could neither prove this fact nor change it. Likewise, I had utterly failed to prove the truth: that Venita had committed suicide and framed her husband, an innocent man now laid out on a slab somewhere, wearing nothing but a sheet and a toe tag.

But oh, how I'd tried.

I'd called in every favor, pressed every button, pulled every lever. I'd helped Oscar find a lawyer in Los Angeles who'd never lost a case in his life until the salacious end of the silver starlet, the "Platinum Pussycat," in West Seattle. The solicitor had returned to California in a rage, his perfect record ruined.

He blames me; he might as well, and he can go to the back of the line.

Oscar's loss was bad enough, but I wished to God that I could quit thinking about little Priscilla. She'd followed me around the house like a duckling every time I came to visit, and I loved her. I would have done anything for her. I would never have harmed her or allowed any harm to come to her.

But not everything is up to me.

The child was dead. She was the first small domino to fall, dragging her parents behind her with such terrible gravity.

I was so frustrated, so angry at myself for telling Venita to do her worst—though I never could have known how literally she'd take this challenge or how thoroughly she would rise to it. Rationally, I was aware of the perilous fury of a mother who'd lost a child; realistically, I could have never imagined her capacity for retribution.

She should've taken it out on me. Just me.

She should've left Oscar out of it. He'd been utterly blameless in his daughter's death, blameless in his wife's death, and blameless of anything except believing too much in a bad man who couldn't help him.

If I'd possessed a second soul to sell, I would've pawned it in a heartbeat to spare Oscar. To spare any of them. All of them.

Starting with that child.

But I didn't. I stood alone in the parlor, surrounded by beautiful things. A glorious round mirror with a gold frame, a marble bust of an esteemed ancestor, curtains made of chartreuse velvet that dripped and pooled across the floor. A rug imported from thousands of miles to the west, furniture carved with whorls and elegant feet shaped like the paws of lions.

There was a fireplace, ornate and sooty despite the regular cleaning. There was a bar cart, but it sat beneath the mirror, and I hated the mirror. I could *not* look at the mirror.

But I needed a drink. I kept my head down.

The crystal decanter was filled with amber-brown hooch, and the sparkling glasses beside it were covered with a fine layer of dust. The bottles on the bottom shelf were all Canadian; legal booze from the north always tended to be of better quality than the bathtub stuff you found downtown with a soft knock on a door and a password.

I crouched beside the cart and used the back of my hand to brush the dust from the labels. My preferred gin was not empty, for I was the only one who ever drank it—and I hadn't been inside the Amundson house in months. No one had. After all the investigators (myself included) had finished combing the place for clues, it'd been locked up by order of the city police.

But now it belonged to me, and I wished with all my life that it didn't.

It had been a mistake to accept Oscar's overtures of friendship. It had been a terrible idea to become a regular guest, a friendly visitor beloved by him and his wife—to say nothing of my duckling: the dear Priscilla, whose demise I caused, if inadvertently.

After the child died, Oscar supported me and struggled to defend me against his wife's wrath.

God, but she became a monster in the end, didn't she? A living wraith, a raging poltergeist with a stained silk smock and bloodshot eyes. Always seething, never resting. Never relenting. Determined to burn down the whole world if that was what it took to punish the men who'd failed her so.

No, I was being unfair.

It was unfair of me to call her monstrous—the pot calling the kettle black, at bare minimum. Even after I'd finished two fingers of my favorite gin, I could see that much.

God, I *hated* that mirror.

I couldn't help but stare at it anyway, taking in the gold frame, its lovely, delicate design circling the round sheet of glass. But I avoided my own face. I already knew that it was gray and sunken. I hadn't slept through the night in weeks, and it showed in every sallow pore. I let my eyes trace the leaves, the feathers. The bits of moth or butterfly—which was it? Hard to tell. In my determination to avoid my own expression, my gaze fell to the bottom of the glass, where I spied a small series of smudges.

Dots. Fingerprints left behind by someone too small to reach any higher.

From some awful, guilty reflex, I flung my glass of gin at the mirror. The drink shattered there, but the mirror itself did not break—it only shuddered on the wall, and only dripped, and only dropped a piece of paper.

The paper was folded several times. It fluttered to the ground.

For a moment, I could not move. I could only glare at the note, which must have been stashed on the other side of the glass, affixed there with tape or twine. I could feel the dark-red flush rising up from my chest, creeping north of my collar, steaming the tips of my ears.

I couldn't clearly see the handwriting that crossed the paper in tight blue lines, but I already knew who it belonged to.

I was torn between the dueling desires to either seize the note or flee the house and return to the East Coast as fast as modern technology could transport me there. It was easier instead to reach for another glass and pour another fat slug of gin, four fingers deep this time. I resolved to sip this one and make it last while watching the contents of the first glass drip down the mirror, over the frame, down the wall, and onto the floor.

Until my curiosity couldn't stand it a moment longer.

When I picked up the folded paper, it was damp. It reeked of juniper and pine.

I took it to the nearest chair, an upholstered wingback with rolled arms and a high crest. It felt like sanctuary. It felt like support enough to unfold the note—carefully because it was so wet around the edges and folds, slowly because I knew who had written it. The sour acid in my stomach told me the contents would only make me miserable. I should have thrown it away. I should have left, locked the front door, and never returned.

But the handwriting was unmistakable.

Venita's script was legendary. At one point, she'd even been called upon to paint the intertitles in the quiet black-and-white movies she'd once headlined. With a fine set of brushes and paint, she'd written her own name on the cards that called her a star, and there was even talk of creating a font based upon it, something to remember her by in perpetuity.

On the exterior of the folded sheet of paper, the letters running slightly, there it was: my own name.

For a moment, all sound was sucked out of the universe. The clock on the wall stopped clicking. The engine growls of a car rumbling past on the street evaporated. The horns of passing ships fell silent. The birds in the trees lost their place and stopped their singing. A faint, high-pitched whine of static replaced them in my ears.

I could hear nothing else—even the scrape of my fingers or the crinkle of the paper where it remained dry.

First, another drink. A big one. Almost enough to empty the glass. It took me three swallows, one after the other, and each one burned harder on the way down than the one before it.

Thusly fortified, and with my heart perched in my searing throat, I read the short, terrible message from a woman who'd been dead for months.

Dear Mr. Sloan,

If you were half the detective the world pretends, you would've found this by now—but we both know you're more coward than investigator. You killed my child. We both know that, too. I don't know how, and I don't expect to understand it. I don't know why, and I shall

> likely never grasp that, either. But you and I, we know what you are.
> If Oscar had only believed me, or if he could have seen you as clearly
> as I do, perhaps he'd be the one holding this letter right now, before a
> roaring fire, having found it while moving furniture or in the course
> of an earthquake that rattles the walls and shakes all the small things
> loose. I might have forgotten it, after I changed my mind about what
> I must surely do next.
>
> Maybe he and I would be peacefully drinking in front of the
> radio, having freshly returned from a movie or a play. We might even
> have a second child by now—not a replacement for my Priscilla, for
> such a thing does not, could not, will not exist. But someone new,
> to mark a fresh beginning. I'm not so old that it's outside the realm
> of possibility. We could've built something new, if only you'd had
> the decency to turn yourself in, confess your crimes, and accept your
> punishment.
>
> For that matter, if you'd only been content to leave us be! If you
> could've removed yourself from our presence and returned to what-
> ever filthy haunts will have you in New York.
>
> But no. You did this. You chose this.

A flush crept up my neck, swallowed my ears, and turned my cheeks into bright-pink flares of fire. It crawled farther, up my nose, past my forehead. I felt each individual hair on my head reacting to the words, smeared but legible. My chest tightened. My breathing went shallow.

> Here's my confession, should you ever find it: We must assume
> if you're reading this that I am dead and gone, and Oscar is to swing
> for my murder. That's the plan, at least. I can't live with a man who'd

choose his lying bastard of a friend above his wife, even in the throes of our shared grief. I can't let him disbelieve me, ignore my concerns, and stay so cozy with someone who has done so much harm to our family.

Here's the challenge, then. If you find this letter before the courts see fit to condemn him, so be it. The world is right, and you're the remarkable genius everyone claims you to be. If not, then here's the truth: I will make sure that people are watching when we go to the overlook. I will see to it that we are witnessed when I cry and fling myself onto the rocks. I will leave him to his fate, as he left me to my sorrow. And here's a secret to accompany this confession: I never liked that gin. We only kept it in the house for you. No one else ever drinks it.

Goodbye, Bartholomew Sloan. I'll see you in hell.

The paper slipped from my hand. I didn't mean to release it. It was between my fingers, and my fingers opened and it fell into my lap. My eyes weren't focusing very well. Everything appeared in doubles. Triples.

I had to close them.

Somehow, I could still see it, the letter atop my legs. The handwriting I knew so well, I had seen on a movie screen, read in a confession, in a threat, in a letter stashed behind a mirror that I was too frightened to touch, in a house where everyone died eventually, and it was no one's fault but my own. The last thought that rattled through my head before the poison took its final hold was short, and simple, and the purest truth I've ever recognized.

I did this.

Ronnie
NOW

When me and Kate got out of the car, the trustee agent was already waiting for us on the front porch. He was jumpy and impatient, then visibly relieved to see us. I didn't know why. We weren't late.

"Veronica Mitchell?"

I gave him a little wave. "That's me."

"You brought a friend," he observed. "Good."

Kate said, "Uh…?" but he didn't elaborate. He only stood there, looking like he'd rather be anywhere else. I had a feeling if I clapped my hands real loud, he'd panic and bolt, so I didn't do that. I just smiled like this was all perfectly normal. Buying a place like this, sight unseen, was surely a sane and reasonable thing for anyone to do.

I climbed the stairs to the house on the side of the ridge, and Kate tagged along a couple of steps behind me. The agent greeted us quickly and with brevity. A hasty handshake for me, a head-nod for my companion. "I'm Jeff Gaines, it's a pleasure, let's get this started." He unlocked the door, shoving it ajar.

"You got a hot date or something?" Kate asked him.

"What?"

I said, "You seem to be in a bit of a rush."

He shuddered in our general direction and declared, "It's nothing personal, but I've always hated this place." Then he took a deep breath and strolled stiffly inside without us, obviously expecting us to follow him. We held back.

Kate looked at me. I looked at Kate.

She said, "Rude."

I shrugged. "I told you, the house has a history."

From inside the house, Jeff called anxiously, "Are you coming?"

"Right behind you," I called back.

"Chickenshit," Kate muttered. "Him, not you. You're the maniac who bought the place, much as it blows my mind, considering." She slipped past me and disappeared into the foyer. "What happened to the woman who couldn't live with a crack in the driveway? A blown-out light bulb? A crooked cabinet door?"

I almost said, "She died in the fire," but that wasn't true. It would've only upset her.

I hesitated on the porch.

It wasn't a huge porch, but it was large enough for a little bit of outdoor furniture, maybe a nice swing. The beadboard overhead was covered in peeling paint and spiderwebs; the columns that supported it all were squared off, not quite in the Craftsman style but leaving behind a slender, more fluid *nouveau* influence.

The place had been built by someone with means, any fool could see it. Every detail whispered money: the fish scale siding that offset the round windows in the attic; the enormous entrance—a huge carved door with dentil molding and a tarnished thumbscrew dead bolt; hell, the size of the place alone was enough to make a flush and flashy statement. If you included the unfinished basement, it was more than five thousand square feet of rotting vintage living space.

And it was all mine. My home. My project. My problem.

Inside, I heard Kate ask Jeff, "Why do you hate this house? It's…lovely."

Something about the way she said "lovely" worried me, so I quit standing there, marveling at my overwhelming impulse purchase, and headed inside for the first time. That's how it goes when you buy a place at auction because the owner is dead and the bank lets you have it for cheap. You roll the dice, and you take your chances.

The foyer was enormous and dark. It smelled like mildew and wet sawdust, fried knob and tube, and wood that had long ago rotted to black mulch. At the back of my sinuses, I detected something else, something dark and sweet and very gross, but I kept it to myself.

I tried to be optimistic. "Once I take all the boards off the windows…get a little light in here, it'll be a really beautiful space. Look at these high ceilings—and that's good quality woodwork around the stairs."

Jeff dropped a set of keys with a clattering thump; they landed on a round table that was covered with a drape. "I'm glad you like it, because the house and everything in it belongs to you as is, with all its mold, asbestos, and, and…everything else…" He petered out.

"It's cool," Kate said with a feeble thrust of optimism.

"Yeah, it is. It'll be a lot of work, but I'm down for it. Even if it takes me a lifetime."

"Oh God, don't put it that way." Jeff took an envelope out from under his armpit, and he held it by the bottom corners to shake out some paperwork.

"Why not?" I wanted to know.

"A guy *died* here, you know that. We had to disclose it with the listing. You signed off on it," he added, finding and waving the piece of paper that had warned me yes, a man had died there. In the middle of a too-hot summer the year before, in a hundred-year-old house with no air-conditioning. He'd decomposed straight through the second floor.

"Yeah, I knew." I nodded idly while I looked around and tried not to think about how much work it'd be to repair.

But that smell. Faint and distinct, very close. Maybe I only picked it up because I knew it was there. Maybe some rat or raccoon had crawled into the place and died since the human being had liquified and soaked and ruined…what was this, three-quarter-inch white oak flooring?

A crinkle around the edge of Jeff's nostrils implied that he could smell it, too. "Dead bodies don't bother you?"

"Have you checked out the Seattle real estate market lately? Everything under a million bucks is a tear-down. That flipper's dead body is the only reason I could afford the place."

"They should've torn it down years ago." He fished around

for a specific piece of paper, some final thing that needed one last signature.

"That's just crazy talk," Kate told him.

Jeff looked up, his face a wild blend of earnest and demented. "Oh? You think so? Did either of you even google the address before you put in the offer? Did you do *any* due diligence?"

I was only half listening to him. I was staring around at a lovely historic house with a grand entryway and sweeping staircase, never mind the boarded windows and drop cloths on the furniture. So what if the wallpaper was peeling down in sheets and the ceiling drooped. It had potential. Right? Good bones and all that.

"Well?" Something in Jeff's voice startled me. I looked up, and he asked again, "Did you look the place up before you put in your bid?"

"No," I admitted. "I saw the picture and the price estimate on the foreclosures list. But I *did* look it up after the bid was accepted. That's how I found out about the guy who died last year. Before you gave me the paperwork."

He snorted. "Hugh Crawford, that's the one you read about. The flipper, right?"

"Right. He bought it from the city, I think? No one was paying taxes on the place, something like that."

"I can't believe you didn't even do a basic internet search first... Jesus. Well, it's your funeral."

I rolled my eyes. "Oh, come on."

He picked up the keys from the table and slapped them into my palm before I was ready. They were cold and sharp, and they stung. "I grew up in this neighborhood, a few blocks south of here," he said with a half-assed wave in a direction that may or may not have indicated the south end of the peninsula. "Everybody knew about this place. Everybody. That's why it sat on the market so long—nobody local wanted to buy it. That's how I knew you were from out of town."

Kate was wandering off while he rambled, running her fingers across the covered furniture, fiddling with the pocket door hardware, tweaking the round light switches that clicked but didn't turn on any lights. I watched her out of the corner of my eye.

"I've lived here awhile, but no, I didn't grow up around here," I informed him. "So do your worst. Tell me a ghost story, I dare you."

He rose to the challenge. It gave him something to do with his nervous energy, and I could respect that. I was always looking for something to do with my own anxiety. Most recently, I'd bought it a decrepit old house to fixate on.

"Fine," he said, as firm and loud as a gunshot. "Hugh Crawford wasn't the first person to die here; he was just the most recent. The first one was a little girl back in the 1930s. She died in the parlor."

I said, "Awe," on principle.

"Where's the parlor?" Kate asked.

Jeff didn't respond. I assume he didn't know.

I shrugged on his behalf. "It's gotta be around here somewhere. Maybe that way, or that way." I pointed to the big open rooms on either side of the foyer.

"Technically, her mother didn't die here in the house," he continued. "She died on the back side of the property, at the overlook. Her husband murdered her, threw her right over the side. There were witnesses and everything. Then her husband was executed for her murder."

I said, "That sounds like two people who died nearby, and only one other person who died in the house. The kid, right? The other two… I mean, they didn't execute the guy here on the premises. That happened someplace else."

"Probably," he admitted with a glum sigh that suggested he agreed but he didn't know the details. Then he brightened morbidly. "But…since there wasn't any family left, the husband's best friend got the house, and he died here, too. *Actually* here, inside the house. Suicide, that's how I heard it."

I wasn't delighted to hear this, but it didn't exactly crush my spirit, either. "You said the girl died in the thirties; so when did the rest of these people die? It can't have been recently."

More sulking from Jeff. "No. It all happened back when the house was fairly new. Nobody's lived in it very long since then. Nobody likes the…the energy," he concluded. Then he changed his mind and kept going. "With no climate control and almost a hundred years of northwest winters? It's a wonder the place is still standing."

"Well, it *is*," I said.

I hoped it was the kind of firm declaration that told him we were done here, and I wasn't afraid of this particular house or these potential ghosts. I'd spent a childhood dreaming of a place like this, plotting with my baby brother—entertaining him with drawings of secret rooms and hidden stairs. Then, as adults, we'd started looking for a place to fix up, this time with grown-up plans for restoration and salvaged upgrades. But that was before what happened…happened.

Now it was just me. Or me and Kate, I guess. I love her like a sister, but it isn't the same.

Jeff sighed loudly. "My point *is*, everybody who ever lived here died."

I snorted. "If you take the long view, everyone who ever lives anywhere dies. I'm going to fix up this house; then I'll have an incredible home. Thanks for dying, Mr. Crawford. And thanks for your time, Jeff."

Thrilled to be excused, he exhaled with relief and patted the envelope's contents on the table. "Great, I'm outta here." He took a few steps toward the door and then paused, turning on his heel and stopping long enough to say, "I *do* think you should google it, though. Not just the house. Run a search for a woman named Venita Rost. They called her 'the Platinum Pussycat.' That'll tell you everything you need to know."

"Venita Rost," I dutifully repeated. "I'll do that. Later."

Then he was gone, yanking the door shut behind himself.

Ronnie
NOW

I listened to Jeff get into his car and drive away, then did my own exhalation of relief and opened the door again. "The Platinum Pussycat, Jesus Christ."

Kate chuckled. "It was a different time."

"Very different, indeed. Ugh, it's stuffy in here. Let's open everything that opens, get some fresh air," I explained myself. "This place has been closed up for too long as it is."

"Sure smells like it." She wrinkled her nose and forehead.

"You smell him too?"

"The dead guy?" she asked, then answered herself. "Maybe, but not really. But a century of mildew? Definitely. Do you have a crowbar or anything, so we could pull the boards off these windows?"

"Not now. Maybe we'll find one lying around if we keep our eyes open. Jeff's boss said the flipper left some stuff inside."

"What if we don't want his stuff?"

I picked at the plywood that covered the left sidelight. It was soft, but not soft enough to peel off with my hands. "That's what dumpsters are for. And what's all this 'we' business? I thought you were just emotional support on this journey of mine."

"I am," she assured me. She poked at the envelope's contents, then strolled into the next space over, past a pair of room dividers with small built-in shelves. "But now that I see the place…you have lots of room here. Plenty of space for a roommate."

"Even if you have to share with a ghost? Or two, or half a dozen?"

She chuckled, then gave me a little side-eye. "Sure. But I thought you'd be more…I don't know. Concerned. Afraid."

"Of ghosts?"

"Yes, of ghosts. You know why."

I nodded. I *did* know why. "All right, here's my thinking," I said, pausing to gather my thoughts, hoping this wouldn't sound any weirder than it felt. "I *hope* there are ghosts here, and I hope those ghosts are particular about their turf, like feral cats."

"Cats," she repeated, adding a note of dubiousness.

"Supposedly, if you start managing a feral-cat colony—trap and release, you know—if you spay and neuter them and then just let them live their lives…they'll keep other cats away. Therefore, you end up with a relatively tame population you can live alongside in peace, and it keeps out fresh interlopers."

"Ah," she said dramatically. "Got it. That makes sense. I mean, it makes sense for *you*. And also for cats."

"Try not to sound so surprised."

"Why?" she countered. She put her hands on her hips, looking like a small, red-haired Peter Pan, if he was a stocky woman in her early thirties. "I *am* surprised. You're afraid of absolutely everything. Why would you, of all people, buy a house this spooky? With neighbors who are clearly terrified of it?"

"First of all, that guy's not a neighbor anymore. He lived here when he was a kid, that's all. Kids tell stories. And second," I said with emphasis, before she could argue with me, "I'm not *afraid* of anything, I just *worry* about everything. It's not the same thing."

She scrunched up her face. "Isn't it, though?" she asked, each word higher than the one before it.

"I said what I said. I worry. I don't fear. Worried is *pro*active. Fear is *re*active. I'd rather be prepared for the worst than surprised by it."

"I still don't get how those two things are different. I don't get why you stopped taking your anxiety medications. I don't get why you choose to live like this, just…free-balling it, from a mental health standpoint."

Of course she didn't. She wouldn't, because I still hadn't told her. I'll probably never tell her. It's not a secret that tortures me or anything. It's not something I feel any compulsion to share; it's something I feel a compulsion to bury.

Same subject, different compulsions.

Anyway, in my experience, most terrible secrets are divulged out of selfishness—and it does more harm than good to share them. This one is *my* sin, for me to live with. It would be cruel to burden her, too.

All I said was, "The meds weren't helping as much as

everybody thought they were. They were expensive, and they had too many side effects."

"Whatever." We'd had this conversation already. She wasn't interested in a retread and neither was I, so we both dropped it. Kate asked, "How do you even get started on a project this big? What will you do first?"

"Not sure yet, but I'll probably start with a general cleanup to get a better look at what I'm working with. The city is sending me a dumpster so I can get started, and I still have Ben's equipment, or most of it. You have the rest, I guess."

"Yeah."

My brother's name hung in the air.

I kept talking, mostly to drag the subject in another direction before things got maudlin. "As you implied, there's so much to do that it's hard to know where to begin—and it's been a while since me and him worked on a project this size. I'll have to sit down and make some real plans now that it's just me. And you, if you want to be part of this. If you're serious, I mean. Do you want to move in eventually or what?"

She looked conflicted, and I couldn't blame her. It was a great house, but I wouldn't really want to live with me, either. "I'm not sure. On the one hand, expensive downtown apartment in a great location…" She held up her hands like they were scales, raising and lowering them as she spoke. "On the other, lots of space to stretch out in a cool old house. But Ronnie, it's West Seattle." She noted this like I was offering to put her up in a van down by the canal.

"It's not the dark side of the moon, Kate. You can literally see the city from the overlook. It's just across the water."

"Via one rickety bridge in a sorry state of repair, and the city could close it again at any time, for God knows how long. It was shut for what, two or three years last time? The commute might be merely annoying, or it could be a colossal pain in the ass. And there's no way to know!"

"This isn't an island, and the Sound isn't a moat. You can drive around the water," I informed her, like she didn't know this already. "It's never *that* bad."

I've never understood Seattle people and their aversion to leaving their own neighborhoods. Like I told Jeff, I didn't grow up around here. I grew up everywhere else, and just wound up here. I stayed here not because I love the place, but because I was tired of moving. Kids from military families do that sometimes.

My brother, Ben, had understood. We used to bitch about it together over whiskey at the yuppie bar around the corner from his place in Issaquah. We didn't love the setting, but it was the only watering hole within walking distance of the house, and neither of us wanted to be the designated driver.

He was maybe halfway through fixing his house up when he started getting sick. But I'm not ready to talk about what happened to him yet.

I'll have to save that for a quieter memory.

Kate was wandering again, touching random dusty objects and wiping her hands on her jeans. Her fingerprints left streaky drag-marks on the denim. "Let me think about it," she concluded. "Maybe once you have a better idea of what you want to do with the place, you know? If there's a glorious little suite, with its own bathroom and a giant closet…"

"There won't be any giant closets in a house this old. If

you're lucky, I'll find you a good-sized bedroom with a smaller one adjacent, and you can use *that* for a closet. There are six of them, you know."

"Six closets?"

"Six bedrooms," I amended. "Six bedrooms, four bathrooms."

"Jesus, how many kitchens?"

I knew she was joking, but I answered, "Two. A regular kitchen on the main floor and a kitchenette in the basement. I think? Someone was going to turn it into an in-law suite a long time ago." I moseyed over to the pile of paperwork left behind when Jeff had fled the scene, and I pushed it around a little. "Listen, for what it's worth, you always have a place with me, here or anyplace else. You know that, right?"

"Yes, and I love you for it. You know it goes both ways, eh?" She stopped wandering long enough to look me in the eye. "As far as I'm concerned, we're family."

"Likewise," I said awkwardly. I meant it; I just didn't say it very well. I changed the subject, kind of. "Hey, how about we take a look around, do some exploring. If you see a room that strikes your fancy, it's yours."

"I like the sound of that!" she declared with fresh enthusiasm. "Now, give me the grand tour."

"I can't. I'm seeing it for the first time, same as you. I don't know what's where or what shape it's in. You might as well give *me* the grand tour."

A big, sly grin stretched across her mouth. "All right, I *will*."

Ronnie

NOW

Kate cleared her throat and strolled back to the front door, which still hung open. I liked the breeze, or at least, I felt like the interior needed it—even though it was downright clammy outside. Technically, it was early June. Realistically, we were still wearing jackets, and it was probably going to rain any minute, goddammit. Around here they call it "June-uary," like they think it's funny.

But the smell, faint and distinct.

Dead things left unattended too long. Or not long enough? How long does it take for a corpse to quit stinking? Or is that why we bury them—because they never really do?

Kate swung her arms open wide. "Welcome to the Mitchell house, home of a neurotic worrier with a disdain for medication, a knack for swinging a hammer, and zero fear of the lingering dead. Originally built in the 1930s for a bunch of people who are no longer with us, it's—"

"1929."

"...built in 1929 for a bunch of people who are dead now. Local neighbor kids suggest the place is haunted to the gills, but that didn't prevent Veronica Mitchell from dropping a huge chunk of change on it. Nor did the house's condition, which could best be described as 'long abandoned,' or perhaps 'condemned.'"

I had to laugh. "Come on, it's not that bad. Let's not use the C-word until I get the full inspection report."

She put her hands down. "When's that again?"

"Ryan's coming out next Thursday. I don't know how long it'll take him to write up the report. Not that long, I bet. He's usually pretty quick."

"Ryan, that friend of Ben's?" she asked.

"Yup." My brother had been a general contractor who specialized in restoration work. I don't have those qualifications, but I often helped out—and I osmosed enough practical information to be pretty useful on a jobsite in a pinch. I also had Ben's stash of business cards and a casual working knowledge of the folks he usually hired around the region.

All this to say, I was better qualified to buy the Rost house than your average yahoo, and I ought to give myself more credit.

"Ben said good things about that Ryan guy." This time I heard the hitch in her voice. Only a little. I didn't hear it all the time anymore, and that was something.

I pretended I hadn't caught it. "He's the one who snaked a camera down a crack in some concrete and found the abandoned oil tank in that one place. Saved Ben a ton of money on the project."

"Yeah, I remember. I'm glad you've got his number."

"Me too," I agreed. "He'll horrify me with his results, but I'll be able to trust them." I didn't want to talk about my brother, and we were doing it again.

I wiggled my fingers at her, gesturing for the envelope and its contents that Jeff had left on the table, since she was closer. She swept it all up and handed it to me. I peered inside. There, along with a bunch of other crap I probably shouldn't throw away, I spied a folded sheet of paper—no, two sheets, folded together, about the size of a birthday card. I unfolded them both and shook them out.

"What's that?"

I grinned over the now-pillowcase-size paper. "Hot damn, I found the architectural drawings."

"Oh, thank God. Please, by all means—now *you* show me around. I was running out of tour ideas anyway."

"Aw, but you got off to such a strong start…" I held the sheets up to the light from the front door. "Okay, let's… Hmm. This is the one for the first floor. I'll, um, I'll improvise."

"Lead the way, madam."

I squinted down at the floor plan drawn in blue ink. It wasn't as old as the house itself; it was left over from an attempted remodel sometime in the 1970s, if I was reading the notations correctly. Somebody had wanted to do a slightly different version of what I'd proposed to Kate: take one of the bathrooms adjacent to a bedroom and turn it into a walk-in closet. Permits had been pulled, plans had been established, and the owner had bailed at the last minute—leaving the city to take the house for unpaid property taxes. It'd been on the market a few times since, but like Jeff had muttered so ominously, no one had lived in it for very long.

Ben would've lived in it. With his help, I'd have gotten it cleaned up in no time.

He would've loved it, and I would never have been able to buy it if he hadn't died. I hadn't known there was a life insurance policy. I'd never had any idea that I was the beneficiary. If he and Kate had gotten married, or if he'd remembered to change it before he'd gotten real sick, I assume he would've transferred it over to her.

But he didn't. And here I am.

It's only a little bit awkward.

I oriented myself to the layout on the paper. Something about it felt almost familiar, though I couldn't have explained it in a thousand years. It might've been as simple as the fact that I'd been inside a lot of derelict houses, and they all tended to be ruined in similar ways.

I turned to face the open front door, which placed me directly beneath a chandelier that was covered in a white plastic garbage bag for reasons that eluded me. Was it to keep the dust off? Maybe? I stared up at it, wondering what it looked like under the covering. Hanging there like that, it might've been a giant spider sac or an enormous cocoon.

"All right, so the house faces north and backs up against the ridge. The east room"—I waved to the left—"originally served as a receiving room, or parlor or however you wish to think of it."

"That's where the little girl died," Kate noted quickly.

"Oh yeah. Okay, so…" I strolled toward it and stopped

before passing the room dividers. "That fireplace is enormous, so it's probably not a coal burner. Nice marble."

"Do you think the kid fell into the fireplace?"

I frowned at her. "What? I have no idea. You have exactly as much information about the situation as I do. Let's not assume the ghost kid is on fire."

"Let's not assume there's a ghost. Or a kid, either. The hell would Jeff know, anyway?"

"Fair point, yes. Let's not take anything he said at face value. For all we know, he was spreading old neighborhood lore that was never true in the first place." I left the parlor entrance and crossed the foyer to the western room. "West room. Here we go."

"A library!" she exclaimed, clapping her hands together. "I'm warming up to this place. Wait, you really own everything inside here? There are still a bunch of books…"

"Yep, the whole estate, baby. It's three-quarters of an acre, and supposedly there are fruit trees somewhere—but we can check out the grounds later."

"The *grounds*," she echoed in a terrible faux British accent. "You're so *fancy*."

"Damn right. I'm living above my raising over here." I poked my head into the library. "Some of the shelves look good, but most of the books are a lost cause. Look, there was a leak around that window before it was boarded up." Light squeaked through the cracks. The books near the window were swollen with moisture, crushing into one another as they moldered down to pulp where they sat. "All of this will have to come out."

A pair of velvet curtains still hung from a rod, a peculiar

contrast to the plywood that covered the outside. I almost wanted to close them to leave myself with the illusion of a closed window, not a broken and boarded one, but they looked wet and heavy, and I had a bad feeling that if I touched them, they'd fall apart.

Kate had wandered off again. "Kitchen's all the way in the back. Weird."

"Nah. Houses this age, their kitchens are usually toward the rear of the structure, and pretty tiny in comparison to modern ones. How bad is it?" I asked.

She hemmed and hawed. "It's…super retro."

"*Good* super retro, or…?"

"Come see for yourself."

That didn't bode well. I pulled myself away from the ruins of the library and passed the wide, fluted base of the stairs. Down the corridor and to the right, there it was. Optimistically, I said, "It's bigger than I expected. And some of these appliances… might be in working order?"

"I dare you to open the fridge. Double-dog dare."

"Christ, not right now." It was a mid-century number with space-aged lines and chrome like an old Cadillac. The stove was of similar vintage, but it was visibly rusted out in a few places and would probably wind up at the dump.

The floor looked like vinyl tiles or maybe linoleum, which might mean wood underneath—or might not. Regardless of their exact composition, the tiles were black and white, lending a checkerboard aspect to the scene despite the grimy coating that muted the shine. The upper cabinets along the wall were sagging off their mounts, dipping down past a bent-up vent hood and hanging by a proverbial thread—or, more literally, a couple of screws.

Kate said, "I like the sink, though. What do they call that, farm-style?"

"Farmhouse," I replied with an approving nod. She hadn't been very involved in Ben's work. She hadn't known him his whole life, been his big sister support system, daydreamed about fixing old mansions with him, or loaned him money to get his now-folded company off the ground. She'd only been his fiancée. But when I say that out loud in my head, it doesn't sound very kind. "Those sinks are usually enamel over…" I didn't want to touch it. It was full of something the consistency of half-dried hair gel and the color of rust. "Either steel or cast iron. These are worth a mint if you can find one in good condition."

"It looks really dirty from here." She stayed in the doorway. Hard to blame her. The whole room felt contaminated, even if it was only in my head. Bathrooms and kitchens get so gross, so easily.

"Dirty comes off. There's a little bit of rust around the drain, but it's otherwise solid," I said, though that was partly a guess. "I can get it reglazed if I have to. They make kits for that. It's not hard."

"Yeah, Ben touched up an overflow drain on the tub at my parents' place. It didn't look too difficult."

I noticed she was saying his name more often, or maybe it was only today. Maybe it was this house. She knew where I'd gotten the money for it, and I'd been halfway afraid that she'd be mad I hadn't shared the windfall or hadn't used it to buy her the place she and Ben had been looking at together before he died.

But if she'd been that kind of person, he would've never loved her in the first place, and if she harbored any hard feelings about it, she kept them to herself. I could respect it either way. The truth was, she came from a little money—or a little stability, anyway—but me and Ben didn't. She understands the difference, and she chooses not to hold it against me.

I'm fairly certain that's why she's stuck with me this long after my brother's death despite the age difference and the gulf in life experiences between us.

I was older than Ben by about a dozen years—he was our parents' last-minute surprise, as they used to put it. Kate was younger than him by two or three years, so I'm almost a whole generation older than she is. She's cool, though—a concentrated ginger cutie-pie, and I genuinely adore her, even though we don't have that much in common.

I mean, except for Ben, and he's gone now. But that's another story, and I still don't feel like talking about it yet—not in the middle of this memory, which is warm in my heart and generally positive, mostly quite happy.

Kate didn't actually want to talk about Ben, either, but sometimes we just can't help it.

We dropped the subject for the umpteenth time and toured the rest of the house.

There was something like a master suite on the main floor, though the bathroom was technically around the corner. The other downstairs bedroom was at the back of the house, dark and quiet, with two small windows up near the ceiling—since it was built so close to the side of the ridge—and a skylight someone had added, probably as part of the unfinished remodel.

I clutched the plans, folded them up, and carried them around. I'd stopped using them for reference once I saw the kitchen. After that, I just plain forgot about them.

I guess I got swept up in the sense of discovery, combined with the sudden understanding that most of the work on the house hadn't been officially sanctioned. I'm not saying the paperwork was useless. I'm saying it was only a partial picture of the situation, and I decided to trust my eyes instead of whatever some guy had told the city of Seattle back when I was a toddler.

It turned out, one of the bathrooms was really a powder room off the main-entry corridor. Something about the framing and flooring implied that somebody'd removed and sold a clawfoot tub, taking the excess square footage for a coat closet. Not a bad idea, honestly.

The powder room had some classic nouveau wallpaper with peacocks and gold trim. It was in such good shape that Kate didn't even have to ask; she just pointed at it and said, "You're keeping *that*."

"Damn right I am."

On the other side of the wall from the kitchen, we found a space that used to be a butler's pantry, I think. I told her I might turn it back into one; it'd make the kitchen feel less cramped. "I hate it when big houses have small kitchens," I told her. "But in old places, that's usually what you get."

"You can fix it."

I agreed. "I can fix it."

The dining room was easily three times the size of the kitchen. It had chair rails and a tray ceiling that retained its natural stain, and so far, it was the best-preserved room of the house. Besides that, there were two separate sitting rooms; one had probably been the formal and fancy one at some point, but now it was hard to say. They were both in decrepit condition: one had a hole in the floor, one had a hole in the wall. Neither one was as big as the front parlor, which I'd already quietly decided to make into the living room.

Ghost kid or no.

Kate opened a door we both thought was a closet. It wasn't. She asked, "Hey, how do you feel about spooky hidden staircases?"

"Hidden?" That got my attention. I poked my head past the frame, and a dangling string tickled me in the face. The string led to a light bulb. I gave the string a tug, and the bulb fizzled to life. "Oh. It's not hidden. It's discreet."

"This place has power? I didn't know you already had power."

I nodded. "I had it turned on yesterday, but I assume that most of the switches and outlets don't work anymore. It looks like you found the basement. Want to check it out?"

"No. I'm not going down there. Are you going down there? Please don't go down there."

A switch with a button was mounted on the inside wall. It almost looked like a doorbell, but I knew better, and I pressed it. In response, something sparked and died with a pop at the bottom of the stairs. "If it makes you feel better, no. I'm not going down there until I get a flashlight, because this little stairwell bulb ain't gonna cut it." I took a step back and pulled the string again to turn it off. "But I do have an electrician coming tomorrow."

"Before the inspection happens?"

I nodded again. "The plumber will be here tomorrow afternoon, too, and I have a roofer lined up as well. Some of this stuff is a given, you know? There's not a chance on earth that the house won't need a re-pipe or a rewiring job. Or a new roof. All of that needs to happen before the fun stuff can begin."

"It's a shame it's come to this. It was a really beautiful home once." She said it almost wistfully, like this was the kind of place she might've wanted for her and Ben to work on—even if manual labor wasn't her jam. The place they'd been talking about buying was already three-quarters restored, and most of what remained to be done was aesthetic, not structural.

I absolutely believed she'd enjoy picking out tile, and cabinets, and paint. I *didn't* believe she had any idea how much work it would be to install them. But there was no point in spoiling her happy illusions. "It'll be a beautiful home again. Eventually."

Kate folded her arms and leaned against the wall. "How long do you think it'll take to bring it up to snuff?"

Thoughtfully, I rocked my head back and forth. "Depending on how soon the crews can get me on their schedules, I should be able to get it up to code in maybe six, eight months. After that, yeah. Then the fun stuff begins."

"Six months? Just to bring it up to *code*?"

"Yup," I said with a firm nod. My estimate was only that low because I knew some folks, I had a chunk of cash ready to throw at the problems, and I'd done this kind of thing before. Or I'd helped Ben do it. Whatever. "A place this size won't be cheap or quick to bring back to life. It'll be even less cheap and less quick because I'd like to keep as many of the original features as I can—and restoration always takes more time than replacement."

"I'm glad you're doing it that way, even if it does take longer," she added, as if it was a conclusion she'd only freshly reached. "You know, the longer I poke around this place, the better I like it."

"You can't be serious. The kitchen is melting into the basement—and speaking of melting through floors…we haven't even been upstairs yet. You know, where the flipper guy, Mr. Crawford…did his thing."

"Well, if I ever do move in, I don't want *that* room. But I could be persuaded to crash in one of the others. Once some of the construction is done, maybe. Don't worry; I'm not canceling my apartment lease anytime soon."

"Oh, Christ, no. You'll want to wait until we have the main structural work done before you make yourself at home. But consider it a standing invitation, eh? It's up to you. Let's go upstairs."

We headed back to the main staircase, a sweeping number with varnish that had oxidized to nearly black. There'd been a runner at some point, but it was long gone—rotted or ripped out. Scraps of old fabric clung to the remaining staples.

At the top of the stairs, we found more natural light.

Most of the second-story windows were not boarded, but the sky was overcast and grim, so the light was the color of milk; it spilled into a wide hallway and a broad landing that was nearly big enough to call a second parlor. Down the corridor to the east, I saw a large bathroom with a claw-foot tub that might've been original.

"Bedroom!" Kate called from the west end. "*Big* bedroom. No giant holes in the floor. The windows are really pretty, too."

I joined her.

"You're right, the windows are gorgeous." Three wide panes of glass had transoms on top, decorated with cut leaded glass patterns. A bed frame with four once-towering posters had collapsed upon itself in the middle of the room, consumed by moisture. Otherwise, there was no furniture.

The next room was another bedroom, this one with a bunch of junk stashed inside it, mostly in piles. Then another bathroom, this one mostly gutted already, and a linen closet with shelves that, according to Kate, "Looked weird."

"This probably started out as a servants' staircase. Eventually, someone wanted a place to put towels, so they took the old slats from the stairs and just…pulled them forward and built a wall behind them."

Across the hall, something wafted through an open door. Not smoke, not an unexpected slice of sunlight through a dusty window. An odor. Not as faint as it'd been downstairs. It dawned on me that I hadn't looked up while I was on the first floor—or I might've had a better idea of where Hugh Crawford had met his demise.

Kate followed my stare and said, "Dare we look?"

Yes. We dared.

I turned the knob, opened the door, and tried not to hold my breath, but it was a reflex—some very primitive bit of my brain that said, No, we don't sniff too deeply of death.

"Holy shit, Ronnie." She put her hand over her mouth and nose, which was overkill, in my opinion.

I stared into the room and saw a giant plastic tarp over the floor, with cinder blocks holding it down around the edges. The tarp was a vivid marine blue, incongruous in a room that was otherwise brown and beige from age or someone else's taste decades before. I detected metallic notes of rust, the stuffy dampness of a room that's been closed without climate control for too long, and the soft stink of a man having died of a heart attack months ago in the middle of the floor.

It wasn't that bad.

Bartholomew Sloan

NOW

The house has sold again, for at least the sixth or seventh time since it was built. I knew it was only a matter of time before we had a new owner, after the man with the tools came alone, and worked alone, and died alone. I honestly expected him to breathe his last in the basement at his little shrine, but he surprised me by dying upstairs, of what looked like natural causes.

I suppose she might have harmed him, sometime when I wasn't looking, but as far as I could tell, he was taken by an old-fashioned heart attack.

He wasn't the first man to develop an unhealthy fixation on Venita Rost, and he probably won't be the last. Every time I think her hold on the popular imagination has finally evaporated, some damn fool comes along to prove me wrong.

I'm not sure what it will take to end her influence. It's mostly relegated to the house and its grounds these days, so perhaps there's my answer: when the house is gone. When the earth is salted beneath it.

I wish I had her strength. If I could reach out like she can, like she sometimes does...if I could manipulate and test and poke and prod...I could twist a couple of old wires, blow gently upon the ensuing spark, and grow a blaze inside the walls that would consume the place, if it could grow undetected. Venita could do that if she wanted. I'm not sure what the limits of her abilities are, but they absolutely extend to small gestures, moving little items. Showing herself, once she's had time to collect her strength afresh.

How else do you think her confessional note went missing?

I remember it fell to my lap. If she hadn't moved it—to Christ knows where—it would've still been there when my corpse was discovered, and my friend would have been exonerated after his death, at least. I don't know what she did with it. She rarely speaks to me except to scream.

Oh yes, she screams.

I used to pride myself on knowing—knowing information and knowing how to find it. Knowing how to do things. It was my stock in trade, even if I'd come by the skill dishonestly. Unfairly. Selfishly and shortsightedly. I deserve whatever eventually becomes of me—or what's left of me—and I know that.

Yes, I know *that*, at least.

And I also know the house has sold again, because in the wake of Mr. Crawford's death, things were very quiet again for a few months. (I think it must have been months, and probably not longer. But time is sometimes strange for me now, so I can't be certain.) Then the antsy young man with the clipboard and the keys had come, muttering to himself as he poked his head into this room here, and that room there—always leaving the front door open, as if he might need to make a hasty escape.

I suppose he sensed Venita. She's been asleep for a while now, but her presence is everywhere. Everyone feels it.

That said, I haven't seen her in quite some time, and I don't know what she's been up to—though I don't go out of my way to cross her path. As far as I know, she can't hurt me. Or she can't hurt me any more than she's already accomplished, I should say…for the simple reason that she has not done so.

If she had the capacity, she would skin me and keep me alive, scoop out my eyes and play with their dangling nerves, smash every bone in my body—beginning with the smallest and working her way up to my femurs, my spine, my skull. She's threatened to do all this, and more. But after a hundred years of frustrated failure, now she mostly avoids me, unless she has some reason to seek me out and harass me.

She doesn't do that as much as she used to. It could be, there's a finite limit to her rage after all. In another hundred years, it might burn out altogether. She might fade away, or drift away. She could settle down into some dusty, silent peace that life never saw fit to grant her.

I used to think there was a chance—since we both were dead, and both were stuck here—that we might one day grow tolerant of one another. Perhaps we might even come to some understanding, if not actual friendship.

But although we are trapped here together, we aren't quite in the same place.

It's as if we occupy different versions of this same territory:

mine depressingly, irrevocably here and now; hers somehow disjointed, neither here nor there, then nor now, only loosely tethered to time or reality.

Often have I heard her talking to herself or to others who are long gone as if they're standing before her, accepting her accolades or abuse. Occasionally she's been desperate enough to ask me if I can see them, or if their presence is only some figment of her mind, more fractured than the leaded glass where the tree came through the attic window decades ago. I don't know the answer, and I quit replying.

Once in a while, though…when her presence is strong and her emotions are heightened, I get some sense that the temporal uncertainty isn't entirely her fault, or not her deliberate doing. I suspect that some piece of her is barely clinging to, or fastened to, or lashed against? another century—where the house is bright and new, the floors gleam with wax, and the parties sparkle with tinny music from the radio or enthusiastic, semi-amateur banging on the piano from whichever drunk has commandeered it.

(I have been that drunk, as the house sometimes likes to remind me.)

Does Venita see me when she claps her hands and laughs and declares, "That was terrible, darling. Have a glass of water and a nap, and give it another try in the morning." I remember her saying something like that once, when I'd spilled my wine across the ivory keys, and Priscilla was delighted. She'd left purple-brown fingerprints on the seat, the sheet music, and the…

I don't mean to think of Priscilla.

Priscilla isn't here, and that's one small mercy. I was afraid the mirror would hold her, or whatever was inside it would trap her there when it...when it did whatever it did. When the bright bolt of shimmering white had lashed out like a whip, clapping her in the forehead. When the child had stood there stunned, petrified, already dead but too confused to fall down. So innocent, just a little girl, just a little question. Just a little push, from something ancient and deplorable. Something I'd brought into her home.

All my fault. Venita is right about that, though she never fully understood the particulars.

So now the house is sold again, and even now—after all this time!—so many things remain that have been present since I was alive. Under the sheets lurk furnishings I've reclined upon, the piano I tipsily played, the goddamn mirror in the goddamn parlor.

Maybe this time, things will be different.

This time a woman's bought the place, and that's different, isn't it?

As far as Venita's reaction to the new owner...I think it could go either way. There's always a chance she'll view this woman as a potential friend or confidante, someone to be wooed and plied. At least, I think it's unlikely she'll be able to seduce this one with her pouts and her whispers, her old photos.

Her diary.

Then again, humans are complex things, aren't they? And I've known of men who seduced men, women who seduced women. *This* woman, this brave fool who's bought this decrepit mansion, she walks with the posture of a man and uses a man's vocabulary. When she speaks, she sounds a bit like Mr.

Crawford, may he rest in peace. She knows that language, the lingo of repair and restoration.

I was never a man who worked with my hands, but I can respect such skill in others. Even a woman.

This new woman is very sad and pretending that she's not. I think it's for the sake of the other one, the woman she has invited to join her in this house. I think they are related somehow. Perhaps cousins? Half sisters?

I'll figure it out eventually.

The new woman is of average height, and she has short, brown hair that's rumpled like a working man. She wears pants like they all do these days, and her pockets show outlines of wallets and keys and tools. She does not wear much makeup, though she's attractive enough, so far as such women go. She must be in her forties. Younger women rarely move with such casual, apathetic confidence or observe random details so keenly.

The other woman with her, she's younger. She's brittle in ways that she's hiding quite well—so well that I can't always see them. From here, from this side of the veil, I do not have access to my old powers…purchased at such a price though they might have been.

Till death do lovers part when they exchange their vows; till death did I have a deal with the devil. Apparently.

The younger woman is a thickset ginger, and left-handed. She's pretty and probably about thirty years of age, and vastly less comfortable in the Amundson house than her companion—though she's eager to disguise this fact.

I didn't catch their names. I wasn't listening for them.

It took me a few minutes to rouse myself from the silence

I'd settled into since Crawford's death. It took me another few minutes to realize that Venita wasn't present. Maybe Venita settles into silence sometimes, too.

Maybe she simply wasn't interested in pestering a fellow female. Mostly, it seems, her fury is directed at men. Even men who love her. Even men who trudge to the gallows with precious little protest, since living without her was merely a formality to be dispensed with at the earliest opportunity.

I don't suppose I blame her.

There's always a chance that Venita will become fond of this woman, and that the sentiment could be returned. Venita needs a friend. Maybe the new owner does, too.

It gives me…not hope, exactly. Something hope adjacent.

Interest, if nothing else. Yes, this might be interesting. The last few owners haven't been.

They've been money men, investors, barely present—merely conducting the symphonies of workmen and demolition and construction. Then there was Hugh Crawford, and he *did* buck the trend, I'll admit. Probably purely because Venita latched on to him before he had time to conduct much of anything.

Like this new woman, he planned to do much of the work himself. And like this new woman, he was aware that he'd need help eventually.

But if what she said about electricians and plumbers is true, the new woman has a much more specific timeline and a much more organized approach to addressing this house and its myriad issues.

It might save her. It might not. It might save the house. Or it might not do that, either.

I don't know if that's what I want or not.

I have no idea what Venita wants anymore.

I have questions about what this new woman wants. She's hiding something important, but I'm not sure who she's hiding it from. Her companion? Herself? If I pay attention, I might be able to figure it out.

Or Venita might.

Now I have the irritating, familiar sensation that I should really warn this new owner, give her some idea of what she's walked in to—but I have no means of doing so. Even if I did, what would I say? How would I explain that there's nothing here but danger and death, and the ghosts who walk these halls are restless and cruel?

Here's a weird little hope: when this woman finds the diary (and she will, they always do)…when she reads it (and I know what's in it, I've read it over many shoulders, many times)…she will spot the dark undercurrent of insanity between those prettily written lines, and realize her peril in a way that every man so far has missed entirely.

Good luck, new woman. I fear you're going to need it.

Ronnie

NOW

Kate stayed in the doorway. I went inside.

"Wow," I said, because I couldn't think of anything else. I pushed one cinder block out of the way and lifted a corner of the tarp. "Oh, wow. They just sawed… yep, straight through the floor. Through the subfloor and the supports. I guess they had to."

"Can you see downstairs?"

"Sure can. Here, come take a look at…" I stopped. "I'm staring down into the… Wait, I think I'm looking down into the library, shit. How did we not notice the big hole in the ceiling down there?"

She stayed where she was. "The library was both very gross and very cool. Also, it was very dark, and there was a lot to look at."

Besides, with the tarp, thick and deep blue, we wouldn't have seen any light coming in from above. It's like she said, there was a lot of other stuff to look at. "The hole's big, maybe eight or nine feet around, and it's cut through several floor joists, *oof*. That's not gonna be cheap. They run all the way…" I gestured to the exterior wall and then past Kate, into the hall. I didn't finish my thought; I redirected it. "I don't think we can sister any of this into the remaining joists."

"What does that mean?"

She didn't really want a tutorial, so I didn't give her one. "It means we're going to lose a lot of flooring up here, and it's gonna get spendy. On the upshot, most of this would have to come out anyway. But the structure of the room—hell, the whole second story, given enough time—is badly compromised. Like 'walls falling down' compromised."

Now I looked up. Water stains oozed across the ceiling, and one corner of plaster had completely fallen away. I didn't have a light on me, but if I'd shined one up there, it would've showed me the attic. Bits of gray vermiculite insulation had crumbled downward, too, all clumpy and wet.

In the northwest, the damp takes everything eventually.

"Leaks in the roof?" Kate asked.

"I told you it was a given. That's why I lined up contractors before I had the full estimate. Sometimes it's both safe and expedient to make assumptions."

"Safe assumptions are your favorite kind."

"Damn right." My eyes snagged on a gaping spot in the eastern wall. "Hey, someone removed a fireplace mantel. So that's two fireplaces; there are at least four, or there used to be. The house still has four chimneys, anyway. Actually…" I let the tarp drop and stood up straight. "I bet there used to be one in the big bedroom with the rotten four-poster, too. That's probably the original master or…"

I don't know what else I meant to say. I was too distracted by the view through a four-panel window that was almost the size of a garage door: it overlooked the Sound and the Olympic Mountains.

The day was grim and gray, like so many others in June-uary, but the scene was still outstanding. A couple of big ships moaned in the water, their horns sounding back and forth between the waves and the ridges; clouds rolled low and flat, smothering the top of the highest peaks and masquerading as fog down closer to the water.

"That's one hell of a view," Kate correctly noted. "And this would make one hell of a bedroom. It's facing west, right? No early-morning sun through the windows."

"You'd get early-morning light all the same, unless you spend a fortune on blackout curtains. Maybe this can be a sitting room—or maybe I'll move the library up here, I don't know. Man, there are worse places to die than a library. Isn't that right, Hugh?" I asked out loud.

"Morbid, aren't you."

I shrugged. "There's a giant hole in the floor and a weird stink in the room. There's no pretending the guy didn't croak here."

"Sensitive, too."

I said, "Meh," and left to continue exploring. Kate tagged along behind me, except when she broke off to check out something alone.

We found the remaining beds and baths, wandered aimlessly

around a few "bonus rooms" that would likely end up as storage in the short term, and tried getting up into the attic with limited success. The pull-down ladder was half-rotten and missing both the bottom step and two of the top ones, so the only safe thing to do was stand halfway up and peer over the edge. But I regret to admit that the attic did not look especially interesting. There wasn't even very much stuff up there: I saw a few crates, a couple of boxes, and enough spiderwebs to stuff a mattress.

"We should go outside," Kate declared.

"Good idea." My eyes were getting itchy from the dust, anyway, and some fresh air would do me good.

We went downstairs and finished snooping around, ending our tour in a large rear room that backed up to the ridge. It felt private and unexpectedly lush. Someone had planted English ivy on the hillside, drat them, except that it hung down prettily over the windows alongside the ferns, brambles, and other assorted random northwest plants that crowded the narrow space between the house and the wall of earth behind it. It was like standing outside a people-size terrarium, or maybe a tropical zoo exhibit.

"I thought the structure would dead-end here. Didn't expect to see these big windows," Kate noted, running her fingers across a small pane of glass and leaving streaks behind in the grime. "This almost feels like, like, what do you call it. A conservatory. Like in the board game Clue, you know."

"It'd make a great conservatory if it got more light." The light that reached the room was filtered through the exterior rainforest overgrowth up the ridge, and it squeezed in through the tops of the windows or oozed in from the narrow landing on the other side.

A Dutch door with a Greek key motif waited at the back. I unlocked it and gave it a shove. It squeaked, resisted, and eventually popped open—only to get stuck in the compost of decaying plant material on the other side. I pushed my shoulder into it. Harder. Again.

I got it open just far enough to let us both out.

"Hey. Since it's not raining yet, I've got an idea," I announced. "Let's check out the view from the overlook."

Ronnie

NOW

What I'd initially mistaken for a landing was a path about six feet wide, running the length of the house's rear exterior. I don't know what I'd expected, really, but I found a drafty tunnel-like space, hemmed in on one side by the ridge—with the whole spot overshadowed by the tops of leaning maples and the sprawling, dark branches of evergreens waving above.

Moss and mildew covered the pathway, making it slick and gross even though it wasn't raining. "Watch your step," I warned. "These bricks are slippery as hell." We were both wearing boots, which felt stupid in June, but what can you do. Even with my heavy treads, I had to be careful where I put my feet.

I started by heading east. The path looked less steep that way, and I wasn't willing to try my luck going uphill.

"It's a jungle back here."

I heartily agreed. "I don't hate it. But landscaping will be next year's undertaking. Gotta get the house's structure stable before I worry about the grounds."

Approvingly, she said, "You're getting good at prioritizing what to worry about. Instead of worrying about everything all at once, I mean."

"Well, I've been practicing."

Around the side of the house, the path ended at a circular landing that wasn't quite big enough to park a car. Beyond that, there were only footpaths, some of which were too overgrown to pass without a machete.

We took the clearest path and made a loop up the property line.

Together we hiked the hill to the top of the ridge, which was set about fifty yards behind the house and to the south. It was exactly as advertised: an overlook where you could stand on the ridge and see the ocean. Look one way, and you could stare at Puget Sound and its nearby islands. Look the other, and there's the Seattle skyline.

Depending on the weather. If the clouds are too low, well. You get the same view everyone gets: a thick blanket of fog the color of dirty snow.

We stood in the usual late-spring weather, squinting against the drizzle that blew in our faces. Kate took a few steps away from me, staring down at the gloomy surf below. "Not exactly crashing waves ready to wash someone out to sea."

"Crashing waves? Who said anything about crashing waves?" I took a gander for myself. The water was fairly calm, the tide lapping against the big rocks and patchy bits of sand. It occurred to me that we were likely standing right where the original lady of the manor had met her demise, and I guess it occurred to Kate, too.

She said, "I just had this idea of that woman going over the side and disappearing into the surf. But there's not much surf to speak of."

The ridge was now laughably guarded by a ridiculous little thigh-high fence.

Her body would've fallen, maybe bounced off the side a few times, and landed on the rocks 150 feet below. She would've broken her neck or hit her head. With this thought, I had an unwelcome flash of a blond body face down on the jagged black stones. I shook my head to clear it out, and it only kind of worked. "It would've been fairly quick," I added. Not the worst way to go.

With a hair too much enthusiasm, she replied, "Oh yeah, it would've been fast. I swear, Ronnie, you really lucked out. This place feels like a private estate in the middle of nowhere. I mean, sure, it's West Seattle, but—"

"Enough with the West Seattle cracks." Too many people had made them already—even me—but I was starting to find them tedious. I'd made my choice, I'd put down my money, and the longer I stood on the property, the more protective of it I felt. "The bridge will be fine. I will be fine. So will you, if you decide to move in."

"All right. No more life-on-Mars jokes. And I get it, I really do. It's hard not to fall in love with the place, even if you're only besotted with what it used to be—and not what it's become."

I, personally, was besotted with the thing in its present state, but I knew that would sound weird if I said it out loud.

And obviously, I did not intend to let it remain in such a state indefinitely. It couldn't. It would fall down around me. "Just think of how great it'll look in a couple of years. This is a long-haul project, Katie. No HGTV four-week makeover, alas."

"Alas," she echoed. And we headed back down toward the house.

With half an hour of poking around outside, we found several cherry trees, a few apple trees, some Italian plums, and a couple of Asian pears. I practically had an orchard, completely overgrown—and buzzing with bees. I assumed there was a hive hanging around somewhere, but I didn't go looking too hard, and Kate kept her distance because she's allergic. Or she talks like she is, but I think for the most part she just doesn't like getting stung. I would worry about it more if she carried an EpiPen or something, but she doesn't.

I stood there for a few minutes in my own personal overgrown, abandoned orchard, watching the runny white light seep through the leaves and listening to the buzzing, happy bees in the softly wilting blossoms that would turn into fruit by fall.

"This is mine," I breathed. "Mine forever. Thanks, Ben. You couldn't have known, couldn't have expected, but…" I wasn't sure what else to say. What was I even doing? Praying? Wishing? Making a statement of intent?

Just being morbid, I guess.

The moment passed and I went back inside, where I found

Kate standing in the library, looking up at the hole in the ceiling we'd missed the first time.

Before I could ask her what she was up to, she started talking. "What do you think it feels like to melt? To soak through something solid, like you're teleporting through a barrier real, real slow. To dissolve, like Kool-Aid powder in water." She looked down at the floor, where a great rectangle of nothingness suggested that a rug had been rolled up and relocated, then undoubtedly disposed of. "He would've dripped right through. But I guess his bones would've stayed up on the second floor."

"Are you all right, philosopher queen?"

"Sure, I was just thinking. How long was he up there?"

"Since last summer, up until a few months ago." I couldn't be more precise.

"Kind of peaceful, right?" she asked, turning to me. "Just a heart attack or stroke, wasn't it?"

"That's what everyone says. I don't think anybody knows for sure. He was alone."

"I wonder if it bothered him. I wonder if he'd rather be here, and if he'll come back to haunt the place."

"He's welcome to do so then."

"Maybe if you were back on your meds, you'd have more brain space to worry about practical things. Like ghosts."

"I don't know how you think antianxiety or OCD medications work, but you've almost certainly got it wrong. And no, I don't worry about ghosts, because even if they're real, it's not like they can hurt you."

"You know that for a fact?"

I did not. To deflect, I told her, "I'm more worried about

the old cloth-wrapped wiring in the walls. I'm worried about an earthquake that sends the house sliding down the ridge, right into the street. I'm worried about foundation problems that cause the structure to settle and collapse, dropping the roof on my head. I'm worried about pipes blowing in the walls and the resulting black mold. I worry about face-planting into some asbestos and giving myself..."

I couldn't finish. She did it for me. "Cancer."

I also worried about stray dogs, war in the Middle East, climate change, coming down with dementia and not knowing it, deadly spiders, wearing polyester and being caught in a plane crash so my clothes melt to my skin before I die, falling space debris, wearing heavy jewelry because what if my necklace gets caught on something and I get strangled, driving off the road into water then being trapped in my car, mass shooters in Costco, meth-heads with homemade shivs, and getting struck by lightning, which is extra stupid because we almost never have thunderstorms out here.

Odds, reality, and probability have nothing to do with it. My brain does what it does, and no, I won't take my medication again. Kate only wants me to because she doesn't know what happened. If she did, she would shut her mouth about it. She probably would never speak to me again, either, so maybe I mean that literally.

But I don't feel like riding that spiral right now.

Me and Kate went to a little bar at Alki Point for dinner, and it was pretty good for bar food. I checked out my new...not *neighborhood*, precisely, because it was a mile or two away from my actual house. But it was the nearest neighborhood with any cool stuff in it, and I felt good about it. There was a beach, or at least a coastline with some sand; I saw a number of cafés, restaurants, and other assorted businesses—most of them indie mom-and-pops—and hot dog carts, ice-cream people, and music stores with old-fashioned vinyls and everything.

The weather was clearing a little, and the sun wouldn't set until nine or so. I was almost feeling optimistic despite the chill and the breeze coming off the water.

I could do this.

I could save this old house. I could start a new life, clear-headed and aware of all the terrible possibilities—but I could hold them at bay. For now.

All I had was *for now*. I think that's all anybody ever has.

Eventually Kate got an Uber and went home, and then I stayed where I was and settled in.

Technically, I still had an apartment in the Central District for another month before the short-term lease ran out, but it was a sketchy little flat in a sketchy little neighborhood in the best of times. I'd never felt as safe there, or as comfortable, or in such familiar surroundings, as I did in the rotting carcass of the ridge house.

I had an overnight bag and a blow-up mattress in my car. I always had blankets and other useful items stashed in there; Ben used to joke that if I found a defibrillator on sale, I'd buy two and leave one in my vehicle, one in my kitchen—and he wasn't wrong. But I didn't have one of those, much less two. I just had everything I needed in case I was ever stranded somewhere without light or heat or power, because goddammit, you never know.

It's the bright side of chronic anxiety. If you're quick and thoughtful, you can be ready for just about any calamity. But see, that's the only thing I'm really, bone-deeply afraid of: not having thought of everything.

So I unloaded my car into my new old home, where I had no close neighbors but plenty of space, no real concern with regards to druggies or burglars, and a whole host of professional tradespeople coming by in the next week or so to address all the things I'd thought of thus far. Or at least they'd let me know how much it would cost.

My life might have been a hot mess, but I had at least this one large portion of it under control.

Yes, I'm pretty good at lying to myself. You have to be, when your brain is shouting at you all the time. I already know it can't be trusted, so it's a bit of a catch-22; but what can you do except find someplace you feel approximately safe, put your head down, and settle in?

Ronnie

NOW

Maybe that means it's time. I could make it time, if you want.
    Okay.

I had a sleeping bag in the car, too—a good one from REI that was rated down to twenty below, and it wasn't supposed to get any colder than the high forties overnight, so I'd be fine. I brought out my mattress with the built-in pump, then spent fifteen minutes hunting for an outlet that still worked. I finally found one in the parlor, where the little girl allegedly died, and I don't know why that didn't bother me, but it didn't. I'd been planning to set up a home base in the big master with the decrepit four-poster bed, but I'd been out of luck. Two outlets in the whole room. One of them had some old smoke/fire damage, so I didn't try it; the other was completely dead.

I suppose I could've inflated the mattress, then moved everything upstairs, but that sounded like a lot of work, and I was both tired and restless. I decided to address the tiredness first, so I set up my bedding in the parlor, and I tried to get some sleep. Restlessness could wait.

It did wait. Until nearly midnight, when I was lying there, staring up at the ceiling with no hole in it, listening to every small sound that pinged, scuttled, dripped, or echoed in my vicinity.

All right. Now.

In this moment of quiet, I can tell you what happened to my brother, Ben.

I moved into his house to help take care of him when the cancer knocked him down and he stopped being able to get back up again. We had hospice care, and that was helpful, yes. He had good insurance—thanks, Obama. Someone came by four days a week to help him get bathed and check all his ports, all his medications, all his machines.

Kate only lived a couple of blocks away, so she was there a lot, too. That's when we got to know each other, sitting around with wine and weed in front of the television while my brother died slowly in his bedroom. We took turns checking on him.

We had to. He had a bad habit of getting up and wandering around, insisting he was okay, and then falling. Once he almost went right down the basement stairs, only catching himself on the rail at the last second. He held on just long enough for Kate to run up and retrieve him.

He hated it. We knew he hated it. He'd been a beefy dude his whole life, ever since he was a "husky" kid; he was strong as hell, and he had the shoulders to prove it.

But once he got sick, he got downright skinny. He got frail.

He hated being weak most of all. Far more than he hated the idea of dying.

Anyway, I'd started taking these antianxiety meds right around the time he started treatment for the stupid little cancer that was just supposed to take one stupid little testicle and call it a day, but no, somebody has to be in that 5 percent fatality rate. Somebody has to feel the odd pain in his back and fear that things are going south again.

The drugs they gave my brother didn't work.

But the drugs that a different kind of doctors gave *me*... those worked *great*.

I went from fretting about interstate overpasses cracking beneath my car to being someone who simply drove to and from downtown when the fancy struck me—never considering that my vehicle could be crushed by the overhead lanes, or I could fall through a hole and crash to the earth, or into the Sound, or the canal.

I just went places. I just *did* things. I didn't wonder every 4.8 seconds if someone was breaking into my house or stealing my identity. I didn't examine every small pain for signs of impending death. I didn't worry about food poisoning or other poisoning by nefarious parties unknown. I didn't check under my car for prowlers who'd slash my Achilles tendon with a knife then rape and murder me before I could even scream.

I had even been thinking about getting a dog, since I wouldn't feel the sickening compulsion to watch it 24/7 for signs of illness or decline, and struggle to brace myself for its inevitable death.

I didn't skulk around my living quarters, or the living quarters of anyone else, looking for potential harm in the form of faulty electrics, carbon monoxide, or radon—not that I could actually see any of those things in the first place. I didn't obsessively check water bills for signs of leaks in the walls. I didn't put goofy tread-stickers in the bathtubs.

I'd like to pretend that medication was a liberating experience, and that it was everything I'd dreamed of and more, but it wasn't.

It wasn't *bad*, I want to be clear. It was nice to have the brain space to not worry 100 percent of the time about 100 percent of the things. I didn't even notice that I wasn't worrying. I just stopped doing it so much.

I found other things to fill the silence. No, not silence. But *quiet*. The volume of the brain-shouting was turned down from an eleven to a three. You'd think it would have changed my life.

It did. But this part was supposed to be about Ben.

And it is. Hang on. Let me get back on track.

This one time, I had some errands to run—I needed to go to the pharmacy and pick up some more supplies for Ben, for one thing; and for another, we were low on groceries.

For a third thing, I kind of needed to get out of the house.

It wasn't that big a deal. With both me and Ben in the house, and all the medical equipment that came home with him because he refused to die in the hospital (and who could blame him), and the constant omnipresent reminders that yes, he was going to die *somewhere*, sooner rather than later…I needed a break. I needed an hour or two for groceries and supplies and maybe some coffee down the street from the drug store.

It was cold enough to leave the refrigerated groceries in the car because it was the end of January at the time, and the city was soaked and frigid. I didn't want to go home. I was medicated and I was not worrying about Ben.

I was not thinking about the load of laundry I'd stuffed into the dryer before I left.

I certainly wasn't *worried* about it, even though *dryer fire* had been on my list of Things to Definitely Be Worried About since I was a teenager, when I saw something on TV about a house that had burned down courtesy of a stray spark and a buildup of lint.

Did you know that some people who like to go camping actually save up their dryer lint and use it for a fire-starter on purpose? Yeah, it's amazingly good at catching fire. It's a scary thing to know.

Before the medication, I would have *never* left the dryer running when I left the house, even though it wouldn't technically be unattended: Ben was home—and Ben was weak, but Ben was present. Ben had a cell phone right beside the bed, and he could call for help if he needed it.

But when it happened, he did not call for help. He'd gotten

up to use the restroom on his own, and he'd fallen—shutting the door and effectively locking himself inside.

That part's not my fault.

Ben damn well knew better than to get up and move around when nobody was home; he had a bedpan and he knew how to use it. We were acutely aware that he didn't have more than another couple of months, not even if we were very lucky. But we were doing our damnedest to make those final months peaceful, safe, and comfortable.

I should've waited until Kate was around. I should've left someone in charge.

But I wasn't worried about it, so I didn't.

I was sitting in the café, sipping a mocha and scrolling around on my phone, when the first fire truck went screaming by. Now, the old Ronnie would've immediately launched into a panic, because it was headed in the direction of our place. But the new Ronnie had pills, and she was Zen as fuck.

Until the third fire truck and the ambulance blew by, headed in the same direction.

That's when I tossed the rest of the mocha; the pills were no match for my sense of rising dread, even though rationally I was confident there was nothing wrong. How could there be? I had groceries and caffeine and useful stuff from CVS in my car. My whole life, everyone had told me to calm down, that I was getting worked up over nothing. Everything was fine. So I should stay calm.

I got back in my car anyway.

I headed home.

I had to ditch my car at the end of our street because the

firefighters had cordoned off the block, and okay. Here's the thing.

Unmedicated Ronnie would have worried endlessly about the laundry in the dryer. Unmedicated Ronnie would have called Kate over at a bare minimum, or waited until she was off work to run errands and get coffee at the little café down the street from the CVS. Unmedicated Ronnie knew she did not hold the reins of the world, but she was confident that she'd fully mitigated as much potential danger as was humanly possible.

But medicated Ronnie was a murderer.

Okay, maybe that overstates the case—or shit, maybe it doesn't. I can only tell you how it feels. Unmedicated Me hates Medicated Me, and I'd prefer it if Kate never finds out why. Maybe on my own deathbed, I'll let it slip, and maybe I'll be high enough on painkillers that I won't be able to stop myself. By then it won't matter. By then, maybe I'll believe in ghosts, and maybe Ben will be waiting for me.

That would be nice. Even if he yells at me, and he probably won't. He'll probably hug me and tell me it wasn't my fault, and we'll both know it's not true, and I'll believe him anyway and we'll go walk into the light together, or however that works.

When the smoke had literally and figuratively cleared, the firefighters found Ben in the bathroom, dead from smoke inhalation.

They thought he'd tried to hide in there, but that's stupid; I know that's not what happened. If he went in there to hide, he would've brought his phone. When the fire broke out, he would've called 911 and then me, but he didn't. A neighbor called when they saw the smoke coming out of a window.

Ben had been sneaking off on short jaunts around the household for weeks, keeping it up while he was still physically capable of doing so—a minor rebellion that made him feel like he still had some autonomy, I suppose. That son of a bitch got up to use the bathroom rather than use the little bean-shaped pan beside his bed—and that's on *him*. If he hadn't been too proud or stubborn, he wouldn't have been stuck someplace without his cell phone.

Ben was not a worrier, and it prematurely killed him.

The charred remains of the dryer clothes all belonged to him, and Kate concluded that he'd thrown them in there while I was gone. It wasn't an unreasonable conclusion. It wouldn't have been the first time he'd done something like it, not by a long shot.

I was too big of a coward to correct her.

I *am* too big of a coward to correct her.

I tell myself that it's for her own protection, that she doesn't need the details and they don't matter anyway—Ben would've been gone by now, even if it hadn't happened. The outcome was always going to be the same.

Kate without a fiancé. Me without a brother. It was written in the stars.

But some things only get worse when you say them out loud, so I keep that story to myself. It isn't even very hard. Lying to Kate by omission doesn't torment me, it's just something I think about every now and again, especially when I'm alone and it's quiet and the night is settling in around me—in a place that's loud like those machines were, in Ben's room. I think about telling her, and then I remember that I mostly want her to know so that I'll feel better, having unburdened myself.

So I keep the burden. It's kinder that way.

The things that haunt me aren't secrets. They're worries, and they protect me. They would protect Kate, too, if she should ever choose to move into the big old house on the ridge.

I hope she does. I'd like to protect her with my neuroses. I'd like to keep her safe. I owe that to Ben.

The moist old mansion creaked and groaned around me.

It soothed me. I fell asleep.

Bartholomew Sloan
NOW

And even now, the house gathers souls.
  I can hear you, Veronica. Can you hear me? If I ask very loudly?
If I say your name the way you like it? If I call you Ronnie? If I keep your secret?

Ronnie

NOW

I woke up with the sun. Not deliberately, God knows. And not a *lot* of sun, either. But around five in the morning, the parlor began filling up with that watered-down white light, that skim milk light. It's all you get out here for months at a stretch. Most of the time, it doesn't bother me. Occasionally, it drives me nuts.

I sat up on my inflatable mattress and was pleased to note that it'd only deflated a little bit overnight—so I considered it forty bucks well spent.

Although I hadn't meant to be up that early, I wasn't mad about it. The electrician wouldn't come by for another few hours, and the plumber was scheduled a few hours after that. For the first time in daylight, I had the place to myself.

I wasn't *glad* Kate wasn't there, and I wasn't exactly happy to be alone in such a large space, but it was a satisfying feeling all the same—to stand there in the massive foyer and know that everything I could see belonged to me. Such as it was.

And it was a wreck, honestly. The place looked every bit as bad as I remembered from the day before.

Using this realization as a lure, I fished around in my psyche, seeking some hint of panic or some flare of anxiety, but I couldn't find one. I was almost as calm as when I was deep in the meds. It works that way, sometimes. If I can give my OCD something big enough to chew on—some place to park itself and idle—I can siphon off enough nervous energy to feel pretty normal.

I wandered the house for a few minutes, my back-brain already chewing happily on the problems, a big gray termite that wasn't happy without a big block of something to gnaw through.

I wriggled my feet back into my boots, then rummaged through my car, retrieving a hot pot and a tin of instant coffee. Suisse Mocha: the gateway java for generations. I had a travel mug sitting in the cupholder. I took that, too.

I hauled all this stuff into the parlor. The single working outlet had not exploded when I used it to inflate the air mattress. It would not explode over a hot pot. Probably.

I kind of wanted a shower, but I didn't trust the pipes, and I didn't trust the floors to hold the cast-iron bathtub on the second floor with anybody standing in it. There was no one else around to smell me, so I resolved to not give a damn, and with that thought, something else flickered in the back of my head. Something about a working bathroom in the basement.

Oh yeah, the basement. The only place I hadn't looked

the day before. One light bulb with a string to illuminate the stairwell.

I grabbed my phone because I didn't feel like going back to my car for the flashlight, and then I went to the little closet-looking door in the main hall—the one Kate had called "hidden" even though it was right there, in front of God and everybody.

I opened it, looked into the darkness, and pulled the string.

It didn't do much. Mostly it turned the corridor a sickly yellow orange, though it also revealed a set of concrete stairs that were riddled with cracks and slick with humidity. A feeble gust of air coughed up the gray-green stink of mildew and wet cardboard.

No death, though. I didn't smell any of that today.

Maybe it'd overloaded my senses while I was asleep, and I'd gone nose-blind to it. Maybe there was nothing dead down there to smell, but a rat or two wouldn't have surprised me. I'd heard them in the walls the night before. Rats and something bigger—maybe a raccoon. Maybe a stray cat.

I put one foot on the top stair and tested it. I didn't feel any shifting concrete or hear any pebbles falling away, so I went ahead and strolled downward—holding the wall to my right with one hand, for there wasn't any rail.

The passage was narrow; I could touch both walls with my fingertips, even when my hands were almost at my sides. I felt cool, damp air wafting up from below.

Okay, so the whole house was full of cool, damp air, but this was colder and damper. It felt like the watery draft from a fog machine, sending tendrils of not-smoke shooting across a haunted-house attraction's floor.

I wondered what the odds were that the furnace still worked.

My feet hit the bottom landing with a slapping thud. Beside me on the wall, there was an old-fashioned light switch with a dial. I pressed it, and the click was way too loud in the large, echoing interior of the unfinished basement. When the light came on, it was abundantly clear that the area had been prepped for a build-out, but the build-out had never come.

The basement was maybe eight hundred square feet all told, and full of both garbage and unlabeled crates. The crates would probably hold useless crap that I don't want, but you never know. I might get lucky one night with a crowbar, or that's what I told myself.

Some of the garbage was contained in big black bags, tied off at the top and looking like lumpy, overinflated balloons.

I turned on the flashlight app and held up my phone. I pointed it from corner to corner, up and down, around the room.

I spied a couple of take-out containers. Half a six-pack of beer, the remainders still snugly seated in their plastic rings. One, two...okay, four empty cigarette packs, wadded up and tossed. I sniffed the air like a beagle. Was that cigarette smoke? Just a touch.

"So you were a smoker, eh, Hugh?" I was glad he hadn't done too much smoking indoors. Or if he had, he'd kept it downstairs.

I shuffled across the floor, pushing plastic painter's drop cloths out of the way and nudging aside rolls of blue masking tape, an empty bucket, and a few racks of nails that went with a pneumatic gun. There, in the nearest corner, I saw plumbing hookups sticking out of the wall and floor.

No toilet. No fixtures.

I swung the light around and spotted something over by the far wall, so I took a closer look. It appeared to be a staging area of some sort: a plastic sheet taped down at the corners, with a bunch of papers and a few stray tools, a sweater, a pair of work boots with worn-out laces that would break within another wearing or two. A big paint-stained flannel had been wadded up and tossed aside. A little improvised hibachi grill, barely more than a light metal tray on a rack, held charred bits of paper and a couple of candles that were burned down to nubs.

"Okay. This is officially weird."

Could Hugh hear me? Would he give a shit if he did? He didn't respond, so I went ahead and poked around.

Even now, I'm not sure what to call what I found down there, or how to describe it.

Well, okay. How about this: I found a shrine. An altar? I mean, I had a wicca phase like every other teenage girl with an unstable home life, I know what they look like. This looked like one of those.

Mr. Crawford had gotten his hands on a photocopy of an old photo. It looked like a Hollywood studio shot—a portrait of a young woman with silver-blond hair that hung in bobbed curls. He'd put it in a cheap brown frame and propped it up against the wall with more burnt-down candles around it and a stack of Classics Collection DVDs, two of which still had library stickers on them.

I picked up the DVDs one at a time. "*The Magic Circus*," I read out loud. The cover had a picture of the same woman, smiling in a spangled costume, standing on a trapeze swing while a ringmaster of some sort waved a whip below her. The text on the back told me that this was "An early silent romp, starring Platinum Pussycat Venita Rost and Michael Payne. A runaway bride tries her hand at circus life, to varying degrees of success. This brief comic romance was filmed in 1922 in Los Angeles, and this reproduction has been created from the only known surviving print…"

The whole thing only ran for eighteen minutes.

I looked around for a DVD player but didn't see one.

"Venita—that's right, that was her name. She was a looker, for sure," I observed. Heart-shaped face and the wide, round eyes of a Kewpie doll—accented with the blocky mascara and tiny, shapely mouth that looked black in the monochrome photos. The other movie was *Goldilocks*, and it involved three potential suitors: One too rich, one too poor, and one with a nice little bungalow in Petaluma. "Thrilling," I declared. The run time was thirty-two minutes.

More library books were stashed beside the framed picture. *Stars of a Forgotten Age. Vamps of the 1920s: Beyond Theda Bara and Clara Bow. And Then What Happened to Them: Lost Celebrities of Black-and-White Cinema. Starlets and Sirens.*

"I'm sensing a theme," I joked to the rats in the walls.

Hugh had become a tad obsessed.

I mean, I understood. He'd bought her house, and she was beautiful, and she was dead. Maybe he'd been a fan before he even found the place. His aborted restoration effort might have been the culmination of years of research, patience, and fundraising…only to end upstairs with a quick and tragic death before he got a chance to do very much to the house.

But he'd made this shrine, and that was something. I wasn't sure what, but it was…something.

A small table was pushed against the wall.

Wait, was it a table? No, a small step stool. Whatever. Same purpose, as it had another candle smooshed into a local bar's coaster—next to a vintage lunch box with a smiling shot of the Dukes of Hazzard and their unfortunate orange car. The lunch box was metal and it was rusting. The buckle that held the box shut was broken, so it popped open when I poked it.

Inside, I found a book. It was the size of a paperback and soft with water damage.

"A little light reading to go along with the short films, eh?" I said as I picked it up, but I quickly realized this wasn't a novel. The cover was blank, and when I flipped it open, I saw that many of the pages were stuck together, their contents ruined by moisture.

I also saw handwriting.

It was *lovely* handwriting. I know that's a dumb thing to note, but it really was pretty—easy to read, smooth, and very uniform. A woman's handwriting, I assumed. I'm not sure why. There was something feminine about it, almost aggressively so. This was a woman who'd dotted her i's with a little heart bubble when she was a tween, I would've bet money on it.

"Ms. Rost?" Another assumption. Who else could it belong to? It was sitting in a place of honor, atop a shrine dedicated to the woman.

Yes. Her name was written on the inside flap, at the top-right corner.

I sat down on the floor. The bare concrete was cold through my clothes. I turned to the first page.

Venita Rost
1932

Oscar was at the station, waiting for the Portland-bound train and probably sighing to himself at top volume, probably very annoyed with me because I was so frustrated over some silly costume jewelry that isn't even worth anything. I know him. He's a sigher. Mr. Sloan overheard his dramatics, and apparently the two struck up a conversation, as men are prone to do when cast together in any given lobby, any given waiting room. For all they complain of women and their gossip, men are the worst clucking hens, I swear it.

But it wasn't just some old costume jewelry; it was my grandmother's wild Victorian stuff that's starting to come back into vogue—at least in small doses. I thought I could give it to Priscilla one day, or even right now, if she wanted to play with it.

Priscilla didn't get to meet her Great-Grandmother Rost. The old woman died when I was a teenager, and more's the pity. She was a lot of fun, once you gave her a couple of cigarettes and at least that many drinks, and I think my child favors her quite a lot. You can see it as plain as day in the old photos, even as dour as the great family matriarch appears in most of them. Victorian to the bone, even down to the widowhood. She liked the weeds, and she wore them the rest of her life as a fashion statement, more than a profession of loss.

Grandmother was funny like that. If anything happens to Oscar, I might wear black forever, too, but it's only because I can't imagine my life without him. I can't imagine it without our daughter, this sparkling elf of a child whose hair is as light as mine for real, the lucky thing. It'll get darker as she gets older. Everybody's does, until it gets lighter again with age, but you might as well enjoy it while you've got it.

My sparkling elf child deserves to play with her great-grandmother's baubles, and that's why I was so beside myself when they turned up missing.

I tried not to shout about the maid getting sick and taking her leave for the month, and I tried not to complain about her replacement, a silent, sallow-faced girl who nevertheless did a stellar job with the woodwork and the dusting. I did my best not to make any untoward accusations when I spoke to her about the little jewelry box—the cheap one in the drawer, beside my stockings and sachets.

She didn't cry, not even a small tear. She got angry at the accusation and threatened to quit on the spot if I didn't retract my words, and I did not retract my words—I told her I would summon the police, and they could search her and hunt around her home. She said that was fine with her, which confused me a bit, but I took her at her word and made the call from the kitchen telephone.

Long story told tightly: she didn't have it. Or she didn't have it anymore? Who can say. I apologized, gave her a week's pay, and sent her home. I don't trust her, so she can't keep working here, but

I'm not a monster and I won't have it said that I am an unfair employer.

I have cleaned houses for people. I have been accused of things and found innocent, and I have been treated less kindly by far.

But I am not like those women. Some things simply won't do.

Melanie will be back in a week, anyway. We can limp along until then, and Mrs. Sumner has offered to help with the laundry, so that's that—but what a pity about the timing. A few weeks ago, the poor old cat started showing signs of decline, and this morning we awoke to find that we'd lost her.

Or rather I awoke to find her. I wrapped her in an old towel and cleaned up before Priscilla came downstairs; the dear creature had released her bladder upon expiring, and there was a bit of a mess.

I couldn't reach the gardener on such short notice, but I found a shovel in his shed out back, and I dug a little hole beneath the old apple tree where the kitty liked to sleep in the shade, during our precious few summer months. Then Priscilla and I held hands, and I said a little prayer. Priscilla read a little poem she wrote. It nearly broke my heart.

When we were finished, we talked about getting a tombstone for Kitty. Oscar will think it's silly, but I might do it anyway. I adored that cat, and the feeling was mutual, I believe. I almost think we should see about getting another one... But then again, Kitty will be hard to replace—in our hearts or in our household.

Wait.

Where was I? Mr. Sloan. That's right. My husband met him at the train station, and they talked for at least two hours, that's what Oscar told me. Some poor soul had flung himself in front of the train and the whole thing was a terrible mess, with police and transit officials and who-knows-what holding up the line. Apparently, it happens more often than you'd think.

I'm terribly curious, as morbid as that may sound. Terribly curious about what would possess a man (or a woman? Sometimes it must be a woman, by the sheer law of averages) to do something like that. There must be easier ways to off oneself, rather than by, well, casting one's body in front of a speeding train. Surely a bullet would be faster and less traumatic for everyone.

Unless that isn't the point? Maybe it's not the point. Maybe the point is to make a big scene, to aggravate as many people as possible, and to go out with a bloody, petty bang—the likes of which shall not be forgotten anytime soon.

If it were me, I'd probably choose poison. Something gentle that would send me right off to sleep.

But of course, I would never do such a thing to my daughter or my husband. It's rude and disrespectful and frankly a little bit mad to even consider it.

Oh dear, I've let my pen wander again, haven't I.

Mr. Sloan. My husband brought him home, since the poor man could not find his way to his own home that evening—for the next available trains were all booked to the gills. So Mr. Bartholomew Sloan spent the night in one of our guest suites upstairs, the room with the wondrous view of the Sound through the giant windows.

"A view of the Sound." What a silly phrase! Well, what can you do.

It turns out, Mr. Sloan is something of a celebrity himself—always a curious and entertaining type to have around for a visit. I don't mind sharing the spotlight in the slightest, least of all with someone from another industry entirely. The man is a detective! A proper one, like Sherlock Jr. or Coke Ennyday, or any of the other detective-mystery films. Or books. I suppose mostly they're books to begin with, or stories from magazines.

But Mr. Sloan is a real detective, not a funny one.

You'd never see Buster playing him, that's for sure. Mr. Sloan is a big man, tall and heavyset, balding just a bit (though he hides it under a hat—like a gentleman, I must say). He has a big voice, too. An East Coast voice, with funny, hard vowels and so much volume, from that huge barrel chest he keeps contained by a waistcoat and the efforts of its heroic buttons.

He's not an unattractive man by any stretch of the imagination. He has nice skin, clear and free of scars; he keeps a short, deep-ginger beard trimmed neatly, and the beard has two short streaks of silver sliding down from the corners of his mouth like vampire fangs.

Oh, Theda would just love it. She'd absolutely scream to see him, I think. She would climb him like a tree, like a little lumberjack.

I think he would be thrilled. God knows most men would.

Mr. Sloan is big man, he's a handsome man, he's a loud man, and he's a brilliant man—not just to hear him tell it. He would never say such a thing out loud; it's too gauche. Too close to telling people you're rich or you're funny. If you have to declare it, it's less true than you think.

But I can read it all over him, and so can dear Priscilla—who has developed what can only be called a crush on the man. Oh, she follows him around and makes the cutest, mooniest eyes in his direction. And he is so kind about her attentions, even though they surely must annoy him. I love my daughter beyond words, but she is eight years old and, frankly, not always the world's most scintillating companion. I look forward to the day that we might converse as adult mother and adult daughter. I yearn for the times to come when we will share clothes and stories. But I have years yet to wait.

Regardless, she's perfect. She's a child, yes. A perfect one. Perfect children are a nuisance to adults, too. It doesn't mean they're less loved or less wanted. It only means they're learning their way around the world, and when you already know how the world works, their daily discoveries are less thrilling than tedious.

Yes, I see that you found a pretty rock. Oh my, that's quite a lovely bug, please put it outside. No, I've never seen a leaf of that shape. I don't know what kind of flower that is, go ask your father. For the love of God, don't put that in your mouth, you're not a baby anymore.

The child is very much mine, though—a natural-born entertainer with a passion for the finer things in life, and I intend to give them to her. Everything I didn't have. Everything I couldn't have, when my mother worked in a factory and my father was drinking away her pay at the nearest bar.

I wanted to go to school and learn how to be an artist. I could've been a great one, you know. For that matter, I might yet become one. There's time, isn't there? I'm not so old yet. I may have left Hollywood land for the moment, but I'm not finished making things. I could take up painting again, or drawing. People can never stop talking about how pretty my handwriting is, and listen, it's not that big of a deal. Handwriting is just drawing letters, over and over again—that's it. There's no magic to it.

But I'm rather good at it all the same. It's nice to be good at things, but I'd like to be good at more of them. Maybe I should go to school. Maybe I'll buy some supplies for Priscilla and let her see what strikes her fancy. I wouldn't want to become one of those parents who forces their child to try all manner of boring things. I'll let her find her own way. I'll let her shine however she shines best.

She will have more choices than I did.

Ronnie

NOW

My phone rang. I'd brought my cell back to bed along with Venita's diary because I didn't have a couch, and it beat sitting downstairs on the cold basement floor. It buzzed violently under my hand and I saw that it was Kate, so I rejected my knee-jerk impulse to decline the call and pretend I hadn't seen it. I picked up the phone. "What?"

"And a very good morning to you, too," she replied with a laugh.

"I never wake up sparkling," I told her, neglecting to add that I'd been up for an hour or two already. It's not like I'd done anything productive with the time, anyway.

"No, you never do. How was your first night in the new old homestead?"

I shifted my weight and stretched out on the air mattress. It squeaked and rustled beneath me. Man, I'd really gotten comfortable again. "Not too bad." I stared up at the ceiling and the array of cracks that sprawled from a broken ceiling medallion. "Though I should move my bed before I spend another night. Woke up covered in plaster dust. Hang on, gonna sneeze."

While I sneezed, she said, "Did we stir it up, walking around yesterday?"

"Probably." Probably, the dust had been falling for decades. But yeah, probably us stomping around upstairs hadn't exactly stabilized anything. I resolved to take pictures: of the ceiling, floors, walls, everything. If anything was visibly falling apart in my presence, I'd give it priority in the restoration work.

I gave up on resting any further and sat up. That's how I discovered that I did, in fact, look very much like I'd gone to sleep in a snowstorm. Well, maybe not a storm. A light dusting, anyway.

"There's no asbestos in that dust, is there?" Kate asked.

"In the plaster? Nah." She didn't know anything about asbestos except that it was bad and you probably shouldn't breathe it. No sense in worrying her.

"Good. I won't have you calling one of those 1-800 numbers on my watch. No bloodsucking ambulance chasers."

"No bloodsucking ambulance chasers," I agreed. I pulled my phone away from my ear and checked the time. It was after nine o'clock. "Certainly not at this hour."

"It's not early. I've already had breakfast, and I'm out and about running errands. From the sound of your voice, you haven't even had coffee yet."

"I don't even have pants yet."

"In your own house, this is permitted."

"Yeah." I could walk around in my underpants if I wanted.

But I didn't. I mashed my head and my shoulder together to hold my phone in place and pulled off my yoga pants, then replaced them with the jeans I'd kicked off to the side. I worked my feet into my boots.

"Are you getting dressed right now?"

"Sort of. I don't have like, a full wardrobe out here. Man, I need to do laundry. Back at my place. My other place. The temporary one." Maybe I'd put a washer and dryer in the basement sooner rather than later. "I'll have to ask the plumber," I mumbled to myself.

Kate heard me. "The plumber? Isn't he coming today?"

"A plumber and an electrician both, yes. Roofer can't make it until later this week. Gonna be a busy day. You want to come over and supervise? Or—" The phone slid off my shoulder when I pulled on a flannel over my T-shirt. I wasn't wearing a bra. Why bother. I didn't have much in the way of tits, and the T-shirt was black. You'd really have to be looking for my nipples, and anybody who goes to that much trouble can get a gander for all I care.

"Or what?"

I retrieved the phone and sat on the edge of my makeshift bed. "Or you could come over, and I could show you the wild-ass scene I found staged in the basement."

"I'm not confident that I'm ready for the basement, but you've piqued my curiosity. Come on. Sell me on this fantastic voyage into the dark, dank depths of your house."

"Okay: I found a shrine."

"A shrine? Oh no, fuck that. I'm *not* game."

"Not like, a shrine to an ancient god or demon or

something," I said with a grin she couldn't see, but might be able to hear. "A fan shrine, to Venita Rost. It was Hugh Crawford's, I assume. I'm pretty sure."

"A shrine to a celebrity who died in your house—no, on the property, right?"

"On the property," I confirmed. "Her husband pushed her off the overlook behind the house."

"Yeah, that's right. I remember now."

"Sounds like you could use some *more* coffee."

"You're not wrong. You want me to bring you some?" she offered.

"Sure thing," I said, thinking of something with more caffeine than my tin full of chocolate dust from the car. "Where are you?"

"At the grocery store, so it'll be a minute. I like shopping first thing in the morning. Fewer people. Better selection."

"Is that so?" I asked idly. I stood up and cracked my back. I took a deep breath, let it out. Tasted the chalky, pale nothingness of plaster, faint on the back of my tongue.

"Yup. You know me, I hate to—"

"Wait in line," I finished the thought right along with her. She could barely wait in traffic, for Chrissake. Waiting was not her strong suit.

"Right, so after I get home, put stuff away, yeah, I'll come over. I'll bring you coffee. Something with lots of sugar and chocolate in it."

"See, that's why I love you."

"Back at ya, babe. See you in an hour or so?"

"See you then." I hung up and looked down at my phone.

The big sweaty cheek smudge on my screen annoyed me, so I wiped it on my jeans and realized that the battery was lower than I'd like. Anything below 30 percent feels like driving around with less than a quarter tank of gas.

Meanwhile, my body felt like my phone's battery, but I was still eager to get moving. I should probably be up and around when the plumber and electrician came by. Then I shook off my bedding and moved the mattress over a few feet, so it wasn't directly beneath the crack in the ceiling that was hemorrhaging plaster dust.

I thought fondly of my instant coffee and hot pot. Sure, I'd have fancy-pants coffee coming in an hour or so, but that wouldn't cut it. I needed calories and warmth *now*.

Bleary-eyed, I wandered away from my bedding and used the stuff I brought in from my car the night before to get myself moving.

In the time it took me to wash my face in the questionable water and pop a Listerine strip into my mouth in lieu of tooth-brushing, several text messages chimed on my phone. The plumber was a woman named Anne, and she'd be by around lunchtime. The electrician was a guy named Terry, and he'd be by around two.

I still had a little time alone, in the light of day, before I'd need to be alert enough for human companionship. Now, what did I want to do with this time?

I kind of wanted to read more of Venita's diary, if I was honest, but I'd left it tucked under the air mattress. Was the diary a secret? Was it something I should keep to myself? It felt like an invasion of privacy on my part, but the woman who wrote it had been dead for nearly a hundred years. Surely its contents didn't matter now, so why was I hoarding the little book like a treasure?

Everyone Venita talked about had been dead for decades, bare minimum. There wasn't even any family out there, no one who might want the diary as a family heirloom, despite its semi-ruined state.

Wait. *Was* there any family?

There had definitely been a daughter, yes. Priscilla, as I had learned via the diary. But she'd died in the parlor, or that's what the trustee agent said—and God knew I hadn't seen any sign of any child having ever lived there. I wasn't even sure what bedroom the kid might have used; they'd all been gutted and emptied except for the master with the rotting four-poster.

I'm not sure what I expected. It's not like a room painted pink wouldn't be painted something else by now, or like any toys wouldn't have made their way to Goodwill generations earlier.

And now I was curious. I'm not sure why, but I was suddenly seized with the desire to find some evidence of Priscilla outside her mother's handwritten account.

Now, where hadn't we investigated yesterday? The basement and the attic, and I think that was it. The attic had a drop-down ladder, and it'd looked less than thrilling, so I'd left it alone. But there'd been boxes up there, right? Some crates?

Maybe it was worth another look.

First, I traipsed back down to the basement—where Hugh Crawford's leftover tools were scattered. I was pretty sure I'd seen a pry bar down there, and I had a Leatherman in my pocket. Between the two, I could probably open just about anything that wasn't locked, like the boarded-up windows...and plenty of things that *were*.

I found the pry bar, retrieved it, and went to the attic hatch and tried the ladder again.

It slid jerkily down on old tracks that were more rust than metal, and absolutely not to be trusted to hold anybody's weight. I stood on the second rung from the top for a minute or two anyway, like I'd done the day before—just staring into the dark.

There was enough rot in the old wood siding to see daylight through cracks; it sliced ribbons of dusty light across the unfinished space, reminding me vaguely of a heist scene with a bunch of lasers guarding a safe. That morning's light was better than yesterday's afternoon light, if for no other reason than the sun was out. A little. Enough for an actual sunbeam or two to creep in, letting the dust flecks sparkle.

I'd had enough dust for one day already, and I also had a phone with a flashlight that was down to a quarter of its battery life. But the attic wasn't that big. I could scan the whole space in a few minutes. Probably. If I didn't fall through it and die.

The floor was plywood laid down over the second-story ceiling beams, and it groaned when I walked on it but held as I poked around.

It was noisy in the attic. Humid, too. The rotten siding let in more than light: it let in mist, smoke from wildfires, and, oh God, spiders. I twitched myself out of a spiderweb and shuddered. I don't hate spiders and I won't kill them, but I don't want them to surprise me, either.

I saw no actual living spiders. They all had the good sense to flee my presence.

But I did see three crates, two cardboard boxes that looked damp-soft enough to sleep on, and a trunk I hadn't noticed the day before. It'd been pushed behind the crates.

I liked the idea of a trunk. It felt more personal than the blank old wood that was guaranteed to give me a thousand splinters if I wasn't careful, and the trunk also looked old. Okay, it *all* looked old—but the trunk looked oldest.

It had a rounded, barrel-shaped top, a vintage-trendy touch that made them uncomfortable for lazy porters to sit on. It also made them difficult for non-lazy porters to stack and ship, but what rich white girl ever gave a damn about such things? Back in the thirties, I figured a safe bet was "virtually none of them."

The trunk had a lock, but the lock had been vigorously picked—no, hacked—open at some point. When I lifted the lid and took a look, I was disappointed to find it empty except for some dead bugs and water-spoiled paper, some of it wadded up, some of it decayed right into the trunk's interior.

I poked at the closest bit of paper. There was handwriting on it, and now I could recognize the handwriting as Venita's, but I couldn't read any of it. She'd done it in pen, and all the letters were runny gibberish.

"This is where Hugh found the diary," I guessed out loud, for the sake of my hiding spider friends. Then I saw a label stuck on the inside, peeling and browned with damp and age. It read "Venita Rost" in her own script, with the house's address scrawled carefully below it. "Definitely hers, but I'm a day late and a dollar short." Hugh had beaten me to the punch.

I closed the trunk lid and checked the boxes. They were

filled with mid-century *National Geographic* magazines. They were riddled with silverfish, and they smelled awful.

Great. Those would be fun to haul downstairs and toss in a dumpster.

On to the crates. Hugh had beaten me to those, too. He'd taken something more violent than a pry bar to them—possibly an axe. The lid to one was completely shattered. Inside I found men's clothes from another era, but which one, it was a little hard to say. I'm not as sharp with men's historic fashion as I am with women's, but the brown suit on top was wool, moth-eaten into rags. No hope for it, whatsoever.

The men's shoes were rat-nibbled. The shaving kit said early twentieth century to me, but again, man-things aren't my specialty. I rooted around in there for a few minutes and gave up on finding anything whole, or interesting, or useful.

Second crate. The lid was loose but not busted up quite so badly.

"Okay, here we go…" Bedding, but the kind that used to be fluffy and pastel. A knitted baby blanket that had collapsed into pieces when someone else had gone digging through the crate (drat you, Hugh). Small shoes, black patent leather, small bites taken out by vermin. A little muff with real fur lining that was long gone (well done, moths). A coat sized for a first or second grader, maybe. Also tattered by neglect and nature.

"Priscilla's stuff. It has to be."

No, it didn't have to be. It could've belonged to any child, really. I was making assumptions, and I wasn't sure they were safe.

But children's things hidden in an old crate? Beside a trunk that definitely belonged to Venita?

I ran my hands through the contents, using my spread fingers to push through the old and ruined textiles like a big fork. I found a few glass buttons down at the bottom, a couple of brass ones, and the buckles for the shoes, rusted and brittle.

I'd hoped for more, of course. Something concrete, ideally with the child's name on it. Or something intact, that wouldn't deserve an immediate trip into the nearest dumpster. I was genuinely disappointed that none of the attic's holdings appeared worth saving.

I tucked my phone into my back pocket and wiped my hands on my jeans.

Someone knocked on the door.

"Plumber must be running earlier than I thought." I shook the cobwebs out of my hair and headed back downstairs.

Bartholomew Sloan
NOW

I saw you thinking, and I could read your thoughts as clearly as if you'd spoken them aloud. You didn't want to answer the call. You wanted to marinate in the house, sleep in it a little longer, get acquainted with its comforts and ailments alike.

I'm afraid there's more to be found of the latter than the former.

You stashed Venita's diary under that balloon mattress, and neither one of us knows why, I think, but I would have done the same. It might be some back-brain, unconscious knowledge that the thing is dangerous, and that it should be hidden away.

It should've been burned as soon as it was found.

For a moment—maybe fifty years ago now, I can't recall exactly—I thought it might actually find the destruction it so richly deserved. The novel-reading wife of the man who bought the place that time—the fellow who'd had a list of plans like you, Ronnie—she found the diary first. She read what was still readable, sensed the danger, and lit a fire in the parlor. Right next to the mirror of such terrible infamy.

But the flue mysteriously snapped shut and the house filled with smoke, and the whole building nearly burned down. I assumed it was Venita, but I could be wrong.

As I said, I haven't seen her since Mr. Crawford died, but I've sensed her. I'm not sure where she goes when she rests; for that matter, I'm not sure where *I* go.

When I sleep, where do I sleep? Do I remain right where I last recalled, as insubstantial as a shadow? Or do I vanish into another, darker realm where horrible things befall me—only to forget it all when I wake?

When I do wake, from noise or disruption, or startlement, or willful harassment…I tend to come around in the parlor. It stands to reason, since that's where I died. Maybe every time I let myself fade into silence, I sit back down at that very same chair—though it's covered in a dust sheet, I can still see it and hold it in my mind—and I close my eyes and the letter falls from my hands, and the drink slides into my lap, and that's the end of me again, for a while.

As for Venita, if I were forced to guess, I might say that she haunts the attic, or maybe her bedroom suite. Or maybe she lurks in the basement, where some of her things were relocated by that man who died upstairs.

But Veronica, you've been to both places, and I've never detected much more than a vague air of Venita-ness in your general vicinity. It's something like nervous anticipation, if you will. It might have been entirely in my own head, if I still had one.

What I mean to say is that she has not made her residual presence known to you. Yet. But she's coming. And when she arrives, you will be thoroughly enchanted like the rest of the people who've tried to live here, I expect. At first, they're always enthralled. At first, they want to reach out and touch her. At first.

I hope I'm wrong.

But no one can sleep through construction, alas—and if that's what rouses her, you'll be in for a difficult time. Venita doesn't like it when people make changes to her home, and she's usually the reason that construction eventually stops. I'll just put it that way.

As for me, I mind my own business.

And yours. I have nothing better to do, and bluntly, I fear you might be in need of some assistance. Or some buffer, perhaps. You'll need someone or something to stand between the two of you if you draw her interest.

Please, listen if you can hear me.

Please, I only want to help.

Ronnie

NOW

I shoved the ladder back up into the ceiling and swiped plaster dust off my nose and cheeks with my sleeve. In my front pocket, I had a hair twisty. I pulled it out and tied up a stubby, rough ponytail as I hustled toward the foyer.

I made it back downstairs before the visitor could knock a second time.

But when I opened the door, the person standing on the stoop was not a plumber named Anne: it was a guy a little younger than me. He was closer to Kate's age, I think, and he was very *Seattle*, if that makes sense. He wore a blue T-shirt under an expensive flannel, and designer jeans with high-top sneakers. His hair was light and wavy, and the way it fluffed in the humidity suggested he wasn't too fond of putting products in it.

"Oh, I'm sorry," I said.

I'd confused him. "What?"

"Sorry," I told him again. "I was expecting the plumber. Or my sister-in-law. Or…not you."

"Sounds like I should be the one apologizing…?" He said it with half a little smirk that was either infuriating or endearing, and I couldn't tell you which.

"No, it's definitely me," I said with a sigh, then I fibbed a plausible fib. "I'm the one who just woke up."

"I hope that isn't my fault? I thought it was late enough that I could…um, well. I'm sorry." On that note, he held out a bottle of Maker's Mark that he'd held behind his back. "Let's try this again. I'm Coty Deaver. And you're new to the neighborhood, so…I'm just saying welcome and, and…hello," he concluded.

I took the bottle, because momma didn't raise no fool. "Oh, wow, thanks! I will definitely make use of this. It's nice to meet you, I'm Ronnie, and yeah. I'm the crazy person who bought the place."

He chuckled and ran a hand behind his neck in a gesture that might've been charming if I were a decade younger and looking to mingle. "It's gotta be a hell of a project. Are you tackling it… alone?"

I read the ellipsis and jumped to a conclusion. "Or with a spouse?" I held up my left hand, displaying no ring. "It's just me. Or me and a crew of dozens of people, when all is said and done."

"Right." He nodded. He was trying to look past me without me noticing it, hoping for a glimpse inside.

If I were in his shoes, I'd be doing the same thing. Even though I knew I wasn't really fit for polite company, I opened the door a little wider. "Do you, uh, want to take a look around? It's pretty wild in here."

He brightened. "Okay, honestly? Yes. I am absolutely *dying* to see inside."

"I feel you. That's half the reason I bought it," I exaggerated. "Come on, I'll give you the tour. Just, um, shit… Maybe I should make you sign a waiver or something. There are holes in the floors and rats in the walls, and those are probably the least of my problems."

Eagerly, he accepted my invitation while refusing precautions. The enthusiasm made him look younger, so I might have misjudged his age on first impression.

Mouth hanging slightly open, he stared around the foyer—toward the parlor, then back across to the library. His eyes ran up the staircase, admiring the woodwork. How do I know that? Because I know what it looks like when somebody admires woodwork, that's how. The guy was a hobbyist of some sort, either ruin porn or old houses, or maybe even urban exploration. You have to be some sort of relevant nerd for your face to light up like that when you see an interior in this sort of condition.

He launched into some chattering that backed up my suspicions.

"This place is amazing! I mean it needs work, obviously—it's been sitting here vacant for ages and ages, so it must need… everything, basically. But there's a lot of original stuff in here, nice wood, nice leaded glass windows. Are you going to keep it? Develop it into a B and B or whatever? Restore it?" I didn't answer quickly enough, so he continued. "They don't make them like this anymore, you know what I mean? When I was a kid"—he shifted gears with a note of conspiracy—"me and my friends used to ride our bikes over here and try to psych ourselves out, tell ourselves ghost stories, you know. We'd hang out over on the side of the house, where the trees are, and count our Halloween candy every year."

"The side yard? Where the little orchard is?"

He nodded. "There was an apple tree back there that looked really gnarly, like it belonged on the cover of a book of ghost stories. We'd sit underneath it and drink stolen beer when we were teenagers and look up at the windows—telling ourselves we saw faces inside. On Halloween, it was easy to convince ourselves that we were intrepid explorers, not trespassers. We took a few pictures, but nothing ever came out. We didn't have real cameras back then, just crappy disposable ones."

"Did anyone live here, or chase you off?" I asked.

"Nah. No one's ever lived here as far as I know. Not since I've been alive."

"What about the guy who died upstairs?" I asked. Surely he would've heard about Hugh Crawford.

"Oh yeah! Forgot about him." He glanced at the top of the steps like he was dying to go take a look, but too polite to ask. "I don't think he was here very long. I didn't know about him until they found his body and it made the news. I live on Beacon Hill now." He cocked his head to indicate a narrow ridge to the east, on the other side of the water.

That was…let's call it a pink flag. If I'd been more awake or alert, I might've called it a red one, but I reserved judgment for the moment—in favor of asking a question. "Then how'd you hear the place had sold again?"

"Oh, I'm still friends with some of the old crew from around here. We gossip. Man, don't take this the wrong way, but I'm *super* jealous of you right now. I would've loved to nab this place for myself, but I couldn't make it happen. I could never get enough money together."

Something about the way he said it struck me as odd. I wasn't in the mood for games and he'd already given me a pink flag, so I pressed for more info. "Wait, which is it? Are you a curious former neighbor kid, or were you a prospective buyer?"

He held up his hands like I'd shown him a gun. "I knew the house was coming up for sale, but I knew good and well I couldn't afford it. You didn't snatch it out from under me or anything, and I'm not here for revenge or vandalism."

"That hadn't even occurred to me." Maybe it should have. Maybe I shouldn't have invited him inside, but he'd looked harmless enough, even skittish. "But feel free to keep talking."

His face locked into a mask of anxious discomfort before he said, all in one breath, "According to family legend, my uncle is one of the people who died in this house." Then he started to say something else, but someone knocked on the door. He jumped like he'd been hit.

"The plumber, I assume. Hold that thought."

But it wasn't the plumber. It was Kate. She was holding a venti something-or-another in each hand, and she thrust one of them toward me. "I finished up faster than I thought, and there wasn't any line. I almost wondered if it wasn't some kind of zombie-apocalypse scenario, but…" Her voice trailed off when she saw I had a guest. "Why, hello there...?" she said to him, or asked him.

He gave her a quick little wave with his right hand. "Hello! Coty Deaver, former neighbor and now, um, curious party, with regards to this house."

"His uncle supposedly died here," I told her as I took the offered coffee drink, then took a mighty swig. I liked this thing, where people give me beverages in the morning.

She pointed an eyebrow at the Maker's that now dangled from my non-coffee-holding hand. "Hey." She stepped forward and offered him her hand. "I'm Kate. I'm Ronnie's sister-in-law. Sorry about your uncle."

He took it and said, "Oh, he died almost a hundred years ago, don't worry about it. It's nice to meet you." He sounded relieved. Kate was good at putting people at ease, even if they'd just shown up at my house unannounced. "I didn't mean to intrude, and I wasn't trying to mislead anybody. I only thought if I show up with a neighborhood-welcome bottle, maybe that would be less weird than opening with the whole truth?"

"That you wanted to get a gander at a familial crime scene?" I think I said it drolly.

Kate was warmer. "What happened to your uncle?"

"My uncle... My great-uncle? Great-great uncle? He died here back in the 1930s. I was going to ask you if I could maybe take some pictures or something; my mom is really into genealogy, and she asked me to try."

"No, I get it. I'm nosy about old houses, too—and if I knew I had a family connection, I'd probably want to see inside." Honestly, it's exactly the kind of thing I would do, so no, I guess

I couldn't get too mad about it. "It's fine, come on. I'll show you around until the plumber arrives, and then you should probably skedaddle."

Kate said, "I want to hear more about this uncle of yours. How did he die?"

"Supposedly he killed himself," he said matter-of-factly. "But my family never quite believed it. He actually owned this place, for about five minutes, but then he—"

Coty was interrupted by yet another knock on the damn door.

It was the third one of the morning, and a personal record with regards to a.m. visitors for yours truly. I wondered if this one had also brought beverages, but I surely couldn't be that lucky. I said, "That's *gotta* be the plumber."

This time I was right.

Anne was a short lumberjack lesbian with a wicked smirk and a buzz cut. She carried a clipboard and a work bag, and she introduced herself as the owner of Westside Plumbing and Rainwater Management. I liked her on the spot and invited her in.

Then I excused Coty by gentle force. "Nothing personal, hon, but the work of restoration and repair is about to get underway."

Kate said, "Aw, I wanted to hear about another death in the house."

I kind of did, too. I'd already found evidence of Venita and Priscilla, and the evidence of Hugh Crawford was concrete enough, in the form of a hole upstairs. When it comes to potential ghosts, you've gotta catch 'em all, right? I wanted to get this uncle's character sheet and stats. "How about this," I proposed. "Come back this evening around six, and I'll order pizza or something. We can sit in the orchard if it's dry, and you can tell us ghost stories about your uncle. Will that work?"

Oh yes. It did.

I couldn't decide whether or not Kate was a little too disappointed to see Coty leave, and I couldn't decide how I felt about that, so I ignored my ambivalence and got down to plumbing business with Anne, who was every bit as thorough, competent, and direct as her plaid flannel and steel-toed boots suggested.

But Jesus, it was a bloodbath. She apologized when she gave me the quote, and apologized further to confess that it didn't include the patchwork to repair whatever walls were cut open for the full re-pipe. "Because you might be able to get that done cheaper by somebody else. I have to subcontract it to a cousin of mine."

I mustered a rueful smile. "I can take care of that myself."

"You gave me that impression, so I'm happy to hear it. I'd hate to think somebody who didn't know jack shit about houses would take on a project like this. But for future reference, you might want to keep your cat inside."

"My…cat? I don't have a cat."

"Sure you do. Pretty white one? Almost a little bit silver? Big green eyes?"

"In *this* house?" I asked, the question pitched too high to sound casual.

"Nah, out there. I kept seeing them out the window. I'd hate for the little guy to get run over by a truck."

Then we spent a few minutes bonding over the challenges

of run-down properties until Kate rejoined us from the kitchen, where she'd been poking around in the cabinets in search of interesting artifacts.

"What's the damage?" she asked when she saw us chatting amicably.

"Only a little north of 15K, so it could be worse," I told her.

Anne shrugged an apology. "Don't jinx it, because you know as well as I do, this number could still go higher. You've got some complicated pipes running through these walls, and I don't think any of them have been in standard use since the mid-century. At least you don't have any Poly-B in here that I could find."

"Nobody's tried to upgrade this place that recently." Then I reconsidered, and reconsidered my reconsidering. "No, the last real remodel effort was in the early seventies, before that garbage was popular."

Anne said, "Good. But if those clay pipes running out to the city sewer are still intact, I'll eat my gloves. That'll be a whole different kettle of fish. You're probably talking bulldozers, excavators, city permits… It could add tens of thousands when all's said and done."

"One bonfire of cash at a time, please," I begged her, and she laughed.

Before she left, I wrote her a check for a deposit and confirmed that I was on her schedule, in the company queue for work starting in a couple of weeks, thank God. I'd been afraid I'd have to wait longer, but hey. It shouldn't take terribly long, relative to some of the other work, so there was a slim (but present) chance that I could weave all these tasks together in a magnificent symphony of restoration.

Or more likely, I'd wind up with workers from different disciplines tripping over each other for months, but what can you do.

Roofing would probably schedule further out, which didn't please me—but some things are out of my control. It was technically summer, and even though it was still fairly cool and damp out here, that's always busy season for the industry. Electricians were a crapshoot.

Oh yeah, the electrician.

Terry Richards from Puget Sound Electric and Solar arrived at two on the dot, mere minutes after Kate and I returned from a late lunch at Alki Point. It took him an hour and a half to meticulously poke through every wired nook and cranny, and while it annoyed Kate, it delighted me. I can work with meticulous. I can even give it permission to punch a few fresh holes in the walls to double-check details or confirm speculation.

His estimate was brutal, too.

"*Thirty-four grand?*" Kate squeaked.

He shrugged at her. "It's a big house, and it needs…everything. Literally everything. I lost count of the small fires that burned out in the walls, most of the wires are still wrapped in fabric, and the knob and tube is still live. Quite frankly, it's a miracle the house is still standing."

"Maybe we should get a second opinion or two," she sulked.

I waved it away. I'd budgeted thirty grand, and I liked Terry for his thoroughness. "That's a reasonable bid, and I'm looking to get started as soon as possible. When can you get me on your schedule?"

"If you'd asked last week, I would've told you September.

But we had a big project fall through for the end of July, so if you want that slot, we can get you on the calendar for right around then."

"That's like, six weeks out? Jesus."

I patted Kate's arm. "Six weeks is fine. It's great. Yes. Put me down for that."

"Why'd the other project fall through?" she asked, as if on a whim.

Another shrug. "The place burned down. You two, uh, are you living here? Right now? Like this?"

Kate pointed at me. "She is. Sort of."

"I'm camping here off and on until my lease in the Central District runs out. Don't worry about me—and yes, I'll be careful." And the plumbers, roofers, and the rest could bring generators to power their tools and lights if they started work sooner. I wrote Terry a deposit check, and we settled on July 18 for a start date.

It was an exhausting and expensive day, and I was glad when the electrician left.

When he was gone, Kate volunteered to make a hasty run to the nearest gas station for paper plates and sodas ahead of our pizza party with the new guy, Coty. She texted happily that she'd even found a cheap foam cooler and a bag of ice to keep the drinks cool.

I stayed back and tidied up to the best of my abilities, but I'm not sure it made much of a difference. At least I'd used an old towel to swipe plaster dust off everything, and that was something, wasn't it?

Except for the bedding, which still collected it like crazy—despite my best efforts.

I picked up my pillow and punched it repeatedly, sending puffs of dust swirling through the air; then I grabbed the corner of my sleeping bag and shook it like a dirty rug. More dust, more debris. Bits of wood chewed to sawdust by termites and plaster as fine as baby powder filled the room and I coughed, then sneezed.

To myself, I said, "I really should've done that outside." It wasn't like I had a vacuum cleaner, or any outlet where plugging one in wouldn't blow out the wall. I didn't even have a broom.

Still rubbing my nose, and then my eyes, I stared at the soft cloud of dust floating through the air and for an instant—no, for a few seconds—I could've sworn it had a shape to it. Almost like a person? No, nothing that clear. Something person-sized, and shaped like…could've been anything.

"The hell am I doing," I asked aloud, then shook my head and put back the bedding. "Imagining stupid shit," I chided. "And not for the first time."

But it still felt weird to me, like I'd gotten a glimpse of something I shouldn't have. Or maybe all the dust and mold was getting to my brain.

By the time Kate got back to the house, I'd stopped wondering about it in favor of wondering about other things, like "Where can I get a pizza around here?"

It was about five thirty, and it was raining, goddammit, so we'd have to hold the party indoors. I ordered a couple of "just throw every-damn-thing on it" large pizzas from a local joint that would probably add something weird like cauliflower, but so what. I was hungry. Coty hadn't made any special dietary requests, and relative to the rest of the day's costs, the pizzas weren't that expensive, even after I tipped the girl who delivered them.

I carried the boxes inside.

Ronnie

NOW

Coty Deaver showed up at four minutes to six, bearing a two-liter of root beer, a sleeve of Solo cups, and a bag of napkins. "I hope I'm not too early?"

Kate exclaimed, "Root beer!" and whipped the door open wider to invite him inside. "We only got Cokes." Over her shoulder to me, she added, "We should've thought about something without caffeine."

"We were in a hurry. Come on in, Coty."

It was still raining, so we skipped the orchard and threw a clean tarp over a crate to use as a table. The smell of sauce and crust and garlic took the edge off the odor of mildew and mold that had become ubiquitous in my nose, and very fleetingly, I wondered if any of us should be inside at all without decent masks.

But everybody dies of something someday, and eventually, me and Kate (and Coty too) will just be three more ghosts with a connection to the house on the ridge.

Me and Kate explained the pseudo sister-in-law thing, and we talked about Ben. We also drank to him. We told Coty about the life insurance policy and everything, and how it should almost, maybe be enough money to fix the house to code. Everything else would have to wait, and would probably get done by me, personally. Eventually.

I don't know why, but the money thing almost warmed him up a little. I wonder if he thought I was just another rich asshole, rolling up to convert a landmark into condos. It would've been a fair assumption. Wrong, but fair. It happens a lot around here.

The sun wasn't down, but the clouds had rolled back in, and I'd had enough Maker's to be the demanding kind of friendly. "So. Tell us about your uncle," I ordered, even though I'd already figured out that he was talking about the investigator in Venita's diary. "We know several people supposedly died here, or near here, but I don't know how much of what we heard is, you know, hearsay. The stuff kids make up when they want to drink beer under a gnarly old tree."

He laughed, either a hair tipsy or pretending to be. Same as me. "No, that's fair. And yeah, I was starting to say when the plumber showed up: technically, Uncle Bart owned this house, but not for very long. He inherited it from the guy who built it."

Something rattled slightly behind me. I wasn't even sure I'd heard it at first.

Kate was visibly, audibly intoxicated. It was adorable. "Didn't that guy go to jail for murder? Isn't that what you said, Ronnie?" To Coty, she added, "She's looked into the house more than I have. She's the one who found—"

I cut her off before she could blab about the shrine

downstairs. I hadn't even shown it to her yet, and it didn't feel right to let this rando in on the secret first. "I found out about Venita Rost, the silent film star who lived here."

The rattling happened again, harder. Now I turned to look and realized that the grand old mirror on the wall beside the fireplace was...not swaying, exactly. But bouncing softly, like someone was shaking it.

"Guys?" I said, trying to collect their attention for the sake of backup. I didn't want to think I'd had so much to drink that I was literally seeing things, but it wouldn't have been the first time.

I don't think either of them heard me. Or more likely, their attention was elsewhere.

Coty's eyes lit up, and even though I'm the one who answered him, he shined them right on Kate. "Right! The blond...the platinum, kitty or something, right. You know about her, okay. She died here too, you know."

I swung my head back and forth. "Nope. She died over *there*." I waved toward the back of the house, and the ridge in which it was embedded. "Her husband murdered her. Threw her off the cliff during a fight."

"That's what the trustee agent said," Kate confirmed for me.

Coty raised a finger and said, "But! My uncle never believed it. Venita's husband was Oscar Amundson, and Oscar was Uncle Bart's best friend. Bart swore that the murder charge was some kind of setup or frame job."

Kate beat me to it when she said, "Lots of men who murder their wives have friends who'd swear the same."

"*Guys.*" I said it again, louder and firmer.

Kate asked, "What?" and Coty said, "Huh?" a fraction of a second before the mirror rattled off its mount and went clanging down to the floor.

We all yelped and cringed up tightly.

The mirror didn't break. It rocked back and forth on its curved edge and then swayed forward as if it were going to fall face down. If the drop hadn't broken it, that follow-up blow would surely do the trick—so I jumped off the mattress with enough speed to surprise myself. I caught it with both hands and let it rest for a moment against my thigh.

Kate and Coty unclenched slowly, and Coty whistled like he was impressed. Well, he should've been. I was impressed with myself, too.

"It…it didn't even crack, did it?" he asked.

"No," I said, before I was sure it was true. But when I looked, yes. The glass was intact. "It's fine."

It was heavy as hell, though, and when I looked up, I couldn't figure out how it'd fallen. The bolts were still in place, anchored with enough insistence to hold for another hundred years.

"What the hell happened?" Kate gasped, looking suddenly more sober.

"I don't know. It was rocking back and forth, kind of shaking. I guess it wiggled its way off the wall." It was a stupid guess and I knew it. They knew it, too. But they'd seen it—out of the corner of their eyes, if not directly, and we'd all been right there when it thudded to the floor with all the finesse of a manhole cover.

The mirror was very, very heavy, and I did not think I could lift it myself.

Coty must've been thinking along the same lines, because he stood up and said, "I can help you put that back, if you want."

"Thanks, man, but if it wants to be down on the floor so badly, it can stay there. For now." I pushed with my hands and leveraged my thigh until the mirror was leaning steadily against the wall, below the spot where it'd once hung.

We sat together in silence for a few seconds before Kate went, "Maybe this place is haunted after all."

I said, "I'd be stunned if it wasn't." But I wasn't as cool about it, this time—not nearly so chill as the day that Jeff showed us around and left us the keys. I wasn't sure I could stand behind my theory of "harmless, and akin to stray cats" if they could move something this...solid.

Coty took a stab at being the voice of reason. "It was probably a small earthquake, the kind we don't notice, hardly at all. Or else, like...weird vibrations."

"Weird vibrations," Kate and I murmured in uneasy agreement.

We settled back down and tried to resume our relative merriment.

I cleared my throat and said, "Sorry for the interruption."

"Why would you apologize? You didn't drop the mirror," Kate noted with a grin.

"Yeah, but it's my house. My mirror. My danger zone. Now, where were we?"

After some floundering, we returned at least adjacently to the subject at hand. It felt like it was important to do so, and I don't know why, exactly. I was starting to feel like the topic itself had prompted the mirror's unsettling theatrics, but that was nonsense, right? Pure crazy shit.

Although. Now that I thought about it...when the mirror had started its shenanigans, we'd been talking about the detective.

"What was his name?" Kate asked suddenly. "Uncle Bart. Was it Bartholomew?"

He nodded. "Bartholomew Sloan. He was from Boston but ended up in New York. I'm not sure how they met out here. I know for a while he was working as a private investigator in Los Angeles. Maybe it had something to do with one of Venita's movies."

"Maybe," I considered, but didn't fill him in on what I'd read in the diary. I didn't know him like that. Not yet.

"He was a PI? In the thirties? Like Sam Spade?" Kate wanted to know.

He laughed again, and this time I was pretty sure he was actually drunk. I assumed he'd driven over and parked on the street, but worst-case scenario, I could stuff him into an Uber if I needed to be rid of him. "I don't know if he was anything like Sam Spade," he told her. "But he was really, *really* good at his job. He traveled the world, solving cases. Finding people. Retrieving property. My grandmother said he once returned an emerald that belonged to a museum in Washington, DC, and he was given an award—or reward? A letter of commendation?" The booze had him a little lost in his own story.

"At any rate," I prompted.

"*At any rate,*" he went along with it. "Uncle Bart became friends with the Amundsons, and he used to visit them all the time. He would stay in one of the spare rooms when he came to Seattle to work or hobnob or whatever it is he did in his downtime. And since Venita and her kid were dead, Oscar left everything to Uncle Bart."

I licked the last of the bourbon off the lip of my cup and set it aside, then held up my hands to slow him down. "Hang on, back up. Oscar was executed, wasn't he? For Venita's murder?"

"Right. The whole time Oscar was in jail, Uncle Bart was scrambling around trying to find proof that her death had been an accident, or worse. He developed a theory that Venita had killed herself and faked the murder to frame her husband. That was his angle, and he was determined to prove it."

Kate asked, "But *why*? Who hates somebody enough to just…*die*, purely so you can send them to jail? Or to their death?"

He pointed one finger at her. "Venita Rost, that's who. She blamed Oscar for what happened to their little girl—I forget her name."

"Priscilla," I blurted out before I could stop myself. I wasn't playing my cards as close to my chest as I meant to. I blamed the Maker's.

"That sounds right? Let's run with that. Priscilla," he decided. "She died in some kind of accident."

Kate said, "The agent told us that the little girl died right here in the parlor."

"This is the parlor?" He frowned. "Oh yeah, I guess… Sure. I hadn't thought about that. Maybe she fell into the fireplace or something."

We all looked over at the enormous fireplace with its expensive stone surround and nodded solemnly, each of us mentally running through morbid scenarios that might have caused the death of a child. She could have choked on a piece of candy; she might have cut herself on a piece of broken glass and the kid could've bled out; she may have jumped onto a couch and fallen, breaking her neck.

We were collectively quiet for too long, and we all got uncomfortable.

Coty said, "That poor little girl."

I said, "Her poor mother."

Kate agreed with us both. "Poor everybody. And poor your uncle, too," she tacked on quickly. "Do you really think the whole thing drove him to suicide?"

He stared down into his Solo cup. "My whole family says no, but you have to take that with a grain of salt. I guess…it would make sense. But you get bored, do some googling, or go to the library—whatever makes you happy—and look up Bartholomew Sloan. He was pretty famous in his time, with a sterling reputation as a mystery-solver."

"Yeah, but if he couldn't exonerate his friend, that might've put some tarnish on it," I noted.

"That's what everybody said. 'Bartholomew Sloan never failed to solve a case, except for that last one.' It broke a streak that was years long—a streak that made him a rich man. *I* think," he said, leaning forward now and dropping his voice like yeah, this was a ghost story after all. "He found out he'd inherited the house after Oscar died, and it surprised him. I think he came here and drank himself to death, maybe by accident. I think he was grieving because his best friends were gone and he couldn't save them."

It was a reasonable theory, and I told him so.

But not long after that, I kicked him out. I thanked him for the stories and sent him on his way. I don't know if he tried to drive home or if he got a car or not; I forgot to look. I was tired and itching to get back to my reading.

I hugged Kate and sent her home behind him.

When she was gone, too, I went back to the parlor and stared back and forth between the mirror and the wall where it'd once hung. I knocked on the studs, but they sounded fine—no soft echoes from water-ruined wood or termites turning the structures to sawdust. When I tugged at the bolts with my bare fingers, they didn't so much as wiggle. I don't think I could've pried them off the wall if I wanted to. It would take one of those extraction tips on a drill to do it.

I checked the back of the mirror again, leaning it against my leg once more to hold it steady.

No, the mountings were fine and undamaged.

"This is dumb," I chided myself. "Sometimes things just fall."

It was true, but it wasn't right. It's just easier to lie to myself when I'm alone.

Bartholomew Sloan

NOW

Can you hear me, Ronnie? Because I need you to hear me—that's why I expended so much effort trying to move the mirror. I wasn't even sure it was possible, but it worked, and you saw it, and now I need to explain: That boy is *not* what he seems. Or rather, he *is*—but his motives aren't what he'd have you believe. Only about half of what he told you is true. He's as bad as me, and likely much worse. That boy will repeat my mistakes with his eyes wide open, and he knows what he's looking for. If we are terribly unlucky, he knows what he's doing.

And here's a bit of truth for the record: he *did* try to buy this house when it went to auction, but he could not scare up the funds to do so.

I know this, because he's been stalking the place for years, and I overheard plenty of his finagling. At one point he even tried to convince that man, Hugh Crawford, to make him the beneficiary of his estate should something ever happen to him. But Mr. Crawford was not a fool.

Allow me to emphasize this point: today was *not* the first time the boy had been inside this house.

It was at least the third, though he might have visited at other times when I was asleep. I'd like to think I would've awakened upon hearing his voice or sensing his presence, but I cannot say for certain—I can only say that it's how I knew of him in the past.

The first time I saw him was several years ago, when the house was vacant but being shown. Since no one has spent any time here in decades, no one has been paying taxes on it, either—and from time to time, the city (or the state? Or whoever?) has tried to unload it on some unsuspecting sucker who sees "good bones" and thinks they'll be the one to save this house.

They're right about the bones, but only in the strictest sense. I think you understand that better than anyone else so far, Ronnie. It gives me hope.

You might be the one who *does* actually save the house.

You're the first woman to give it a try, and maybe that's just what the place needs: a woman with experience, a methodical mind, and the skills of a man. I hope you would not find this assessment offensive. I think you probably wouldn't? You don't strike me as the touchy sort.

And if you are, well...there's nothing I can do about it since you still can't hear me.

It hardly seems fair. I hear so much from you that I feel like I'm eavesdropping on someone's life. It feels intrusive and rude.

Not that I can look away.

But my nephew. My great-grandnephew. *He's* the one I mean to warn you about.

The moment he set foot in here, I knew that he was mine somehow.

Or not *mine*, per se. But some extension of me—some continuation of life, of family. Some persistence of essence, that's as near as I can pinpoint the sensation.

He was accompanied by a young woman I eventually figured out was a real estate agent, acting on behalf of some bank or government entity. She went through the motions of showing him the sights, though she did so with an air of futility. The state of the house has fallen so far, so low, it takes a certain kind of person with a certain bank account to take a chance on something in need of so much work.

Coty did not look or act like such an account holder.

It's a good rule of thumb when dealing with an agent who wishes to sell you something, to be reserved in your expressions of approval lest the price go up. If Coty is aware of this universal truth, he was very bad at presenting it. His eagerness was palpable. It did not stop short of being embarrassing.

When the woman's back was turned, he took photos with his handheld phone. He'd silenced the little device so that it made no sound, but I saw him holding it out of sight, pressing the screen, collecting snapshots.

She declined to show him the attic or the basement, on the grounds that they were unsafe, and she was wearing high heels. I think she was afraid of them. I think she was a little afraid of *him*. Wary of him.

She was as alone with him as she wished to be, that's what I mean to say. Women have always required an excess of caution to survive.

Regardless, the first time Coty saw this house… When the agent was finished with him, she locked up behind them both and wished him well. He promised to be in touch within the next day or two.

I doubt he ever reached out to her again, but he did in fact return to the house a few days later. It was very early in the morning; the sun was barely up and it was overcast, so it might as well have been nighttime still.

He pried open one of those windows behind the moldering curtains that once were a vibrant green, and he slithered inside on his belly; the window would only open by a foot or so, and it took some wriggling on his part to breach the threshold in that manner, but it was a more discreet entrance than if he'd forced the front door. The front door faces the street. His chosen window faced nothing but the shadow of the ridge and some trees.

He made a disgusted little sound when he hit the floor because he'd landed on the edge of the rug, which had all but dissolved into mildew and rot. The floors around that window were soft under his feet.

When he stood up straight, he was holding a large metal flashlight—the kind you could use to bludgeon someone, if you were so inclined. Not that there was anyone present to bludgeon.

Nobody here but us ghosts.

I was upstairs that day, in the room where Mr. Crawford would later meet his end. I saw Coty sneaking through the trees, darting back and forth as if he were being pursued. No one pursued him. I only went to meet him, and to discover the nature of the peculiar pull I felt toward his presence.

Many trespassers had come and gone over the years. People broke in all the time, wanting to get a look at the interior, or raid it for antiques, or hunt for shades like myself.

But this one.

He was alone and carrying a backpack. He shouldered it again and shined his light around. It went right through me. I did not feel it. He did not see me.

Coty began to explore.

He lifted the hems of the furniture drapes and flipped through the books on the shelves, such as they were. Too many were stuck together—moisture and time turning their pages to glue, their covers to mulch. He aimed his light into every room, even climbing down into the basement, which was brave of him.

I suppose I cannot call him a coward. A fool, yes. A lazy fool. But not a coward.

I do not know if he knew that I lingered. He couldn't have, could he? I believe that this trip was an exercise in optimism on his part.

"Hello, you crazy old house." He stood in the foyer with the light aimed forward. He swept it from side to side as if he were looking for something, and he wasn't sure where it was or what it looked like. "Hello, ghosts."

I was startled. Had I been mistaken? Could he sense me after all? Or even see me?

No.

"I know there are ghosts here. There *must* be. Where else

would Oscar go, once freed from his mortal coil?" I had no idea whatsoever. I hadn't seen any sign of him since the day he died. "Or if not him, then the daughter. The little girl. Little-girl ghosts are always spooky, right? They sing nursery rhymes in half the horror-movie trailers, swear to God."

I didn't know what he was talking about. Still don't. But Priscilla isn't here, either, so now I knew he was grasping at straws.

"Maybe even the late, great Ms. Rost herself. That would be something, if she's hanging around. I'd love to meet her. Better yet," he said slowly, connivingly, as if he knew he was being overheard and intended to perform accordingly, "I would *love* to meet my dearly departed uncle, Bartholomew Sloan."

If I'd had a heart, it would have stopped.

"That's right. Uncle Bart. Can I call you Uncle Bart?"

I'd rather he didn't, but I could hardly prevent him from doing so.

"I know what you did, Uncle Bart. I know who you were, and I know you weren't *that* good a detective—not on your own. Not without help."

If I'd had a stomach, it would have sunk. At first, I'd thought he was talking about Priscilla. Then I realized he wasn't.

"I know who you talked to. I know what you bought and why I can't find it. You took it to the grave, I assume. It was information, a spell rather than an…an artifact or anything like that. It must have been a ritual. You must have destroyed every trace of it. Did you destroy him, too?"

No, you little shit, I tried to say. *He destroyed* me.

I saw no sign that he heard or cared. He was speaking of

a man I dare not name, the only mystic Harry Houdini could never unmask as a fraud.

Because the man was not a fraud. God, I wish he had been.

I wonder what became of him. Last I heard, he was in Bohemia, on the trail of some exciting new discovery he never publicly named. Whatever it was, I do not know if he found it. He masked himself as an archaeologist and historian for his travels, and sometimes wrote articles he'd wire back to American newspapers. They were popular reading from coast to coast.

Well, I don't know. Let's say it wasn't a mask.

Let's say it was a cosmetic truth, and let it lie there. I do not know what guided him. I do not know who or what he answered to. I do not know if he died, or how he died, or if he was even capable of dying. After our bargain was completed, I never saw or spoke to the man again.

But how did this boy know? *What* did this boy know?

"I want what he gave you," my nephew announced. "The world is stacked against me. Everything is rigged. I can't get on my feet like this," he complained. No, he whined. "I need help. Extraordinary help. I need *you*. I want to know how you killed that little girl and if I'll need to do something similar. I can do it if I have to," he said with appalling earnestness. "But you screwed up. You didn't know what her mother would do."

He had me there. I sure as hell *hadn't*.

In a peculiar singsong voice, he said, "I don't think you killed yourself."

Fine. He was right about that, too.

"I think you're still here. I mean, I think *somebody* is. I hope it's you. Or someone who knows you and knows what you did. One way or another, I'm going to figure it out."

Jesus, I hoped not.

Even this terrible excuse for a descendant—obliquely, via my sister—I would have dissuaded even *him* from such a path if I'd been able. Perhaps I should have tried harder. I owed his grandmother that much.

I owed Eva, too. Even though... Christ, Coty should've been hers—not Maggie's.

My sister Margaret was of a type: capable, tough, practical. She was talented, too, of course. She had the mind of a mathematician, and she used it to design the most remarkable articles of clothing, to such success that I concluded that math must be art after all. Numbers must be the language of the structure of the universe for her to bend them so keenly to suit her will.

Eva was...not. She was brilliant in her way, of course. I'd never suggest otherwise. I loved her and would have cared for her spinster self into her old age, if I'd been able. She never had children of her own, and that's likely a kindness on the part of some fate, somewhere. I do not think she would have done well with a child.

Then again, Venita always reminded me of her a bit, so there's every chance that I'm wrong. Venita was a marvelous mother. She was protective without hovering, encouraging without being demanding, supportive without being too controlling. I think it surprised everyone. She had such a reputation for flirtation and frivolity, but there was a savvy undercurrent to her mind, I understand that now.

I understood it then, too.

But I *see* it clearly now, in a way I did not at the time.

Can you hear me, Veronica? Do you mind if I call you that? I like the name, even if you don't. You must not care for it, or you'd use it. Unless...if you're a woman who operates in the spheres of men, it may be of some benefit to wear such an ambiguous name. A "Ronnie" could be man or woman. The more I consider it, yes—the more I suspect it makes your life easier. You've made your decision, and I can respect that. What kind of gentleman refuses to call someone by their chosen moniker, after all?

But I hope you can hear me, if not now, then someday.

Or for the love of God, can *you* hear me, Venita? I'd even settle for you if you're listening. You hate me, yes? Then by all means, return to wakefulness and hate my flesh and blood by extension. Chase him away! Send him packing the way you sent the others when you were bored with them. Don't let him gain a toehold in this house.

He's worse than me, Venita. I want you to understand that.

I need for you to know: I would've sooner committed myself to the darkest regions of hell than harm your precious Priscilla. But this horrible boy... He would have killed her on purpose, thinking it was necessary and worth the trouble.

Ronnie

NOW

First things first: the house must become structurally sound, and it's a pretty far cry from that. It's nothing short of a miracle that it's still standing so successfully and that the second-story floor hasn't collapsed through the first-story ceiling. I'd like to smack whoever cut that hole around the remains of Mr. Crawford. It could've been done with planning and finesse, so as not to be a huge problem for the next person to come along.

Come morning, I tried to get myself some water for my instant coffee, and the pipes just shrieked dryly. With this aquatic rejection, I had to go "home" to take a shower and change, and honestly, that might've been for the best. It'd been a couple of days since I'd bathed, and I was starting to smell like the house, like it's been absorbing me, or infecting me, or… whatever metaphor makes you happiest, I guess.

I love this house, but it smells weird and it is not quiet—and

I don't think it's empty, either. I am never alone here, and I'm more confident of that than I would ever say out loud to Kate. She already thinks I'm nuts.

I mean, she isn't wrong.

Besides, I had plenty of real-life, living flesh-and-blood people to deal with that day, so I finished cleaning up and packed myself a fresh bag of stuff for the new old house and returned in time to meet the guys who were dropping off the dumpster. I didn't really have to be present for that, but it's good that I was; I got to tell them exactly where I wanted it, rather than let them leave it wherever they found it easiest. I had them leave it higher up the slope, as close to the house as they could get it, because that was easiest for *me*.

Look, I'm not an asshole when it comes to dealing with hired people. I've *been* hired people half my life, and I know how it goes. But when I'm spending my own money, I want to get what I paid for and not have it thrown at me, as my brother used to say.

While they were there, I chatted up a couple of the guys about finding day laborers to help me with the heavy shit. When I was younger and broker, I used to just drive down to the Home Depot and pick up whoever was at loose ends that day, but these days I'd rather go with referrals. Once or twice I accidentally nabbed a real weirdo.

The delivery driver told me he had a couple of guys in mind, a father and son who he'd trust with his life or his house. He gave me their card. I thanked him, and they left.

Now I had a dumpster and a lead on two guys to help me fill it.

I was perhaps unreasonably pleased about this, but you have to understand: a dumpster means your first step is in place. The second step is to remove all the stuff you can't save, or don't care to save. The rotted wood, warped trim, the boards from the windows, the old curtains, most of the library (alas), anything else you can imagine. The third step is to clean like a motherfucker, and then—*only then*—you'll know what you're really working with.

It's one thing to know an old house is in rough shape, and another to see it stripped down and empty. That's when you find out how good the bones really are. That's when you find the breaks, the fractures, the weak spots that need shoring up.

I called the number and talked to the dad, I think. His name was Carlos, and he said he'd come out next week to give me an estimate, which delighted me. I wanted to get started as soon as possible.

Kate was at work, so she wouldn't be around until the afternoon—if she intended to come around at all. I felt like we'd spent a lot of time together in the last few days. Maybe she could use a break from me.

I didn't really need a break from her, but I wouldn't be mad at one, either. I was still getting all my house-sorting ducks in a row, and I kind of liked being alone in the place anyway. Or... not alone, as the case may be.

No other living people, at least. Just me and the ghosts.

I strapped on my work gloves and got started with the smaller things I didn't want, throwing them into a wheelbarrow I'd found outside behind the house. The kitchen felt like a good place to begin, so I pulled everything off the counters and tossed it into trash bags. It was all garbage, including a stack of broken plates, a bread box that had collapsed into matchsticks, some soft stuff that might've once been rolls of paper towels but God only knew, and a moldering toaster oven with a cracked window and a Bakelite outlet plug as big as a crab apple.

I was mildly surprised to find the cabinets were empty, or almost empty. I scraped out three rat corpses that were somehow both desiccated and soggy at the same time, a smattering of old silverware that wasn't silver or worth anything, and a set of *Southern Living* cookbooks that had become a solid boulder of moisture-glued paper and cardboard.

Once, there had been a backsplash, but half the tiles had fallen off the wall. I didn't even need a pry bar to pick off the rest, so I tackled that next.

And so forth, and so on.

The last thing I did was pull down the half curtain and rod that served as a privacy screen for the window over the sink. No one was back there anyway. I tugged the mountings free with my hands; the walls around the window were the consistency of damp chalk.

I tossed the whole shebang back into the wheelbarrow and stared out the window to see what kind of view I had. It didn't overlook the Sound; that was the other side of the house. This was mostly facing the ridge, and some trees, and a lot where another house had burned down decades ago—but nothing had been built to replace it.

Something pale moved at the edge of those trees.

I did a double take and squinted. It was small, whatever it was. And it was gone. "Must be the cat Anne was talking about," I told myself. People often let them come and go, which I don't like, but hey—they're not my cats, and it's not up to me. I hadn't gotten a good enough look at that one to tell if it was wearing a collar or tags, but the plumber was right. It was pretty.

I thought about the rat corpses I'd swept into the bin, and I considered putting out some tuna. If a cat's gonna hang around the house, it ought to make itself useful.

Finally, I took a break for lunch. I went to a sandwich place that was pretty close, and while I was out, I stopped by the storage unit where we keep a bunch of Ben's old stuff. Well, Ben's and mine. We pooled a lot of equipment, and I was going to need tools. I also grabbed a box of extra-strength trash bags for good measure.

Back at the house, I decided my next priority would be turning the water back on so I could use the bathrooms again. I don't know that much about plumbing, but I had a water key and I'd been paying attention when the cute flannel-butch-plumbing woman was making the rounds.

I pried up the cover to the city-water connection by the street, turned the valve, and then I had...well, it wasn't *good* water, but it was water. And just in time, because I'd gotten a thirty-two-ounce soda with that sandwich, and it'd gone right through me.

The powder room was closest, so I went inside. I didn't shut the door. I've lived alone so long that I have to remind myself to close it when other people are around; besides, the room was barely big enough to turn around in, and very dark—though God, I loved that peacock wallpaper.

While I peed, I ran one hand along a feather, feeling the texture catch the edge of my nails like the wall had fingerprints of its own. The paper was good quality, and it'd been installed by a pro who knew what they were doing. It never would've lasted so long otherwise.

When I finished I stood up, fixed my jeans, and turned to the sink by pure habit—flicking the hot water lever because hope springs eternal. A thin, dirty stream dribbled from the faucet. I don't know why I bothered; it was just the habit of muscle memory. I didn't have any soap in there, anyway. I added soap to my mental list.

And since I was there, I looked in the mirror to see how wild my hair had become over the course of the day thus far.

It was bad. Real bad.

I ran my hands through it and wondered if I had a bandanna in the car. Wait. Did I have some schmutz on my face? Had I left the house like that? Gotten food like that?

I flipped the light switch to get a better look. Nothing happened. I opened the door wider to let in more light from the hallway and drew my face up close to the mirror. Yup, I had a streak of something dark across my forehead and dusting one cheek. I hoped it wasn't mold, but it probably was.

Something flickered behind me.

I whipped around. Pure reflex. Left one hand on the side of the ceramic pedestal sink and raised the other one to...to...I don't know. Push back. Hold at bay. Something. Someone.

No, I was still alone.

The room was too small to hide anyone, and no, the light wasn't working, but yes, the door was still open and I could see just fine from the light out in the hall. I looked at the mirror again. Around the edges, it was cloudy with age. I'd probably gotten a glimpse of my own elbow.

No. There it was again.

Someone standing behind me. Just the shape of someone, barely an outline, only a trace of a shadow to fill it in—a more evolved version of the figure I'd seen in the dust from the tarp. My heart rate spiked. I felt a warm pink flush creeping up my neck, seeping past my collarbone.

I forced myself to stare straight ahead, into my own eyes, not flinching away or looking back. I said, "I see you," and my voice hardly shook at all.

But I heard nothing in reply, and the figure did not move. It didn't shift like it breathed, and it didn't loom or threaten. I got the funniest sense that it was confused. Did it want my attention? Could it see me? Was I losing my mind? Misinterpreting the age-fogged mirror and a slight bend in the glass?

The head shook. Back and forth. Slowly and slightly, but perceptibly.

I fought the twin urges to scream and run. My anxiety waged war with my curiosity, and neither one was able to strike a killing blow. Both ran rampant between my ears, settling in my stomach like a hot slug of lead.

The thing that had joined me in the powder room was taller than me, and wider, too. I guessed it for a man by likelihood, and maybe by some instinct about its posture or shape. The longer I stared at it, the less I could convince myself that I was only seeing things.

I should've left, shut the door, locked it, boarded over it, and put up an Out of Order sign.

Instead, I whispered, "Hello?"

And I heard nothing in return. I couldn't even tell if the shadow was trying to reply.

"Hugh? Mr. Crawford?" My gut said no, but I didn't know why. My gut is a fool at times, and it's not to be trusted, but every now and again, I trust it anyway. When you're alone, you take the advice you can get. "Someone else?"

I thought the head nodded, but it was getting hard to tell. It was fading. I was losing it, whatever it was.

"Hello?"

It evaporated. If it'd ever been there in the first place.

No. Too late for that.

I don't get to second-guess these things when I've stared them down long enough to be sure they're no illusion. "All right," I said, planting my hands on either side of the sink. They were clammy with sweat, and they slipped when I leaned forward.

I looked at the mirror again, locking on to my own eyes, and telling myself, "All right, someone's here in the house with me. I figured that out already." As if that meant it wasn't a problem and I shouldn't be afraid.

I shouldn't worry.

"Fuck," I concluded. I left the powder room and let the door swing shut behind me. It clapped loudly, slamming against the frame. I jumped at the noise but kept moving. I refused to be intimidated in my own house. Someone had been standing there with me, in the powder room. Behind me.

Whoever I'd seen, it hadn't been a starlet.

According to the internet, Venita Rost was a petite thing, maybe a hair over or under five feet. I'm several inches taller than that, and whoever I saw was considerably bigger than me.

I paused by the staircase landing. I gripped the banister. It creaked, but I didn't let go. I needed it for support.

Yeah, my ghost was a guy. A large guy, with the posture of a man who knows he's big and who does not wish to frighten anyone with his size. There was a slouch to it, an inward hunker of the shoulders. It was the posture of someone big speaking to someone small.

An obvious suspect sprang to mind. After all, Venita had described the investigator as a large, handsome man. "Was that you?" I asked the empty landing. "Bartholomew Sloan?"

Nothing and no one answered. Nothing rattled on the walls, seeking attention.

I wondered if I could find an actual photo of the guy online and get an idea of what he'd looked like in life. After all, everyone knows all knowledge is contained within the internet.

"I know you were a big guy." Then I said the thing I really meant, when I circled the thought with questions and theories. "I hope you were also a *good* guy."

Because, real talk: Even if he solved crimes, found lost property, located missing people, and struggled to defend a friend he believed to be innocent…when it comes to a big man's intentions, there's no telling—so you'd better play it safe when you can and hope for the best when you can't.

I did not like the idea of a big man's ghost lurking in my house.

Never mind what I'd told Kate about stray cats and stray spirits; never mind everything I'd ever heard about ghosts not actually harming anyone. Never mind my itchy brain that worried and worried—it wasn't the kind of brain that made things up, and I have never been the kind of mentally ill that "sees" things. No matter how hard I tried, I could not convince myself that the incident had not occurred.

I am anxious, yes. I am *not* delusional.

I tried to soften the thought of sharing my house with the dead instead, chewing on it until I could swallow it as easy as oatmeal. I had to. I felt like I was choking on glass.

The one saving grace of a *bad* big man is that he's probably slow. You can probably dodge and outrun a big man if you have to. Yes, push come to shove, I'd rather deal with a big, slow man than a small, fast one.

This thought let some of the air out of my anxiety bubble. Not much, but a smidge. Where else could I poke it? Where else could I release some pressure?

I reminded myself that there were no credible accounts of ghosts doing physical harm to a person, never mind the oddball TV shows that swear to scratches and pushes. I could handle a scratch or two. (More air went out of the bubble.) I could be extra careful around the stairs and the hole in the floor in the room with the view. (More air, a soft mental hissing.)

Shit, he might even be friendly. (That one didn't help much.)

Still twitching slightly, still looking for clues and comfort, I burned off nervous energy by checking up and down the hall, then pacing into the foyer, the library, the parlor with my air mattress, and back into the kitchen—which seemed very bright, now that it was mostly empty and the curtains were gone. I stood at the sink and stared into the yard.

Outside, sitting still beside a tree, was a light-colored cat with eyes so green I could see them from across the lawn. It blinked at me, licked its paw, and disappeared back into the orchard.

Venita Rost
1932

It's been a highly entertaining couple of days in the big new house: we've had an unexpected guest! Sometimes an unexpected guest is not the first thing you want, or the precursor to a good time at all—but in this case, the guest in question is Mr. Sloan, who had fully intended to stop by for a day or two to visit with my husband. However, my poor husband is stranded in Portland due to a surprise snowstorm that's thrown the whole region into disarray.

You'd think that being so far north, Washington and Oregon would be better prepared for such weather—but you'd be wrong. We don't get snow here, not more than a few flakes at a time, and those come none too often... So when they do, people absolutely lose their minds.

We got five inches in Seattle, but we got them just late enough to allow Mr. Sloan to arrive and become trapped here. With us. Me and Priscilla, I mean.

I know it's not the interlude he expected, and I might've assumed he'd be annoyed at the inconvenience of it all, stuck indoors with a friend's wife and a little girl who hovers at his heel, asking him a thousand questions per hour.

But he's so patient with her, it's so adorable. Maybe he thinks of it as a respite from asking questions himself, since that's much of his job, to hear him tell it. He says it's all "legwork and jaw-work," walking around and talking to people. That's all it takes to solve mysteries, find missing people, and track down stolen property. I know he's filing off the edges to make it easier for Prissy to understand, and I appreciate how he muddles details that might be above her head or things that might upset her (at her tender age).

For dinner this evening, I made a quick meal out of what we had on hand: a rich potato-and-corn stew like my grandmother made; it's perfect for throwing in all the odds and ends that linger in the kitchen, and it's hard to mess up. I added some good French bread that was starting to go stale but was revived with some garlic and butter and a few minutes in the oven. We finished off the meal with some baked apples I'd made on the fly with some brown sugar, cinnamon, and the season's last offerings from the orchard.

I love that orchard. I'm so glad we bought it, and the land next to it. I'm so glad we put our house here.

I'm not hopeless in a kitchen, you know. I didn't come from money, and I don't need a housekeeper or cook to feed myself or my family. It's just as well. The streetcars weren't running and neither were the cabs. The city on the other side of the Sound is a quiet white ghost town, and here in West Seattle, it's much the same.

But I can make do, and Mr. Sloan did not complain. He helped himself to a third serving, I believe, and polished off the last of the garlic bread while he was at it. I'd like to think that Oscar will be proud of me to hear it. He doesn't quite treat me like a hothouse orchid, but sometimes he's too eager to pay someone else to do something I can do just fine for myself, thank you very much.

He means well. Most people do, I think.

Mr. Sloan certainly does. I've never seen a childless man quite so taken with a child—and not in the way that makes a mother wary. He seems to genuinely enjoy her presence, her energy, her incessant questions. He makes room for her in a conversation. He is never short with her, and never unkind.

After we ate, we played some board games in the parlor while the Victrola played the new records I got from the shop downtown last month, and when we'd listened to those, we turned on the radio.

Priscilla, invigorated by the presence of an audience, decided that she wanted to put on her coat and hat and muff, and go play in the snow—but I declared that it was getting too late for that, because it was, and honestly, I know that little stinker: she wanted to go up to the overlook on the ridge and watch the boats pass by below. And I simply don't trust it. I trust her motives, of course, but I don't trust the weather. I don't trust the snow, how it sometimes sits on top of ice. It's too dangerous.

So we played one more game—gin rummy, this time, and Mr. Sloan taught her how. She sat beside him and squinted at his cards with intense concentration and a seriousness that makes me giggle to think of it, even now. He called her his "consultant," and she helped him play his hands.

Finally, it was time for bed for the baby, and a nightcap for Momma.

Mr. Sloan joined me in the parlor in front of the fireplace, which was absolutely blazing because that's just how I like it. It's the only thing that makes the cold tolerable: an excessively lovely heat source, preferably one that looks and feels like a blast furnace with a marble surround.

I had some bourbon, the good stuff that Oscar brought me from when he passed through Kentucky. You know they still let them make it there, during Prohibition? One place stayed open, anyway. Something about industrial or medicinal uses, and I'm absolutely confident that no one, anywhere, ever used industrial or medicinal bourbon for anything like leisure.

Christ, that was a silly decade. I'm thrilled that it's over.

But Mr. Sloan, he had gin. I can't stand the stuff and I don't keep it around for myself, but Mr. Sloan arrived with some of his own—and I can appreciate a fellow who travels with his own vices, rather than feeling the need to seek them out everywhere he goes. Not that discretion has ever been one of the greater parts of my personal valor, but I can admire it in others.

I told him to leave it on the bar cart, and when it was gone, I'd see about having a bottle for him next time he comes.

"Even though you swear it smells like turpentine?"

"Well it does smell like turpentine, and you'll never convince me otherwise. I don't know how you can drink that stuff; I'd use it to clean grease out of a rug, myself." I'd already had a swig or two from the Kentucky bottle, poured into one of the little crystal glasses that feel too fancy to use when I'm alone, and that's silly. Maybe I should use them more often. Maybe I deserve nice things, and I can afford nice things, and I don't have to save nice things for guests or special occasions.

As if to show me how wrong I was about the gin, Mr. Sloan

downed half his drink in a swallow or two and licked his lips. "If it makes you feel any better—and why would it, but let's try—I think bourbon smells suspiciously like horse piss and smoke."

"Even the fancy stuff?"

He cocked the glass and an eyebrow at me. "Especially the fancy stuff. That's Thoroughbred horse piss and smoke, right there."

He was only being funny, so I laughed. It's always best to laugh when men are being funny, or even when they only think they are. That's something I should probably teach Prissy, for the sake of her future self-preservation. Not all men are as easygoing as Mr. Sloan, or so open to being gently teased about their preferences.

I suppose it sounds nearly suspicious, to say that I drank late into the night with Mr. Sloan, in our lovely parlor with the tremendous fireplace, while the snow fell outside and collected along the ridge, while the radio played quietly.

But there was nothing salacious about any of it. We only talked, and there was never any suggestion of anything untoward.

I think he must be a very good man, this Mr. Sloan. He's helped so many people, and he's such a good friend to Oscar that he can even be trusted to stay the night with Oscar's wife, without any hint of impropriety.

On the contrary, we chatted about Oscar, first and foremost, as he was the primary interest we held in common. But when we'd exhausted our store of anecdotes about the man, we wandered to more personal topics. He asked about my family, and I told him just enough. I'm not embarrassed to have grown up poor any more than I'm embarrassed to be rich right now—but once or twice, we had times that were too hard to talk about, even among friends. I kept it shallow.

"After my father died in the threshing accident, we moved

west—out to California. I started working at a deli down the street from the big new studio that had just opened up."

"How old were you then?" he asked.

"Not quite sixteen when I started the job, and just a hair over sixteen when one of the executives came inside for a sandwich. He saw me, asked if I ever thought about being in the pictures, and the rest was history." I said it breezily, leaving out the parts he wouldn't have enjoyed hearing. It's never really that simple, when a grown man offers something nice to a teenage girl, but that's how the world works, isn't it?

"What a fortunate fellow, stumbling upon a beautiful young woman who turned out to be so talented," he said graciously.

"I wouldn't say I was talented right off the bat. It took a good deal of hard work and long hours. God, the hours were long," I moaned. "Twelve-hour days or more, sometimes. It took forever to get every shot set up, and if somebody blew a take? I tell you, I burst into tears the first time a director shouted at me for something that wasn't my fault—and I almost died the first time I was shouted at for something that was."

"Sounds like there was a lot of shouting."

"So much shouting," I happily confirmed. "Everyone trying to be heard, every moment. Shouting through the megaphone, shouting to the grips and the cameramen, and the scriptwriters and the extras. Good God. It was chaos at times."

His cheeks were pink with the warmth and the booze, and he'd melted down into his seat quite comfortably. He swirled the surviving contents of his glass—though they were not long for this world—and he let it rest atop his knee. "Surely there must have been good times. You can't have stayed in the industry as long as you did purely for the money."

He was right on the former, and wrong about the latter. I would've absolutely kept at it for the money. Twelve-hour days and a gauntlet of fanny-grabbers still beat being a hungry hobo living out of a train car.

But I didn't bother him with that.

I said, "Good times? Plenty of them, yes. Do you have any idea how many handsome men I kissed before I met Oscar? How many exotic locations I pretended to visit?"

"Did you ever visit any real exotic locations?" he asked curiously.

"Only a couple of times. I'd generally prefer to take the sound stages above the locations."

He killed off the contents of the glass and set it on the little table at his elbow. "And why is that?"

"Pure practicality. A good studio can build a jungle or a desert, a mountaintop or a ship. But if you tried to film a movie in such a place, you'd have to consider the needs of the production and the needs of a crew. It takes a small city's worth of people to complete any project, and they all must be fed and sheltered, and the film itself is fragile—so many things can ruin it..."

I might have rambled, but it's a subject on which I have some expertise. Or some experience, if you can call those two things different. But Mr. Sloan was very patient with me, and when I realized that I'd monopolized the chatter, I turned the tables on him.

"Now it's your turn, sir. How did you decide on detective work? Where did you come from, besides 'New York'?" I said the city with the accent Oscar liked to use, poking a bit of fun.

"I did not come from New York," he repeated it back at me with a twinkle in his eye. "I came from Maine, if you must know. The accents are different, but I've worked hard to file mine off. I find that a more *neutral mode of speech works better when gathering information for the purposes of crime-solving."*

"I suppose that makes sense. Unless you're solving crimes in Maine. Then you might want to remind them you're a hometown boy, right?"

"Right," he agreed. "But I have solved suspiciously few crimes in Maine, now that you mention it. Either it's an upstanding state, or the criminals are so successful as to go undetected."

"Truly, the money must lie elsewhere."

"Correct, and that's why I headed for the big city. New York was overflowing with crime of every color, every kind, every level. To be frank, it was quite easy to build a reputation there. It was the easiest-possible location to establish oneself as a righter of wrongs, a solver of puzzles. After all, there are so many to go around."

I was fishing for more personal details, so I said, "Your family must be very proud of you." But I regretted it immediately.

He did not darken, exactly, but the twinkle left his eye. "My mother died when I was young. My father worked himself to death in the cannery before I finished college—and I was the first to do so. In the family, I mean."

"That's something to be proud of! I never went," I admitted. "Didn't finish high school, either. Stopped at seventh grade because that's when Daddy died, and I had to go to work."

"I'm afraid that's true of so many promising young people. You would've been a brilliant student, I'm confident of it."

There he went again, turning the topic back to me. I wouldn't let him get away with it that easily. "Thank you for the vote of confidence, I honestly appreciate it. Now, tell me, do you have any siblings? Any family left at all?" I would have asked about children, but he doesn't wear a ring and I didn't want to make assumptions.

"I have two younger sisters, yes. Eva and Margaret. Margaret is a brilliant dressmaker and has her own shop out in Syracuse these days. She's married with four children of her own, two of them gingers like the rest of us." He said that part with a faint smile. "Eva never married, but she helps at the shop. She's a fine seamstress herself, and I suspect that Margaret appreciates the child-rearing assistance."

"I could hardly blame her! Merely one child is exhausting enough. Even a very good one, like Priscilla—and she is very good, you know. Such a brilliant and charming thing; she's rarely any trouble at all."

Now he struck an indignant pose, as if I'd compelled him to defend her honor. "Madam! You malign that precious creature with your implications! I'd be shocked to learn that she's ever any trouble whatsoever!"

I laughed and finished my own drink. "She's not the bad mischievous sort, is what I meant—or not the difficult variety of mischievous. She's full of questions and opinions, and she's not yet old enough to know when it is—and isn't—appropriate to apply them, and that's troublesome at times. Just the other day, she hassled the grocer about the state of his stock because the apples were bruised... when she's the one who knocked them off the table. By accident," I assured him quickly.

"Oh no, she'd never do such a thing on purpose. I'd never stand for such slander on her behalf."

"She's a lucky girl, to have such a champion," I told him warmly. Actually, by that point in the night, I was doing everything warmly. I was already warm from the booze, and the fireplace was dying down but the parlor was practically an oven. I yawned, stretched, and rose from my own seat.

He said, "Yes, I do suppose it's about that time."

"Time? Good heavens, don't tell me what time it is. I know it's late, and there's a reason we've called Priscilla 'the rooster' since she was born. If you'll excuse me, Mr. Sloan, I'm afraid I must call it a night. I trust your room is set up according to your needs?"

"Madam, the room is perfect—and I cannot thank you enough for your hospitality, and for the joy of your company on an otherwise dreary winter evening."

He was laying it on a little thick, but I'm not the kind of girl to let a compliment go unappreciated. I thanked him, wished him good night, and went back to my own room—stopping by Priscilla's before I settled in.

I cracked the door open and peered inside to see her perfect, round, sleeping face lying so sweetly on the pillow that I thought my heart would burst. She snored very softly, almost a tiny whistle. It was the most precious thing I've ever seen, but I closed the door and tiptoed to my own quarters, where I slept alone.

Ronnie

NOW

I've always been more of a dog person.

The pale, roaming animal is definitely a cat, and a funny-colored one: it's not quite white, not quite silver... almost a very pale blond. You might even call it "platinum."

I've never had a cat of my own, but I know plenty of people who keep them. I wouldn't hurt one, and I would stop anybody else from hurting one, so it's not like I hate them or anything. It's nothing personal. I just don't like being responsible for anything other than myself.

I still thought about putting out some tuna, though. Maybe I'd grab an extra can or two on my next trip to the grocery store. I like rats a lot less than I like cats.

In the throes of my panic spiral, I'd missed a call. I checked my phone, and it was just the dumpster-company manager—or office person, or whatever—confirming that I'd rented the dumpster in two-week increments and reminding me of the payment schedule and all that. No big deal.

I took a deep breath and shook off the lingering shudders as best I could, and I considered calling Kate—just to tell someone what had happened. But I wasn't quite ready for that. The shudders weren't all the way gone, and I didn't want to subject Kate to my presence when I'm...not on an even keel, shall we say.

She's aware that I have issues, obviously, but I've protected her from the worst of them. Or...let's be honest, now. I've protected *myself* and my dignity by not letting her see the crying, the shaking, the spinning brain that fires stupid thoughts out of my mouth and snaps at people who only want to help.

I really, really didn't want her to see me like that.

I looked at my phone. I didn't want her to hear me like that, either.

Even though I was much calmer than half an hour before, I was pretty sure that if I tried to hold a normal conversation with anybody, I would fall apart. So I didn't call her. I didn't text. I needed more time to get my shit together.

I needed to get moving. Get self-distracting.

I snapped open some trash bags and got back down to business. It was either that or curl up into a ball somewhere and let the rest of it pass—and I had stuff to do. Might as well put the nervous energy to work rather than let it eat me up while I hid under a blanket.

I cracked my knuckles and tackled the butler's pantry, but that didn't take long; I just scooped things off shelves and into a bag, then tossed all the bags into the wheelbarrow and ran them outside to the dumpster. When I was finished you couldn't call it clean, but you could call it empty. I moved on to the upstairs bathroom, then quit when I had it stripped down to the fixtures. The water was still barely functional and very brown, and not at all warm no matter how long I let it run. I left the tap open as long as I did as a thought experiment, I guess. I didn't really think the heater would magically kick on.

I stared in the mirror up there for longer than I ever tend to look at myself, wondering if I'd see someone behind me again, or in front of me, or however that worked—but no. Maybe it only happened in the powder room.

But I was thinking about water and thinking about the Sound, and I turned off the faucet, then left the bathroom and crossed the hall, letting myself inside the closed-up room where Hugh Crawford had died the year before.

It's a beautiful room, if you can ignore the hole in the floor—but you can't, because you have to give it a wide berth. The edges of the hole are rough and weak; I probably weigh 150 pounds or so, and I don't trust any flooring that's missing major sections of its joists. But there's still space to walk around, and the huge panoramic windows are really something else.

I tiptoed as lightly as possible around the tarp-covered floor and cringed with every creak, groan, and whine from the wood underfoot. It was only my imagination, the way it bowed beneath me. It wouldn't even kill me if it gave way, I bet.

It was a stupid thought, but it made me grin, anyway, and it distracted me until I could reach the window. I saw a ferry and a cargo ship crossing the smooth, gray expanse of the Sound, and it was both peaceful and creepy, the way they barely seemed to move at all from this distance.

I've been on a ferry before. They move faster than you'd think.

"Hey, Hugh, was that you, in the downstairs powder room earlier? You're the most recent ghost on the premises, I guess. Does that mean you're the strongest? I don't know…" I started to say more, but my head was still a little scrambled from the powder room panic attack, and I'd lost my thought as I suddenly remembered I'd meant to look up the late, great Detective Sloan.

I pulled my phone out of my back pocket and went to the world's *actual* greatest detective: Inspector Google.

In a matter of seconds I had dozens of articles about the man himself, as well as some photos—one of which showed him standing in a group of other men, and yes, now he was suspect number one for the man in the mirror. He was at least half a head taller than everyone else in the photo, with a barrel chest and a tidy beard.

"Helloooo, Mr. Sloan. You were a handsome gent, I must say. Good fashion sense, too." He was wearing a very nice three-piece suit, tailored perfectly. Couldn't tell what color it was, of course, but I recognize a good cut when I see one.

I let myself get distracted by the articles, most of which were either general biographies or selected cases via "lesser-known cool people of history" websites, plus a couple of pieces about his death in the house I'd just bought. I read through one or two of those while I was standing there, and then I felt something shift under my feet—which reminded me where I was, and why I shouldn't be hanging out there.

"Whoops…" I declared, and I skirted the edge of the hole

all the way back to the door. "One of these days, I oughta put a reading nook up here or something like that. Eventually." It was too nice a space to leave as a guest bedroom.

I liked talking out loud. My voice didn't quiver anymore, and I didn't feel the mottled pink heat around my chest and throat. I sounded normal. I had successfully talked myself down from a pretty hardcore freak-out, and expended enough anxious energy that I was now a little tired but otherwise feeling all right.

A "little" tired, who am I kidding.

A final, small yelp of anxiety shouted from the depths that the house was so big, too big, I-had-bitten-off-more-than-I-could-chew big. I would surely go broke and die in this house like everyone else.

But it was a tiny yelp, and I knew to ignore it.

This house has more space than I'll ever need, for anything. I'm half afraid that when all's said and done, I'll wind up with a bunch of empty rooms I have to pay to keep heated all winter, but I'll cross that bridge when I get to it. Likewise, I realized I'd have to go shopping eventually. I didn't feel the need to populate the whole house with wild furnishings, but it'd be nice to someday furnish some of the space, even if I wasn't using it.

I don't really enjoy shopping, unless it's thrifting or yard sales. Nothing new is quite so cool as an object with a story.

Speaking of.

I swallowed the last of my simmering anxiety and considered that I might have some options within easy reach.

I'm not really a furniture girl, if I'm honest. I can't tell an antique from a reproduction; but this house still had some of its furnishings, and none of them could possibly be any newer than the seventies—since I didn't think Hugh had brought anything with him. They were all covered and stationary, scattered around the house in various assorted corners. I'd been ignoring them because, like I said. Furniture isn't my thing. I want something comfortable that won't fall apart when I use it. That's the sum of my furnishing requirements.

In general, with clothes, furniture, and everything else: If it isn't vintage, I don't much care what it looks like.

But now I was curious.

Had Bartholomew Sloan, or Venita Rost, or her husband or child…had any of them ever touched any of those things? Sat in those chairs? Played that piano?

Piano? Wait. Yes, I knew there was a piano; even under the sheeting, it was immediately recognizable in the otherwise unremarkable "music room" on the first floor, but it wasn't like I could play it. I can't even read music. But that's not what made me think of it. I could hear music very faintly. Maybe? It must've been coming from outside—or that's what I told myself. I'm such a terrible liar that I didn't quite believe it.

Since I was thinking about the piano, I followed the music downstairs, down the hall, to the nondescript room at the end. I could still hear it. A little louder now. The soft plunk of keys being depressed, of hammers striking wires. Not quite a tune, but not quite…*not* a tune, either.

When I reached the music room, the music stopped. Or I stopped hearing it, if that's what happened.

I'm not sure. I don't really think it was coming from outside, but there I was, and the piano was covered with a sheet. The sheet was covered with a layer of dust thick enough to muffle sound, and I powdered the whole damn room—myself included—when I shook it free. I squinted and wiped my eyes, but they went on itching anyway.

It was grim in there. I hadn't opened the curtains the other day because most of the interesting stuff was down the other wing. So I did that now, and it improved the situation a little. Kind of. It certainly gave me a better look at what I was working with.

The instrument looked like it might have been expensive once, and it was in one piece, so that was something. I ran my fingers over the surface and left shiny trails behind in the grime. There was a label over the keys: Sauter. "Never heard of it," I muttered to myself, then I pulled out my phone again and learned that it was a European company of considerable repute.

I wondered if the piano still worked, so I pressed a few keys and let the notes ring out. They were janky notes, all off-key with a muted, mournful tone. Lying on the floor, I saw a music stand that was rusting into crumbles, and with that, I'd officially covered all the room's highlights.

I left, opened the rear door wide, and grabbed my wheelbarrow to start cleaning things out in earnest.

By the time I'd worked my way back to the parlor, I'd decided to tidy up my sleeping area and the rest of the room. It wasn't clean but it wasn't that cluttered, and there were three shrouded items that I'd left covered out of laziness and lack of interest in furniture. But now I pulled down a sheet and discovered a moth-eaten chair whose wool upholstery collapsed when I touched it. Coiled metal springs stuck out from the empty spots and the worn places, and one of the wooden legs had gotten wet and rotted.

The chair was trash, which made me sad. I liked the shape of it.

Under the next sheet, I found an honest-to-God Victrola. The cabinet was a work of art, and I found the trumpet stashed inside a compartment beneath the record holder. Not a crack in sight. If I could restore it, get it to play again…that would really be something. Or I so thought. I already knew it wasn't worth much. Those things turn up in antique malls and junk shops all the time. It's hard to get (or manufacture) parts for them these days, so people tend to toss them—or hipsters turn them into bar cabinets, something like that.

Not me. I like to fix shit.

I figured that surely somewhere in the greater Seattle area, I could find someone to tell me how much trouble it'd be worth to save. And by "trouble," I mean "money." Maybe I'd stumble upon a vintage-musical-equipment enthusiast with a 3D printer or something. You never know.

Then, under the third sheet, I found actual treasure. Not buried, just covered.

"Well, fuck me running," I marveled.

It was a bar cart, a nice one made of brass and glass and in need of a good polishing. It still had a full crystal serving set, a decanter and tumblers, and some old bottles of booze with labels that were absolute artwork, if you asked me.

Most of the bottles were Canadian, and some of the labels looked like they might have been, uh, independently produced—which would make sense, considering the age of the house and when it'd been occupied.

Canadian booze-running during Prohibition isn't exactly a regional secret.

I also saw some good ol' American standards: representatives of Kentucky and Tennessee, and some gin that came from Brooklyn, if the label could be believed.

"Never heard of any gin from Brooklyn," I admitted to the empty room.

But someone replied anyway: *Don't drink that.*

I whipped around, dropping the drape back over the cart. I was too shocked to guess where the voice had come from, or from whom. A feeble ray of light shined in through the east window, stretching down from a break in the clouds; in it, I saw sparkles of dust flickering in the air, spinning slowly, and the shape of something. Someone.

I watched it, or I watched its absence—trying to convince myself there was nothing to see there, because I'd only recently calmed myself down from the powder room incident and I did *not* need the bonus jump scares to set me off again. But there was a gap in the dust the same as before, a space in the shape of a person. They stood beside the old chair that no one would likely occupy ever again.

I heard the voice clearly but barely, like the shouted words of a friend at the other end of a crowded bar. *It's not for you*, it said, and then the tragic excuse for a sunbeam was gone—and so was the unexpected shape of someone lingering in the air, in the parlor.

Outside I heard a little noise that was almost a cry, almost the yelp of a baby.

I looked out the window and saw the platinum cat again,

but only for an instant. It didn't run off. It didn't fade like the Cheshire cat, leaving only a smile behind. It was there beside the dumpster, and then it wasn't.

And I hadn't even blinked.

Ronnie

NOW

Hands shaking, I only dropped my phone once in an effort to call Kate. She picked up on the third ring, and I immediately started babbling at her. "Katie, this place is haunted. Like, *super* haunted, and I think the ghosts are trying to get my attention, and it's freaking me *out*."

"Whoa, there, Dr. Venkman…slow your roll. I thought you liked the idea of resident ghosts? Like feral cats, remember?"

"And there's a *cat*," I added insistently. "Except I don't think it's real. Or it's real, but it's also a ghost, maybe. You know what they called Venita Rost, right? The Platinum Pussycat?"

"Is…is the cat platinum colored? Do cats come in that color?"

"This one does," I said, almost embarrassed to be so breathless. I was still in the parlor, now milling around in the spot where there was plenty of dust and no ghost to speak of, and no cat outside the window. I can't sit still while I talk on the phone during the best of times, and now I was pacing in circles at top speed, practically wearing a ring into the floor. "It's that silvery-blond color, just a hint of yellow to it. Green eyes. Big green eyes."

"Did Venita Rost have green eyes?"

"Yes," I said more confidently than I should have. I didn't actually know; it just sounded right to say so.

I heard her shift the phone in her grasp. "You want me to come over? We can do lunch. Maybe you and that house could use a little time apart."

"Yeah," I said, and the thought calmed me. Just enough to stop me from babbling about the spirits of big, handsome men in powder rooms. "Yeah, we can do lunch and look for the cat and, uh…" I reached for a normal subject, free of spooks. The only thing I could think of was: "I can show you my new dumpster."

"You bought a dumpster?"

"I'm renting one," I confirmed. "For a whole month, and I might need it for two. Don't know yet." My blood pressure was dropping as I talked, and I forced myself to sound normal. Fake it till you make it, they say—and fuck me, but it works. The more I talked, the more I settled down. "I'm trying to clear out all the stuff I can by myself. Before I have to hire people, you know. I've got a lead on a couple of guys, though."

"You're working by yourself? When *I* exist? Let me just grab some takeout, and I'll show up, and I'll help."

"Don't you have a job?"

"I can knock off early. I finished the only project with a pressing deadline," she assured me. Kate was a freelancer who wore many hats; she'd gotten her start volunteering on local political campaigns, and it'd parlayed into her own little cottage industry of website management and PR consulting at the local level.

"If you're sure." I didn't want to dissuade her, but I didn't want to beg, either. And I desperately wanted takeout. Who knew seeing ghosts could make you so hungry?

"Give me an hour, and I'll see you soon."

We both hung up, and by then I'd even quit pacing around; I'd come to a stop in front of the gorgeous decorative mirror that used to hang beside the fireplace. It was important, and I knew it, but I didn't know how. Sure, it was beautiful, but that didn't mean *important*. It appeared heavy and vintage, and that might mean *valuable*—or then again, maybe not.

But something about it held my attention. It felt less like a mirror than a portal, which sounds like a stupid thing to say, I know. Every mirror feels that way, doesn't it? Even the one in the powder room.

I shot a glance toward the hall past the stairs, and toward the spot where the powder room was out of my line of sight.

No, I was alone again. Or at least, as alone as I ever was—so I ought to say that I felt the absence of any other distinct, concrete presence trying to get my attention.

"Don't drink it," I recalled out loud. "It's not for you." I'd remember the voice if I heard it again.

I went back to the bar cart and picked up the bottle again. I turned it over in my hands and read every line of the faded label. I swished the contents around. About a quarter of the contents remained, and they'd turned an odd color. When I removed the stopper and gave it a sniff, I didn't like the odor—but then again, I don't like gin.

I made a face and a sound to match, stopped the bottle up again, and tucked it back onto the bottom shelf of the cart. "Don't worry," I informed any ghosts who might be lingering in the corners, in the dust, or in the mirror. "I won't drink it. I've never liked the stuff. It's a pretty bottle, though. Love the label. Maybe I'll…turn it into a vase or something."

A loud knocking echoed through the foyer, and I almost jumped out of my skin.

It was Coty.

When I opened the front door, my face must've declared my shock and confusion, because he immediately gave me a small, friendly wave. "Hey, it's just me. Listen, I got a text from Kate a few minutes ago, and she said you were, uh, having a real time over here. Is everything okay?"

Now I was somehow both less confused and more. When had Kate given him her number? And what made her think I needed immediate company, rather than food?

I said, "Yeah, I guess? It's only—there's, um…" I tried and failed to think of a good reason to chase him away.

I didn't exactly like him, and I didn't trust him. Something was starting to seem a little too easy, a little bit "off," if you feel me. Even the bottle of Maker's couldn't put all my concerns to rest; the guy was just a little too good at looking harmless, a little too eager to ingratiate himself. It made me suspicious.

He said, "If you're in the middle of something, or, I don't know. This is just a welfare check, I swear. I'm not trying to insert myself into your day or anything."

"No, it's fine. I assume Kate's getting you food, too?"

"Is she?" he asked, but did not answer.

"Doesn't matter," I concluded. My solitude had ended, Kate was on her way, and I didn't dislike him enough to be rude. Besides, I kind of wanted some other definitely alive person inside the house with me. I stood aside and held the door. "Come on in. There's nothing to see right now, but an hour ago…things got *real weird* in here."

As if I'd snapped my fingers, I had his immediate and total attention. "'Weird' how?"

I led him into the parlor and gestured at the chair I'd uncovered, then flopped down on my air mattress; it bounced and hissed a little bit of air loose, but mostly kept its composure. "Oh, you know. Ghost stuff," I said with a dismissive wave of my hand, which surely underscored how totally unflapped I was by this development. As if I'm that good of a liar. "It's fine, really. Me and Kate talked about it already."

He took the recently uncovered vintage chair, despite its uncomfortable state, and I explained my "feral cat colony" theory of hauntings a little too earnestly, with considerably less confidence than when I'd laid it out for Kate. He nodded along as if I were making the utmost sense.

"But something happened today?" he prompted. "Not long ago? Nothing personal, but you seemed pretty rattled when you opened the door."

I filled him in on that, too. The figure in the mirror. The dust. The voice. The cat.

Once I got talking, I couldn't stop. It's easy to have a theory of hauntings when you don't ever really encounter any; it's somewhat less straightforward when it's *your* house and *your* ghosts, and *you're* the one they're trying to reach.

I know I'd told Kate that I didn't believe they could harm me, but the more I thought about it, the less certain I was. After all, the mirror on the floor was a sharp reminder that there was some agency at work besides my own. Maybe I'd only thought that my ghost theory was likely, or I told myself that much because I like old houses—and that's where ghosts tend to congregate.

"I thought I had it under control. I thought I could coexist comfortably with the lingering dead," I said dramatically. "Now I don't know." An old quote flickered through my head; I think it was Mike Tyson, of all people: "Everybody has a plan until they get punched in the face," or something like that. Well, I'd had a plan for ghosts until I found out I actually had some ghosts.

Now I was a little lost.

Coty's eyes widened at the cat bit. He got up from the chair, which groaned and squeaked even louder than my air mattress, and went to the window to squint outside. "And the cat disappeared? Into the trees?"

"No, it just *disappeared*. It was there, and I was staring at it, and then it was gone—and I wondered if it hadn't been in my head all along, except I've seen it several times now. It's... You know what? It's probably a perfectly normal stray that hangs around, catching rats. It's not a ghost. There can't possibly be such a thing as ghost cats."

He was stuck on the vermin bit. "You have rats?"

"I'd be stunned if I didn't," I confirmed. God knew I'd

already swept up a mountain of the telltale brown jelly beans they left lying around. Then I softened it for him, because the sudden panic on his face said that rats were not his jam. His sudden angst was almost—but not quite—endearing. "I haven't seen any living ones yet, so don't get too worked up about it, okay?"

"Okay," he said, eyeing the walls with a wariness that said he didn't believe me. Then he was distracted by the bar cart. "Oh, is this the gin? The stuff the ghost told you not to drink?"

"Yeah, and if I were you, I wouldn't drink it, either. To be on the safe side."

He collected the bottle and stared at it from several different angles, holding it up to the light in case it could tell him something it hadn't told me. "Supposedly my uncle Bart liked gin."

"Man, I don't even know my great-great-uncle's name." My family had never been very big, always a unit of one or two kids at most; we weren't the kind of wildly long-lived folks who stacked a few generations deep at a time.

"Yeah, but *my* uncle was famous. Kind of famous. In some circles."

"And you're the king of the fanboys." When he flashed me a look that said he disapproved of this assessment, I shrugged a half-assed apology. "Don't get me wrong. If I had a famous relative or ancestor, then sure—that relative would become infinitely more interesting than the ones I know about already."

"I heard stories about the guy for my whole life, and it's like…" He held on to the gin, carrying it with him like a teddy bear. Then he flopped back down into the old chair with enough vigor that I cringed for the poor antique as well as his ass, considering the exposed springs, but it held steady. "You gotta understand. In my family, nobody really *does* anything. Nobody is successful, nobody is important."

"Sounds like my family."

He shook his head at me. "Kate told me about your brother. He owned his own company and everything. That's something. It's more than anybody in my gene pool has done, that's for sure."

I was strongly tempted to ask him when the hell he and Kate had been talking about me and Ben, but that wasn't really my business, now, was it? Not only was it none of my business, but there wasn't a damn thing wrong with the two of them having a private conversation—and I'd sound like a psycho if I objected to it within anybody's earshot. So I kept that to myself, not least of all because I didn't like what it said about me, if I was jealous.

Was I jealous? Or was it something else?

"Ben was the family shining star," I said, not sure how else to spin it. "He worked his ass off to get that company off the ground, and he always had a head for business that I missed out on. I don't know who he inherited it from or if he just learned it somewhere along the way."

"Right. But in my family...well, shit. My dad drank himself to death when I was in high school—which I dropped out of, by the way, though I got my GED. My mom really checked out after he died. We were on welfare for a while, but then she ran off with some older guy about ten years ago, and last I heard she was in Alaska."

I didn't know what to say, so I said, "Wow."

"Tell me about it. My sister got knocked up at sixteen,

married the father, and now has a restraining order against him."

"Jesus, you guys *are* cursed."

"Feels that way." The way he looked at the bottle was almost…lovingly, yeah, that's how I'd put it. He looked at it like he adored it, this hypothetical relic of his ancestry. "The only guy who ever did anything was my Uncle Bart: East Coast investigative legend turned West Coast celebrity detective."

"But then he died. After this whole family died," I said with a vague gesture that indicated the house at large, but really just meant the people who'd built it. "Maybe your family curse didn't miss him after all."

"Shit, you don't think it's contagious, do you?"

"I don't believe in curses, so…no. I don't think yours is contagious."

"What about luck?" he asked curiously. "Do you believe in luck?"

"Luck amounts to random chance, if you ask me."

With just a hair more calculation in his voice, he asked, "But do you think it can be manipulated?"

"Manipulated?" I flashed an eye at the bar cart. This conversation was making me want to drink, and I was almost out of the bottle he'd left us. But no. I wasn't quite brave enough to try century-old booze.

"Sure," he nodded. "Don't you think some people are luckier than others? There must be some mechanism to it."

I disagreed, and I had a feeling that if I said so, it would lead to an even stupider train of conversation, so I only shrugged. "Sure, why not."

He was staring down at the bottle again, cradling it like a doll. "You think he drank out of this?"

"Maybe." I shrugged. "Venita Rost didn't care for it."

"She didn't? How do you know that?"

I shrugged at him again. "Read it someplace." Outside, I heard a car pulling up. It was Kate's; I knew the sound. I also knew what the look in his eyes said, so I told him, "But for real, you shouldn't try to drink that."

"Why not? It's alcohol. Alcohol gets fancier and more expensive as you age it."

"Not all of it," I told him, even though I didn't know if that was true or not. "That shit will make you sick, you mark my words."

"Or the *ghost's* words." He said it with a wink, but it irritated me anyway. "You know, I think this might be as close as I've ever been to Uncle Bart, touching something he probably touched."

"No family heirlooms left behind?"

He sighed happily. "Nope. Just this mostly empty bottle of gin that a ghost told you not to drink."

"Listen, I don't take much advice from living people, but if a dead person goes to the trouble to warn me? I feel like I should probably heed them."

Kate was coming up the steps; I could hear her boots stomping along, heavy as always, for someone so relatively petite otherwise. I've never heard anyone so small walk so loudly in my life, I swear.

I got up off my air mattress/couch and opened the door before she could knock. "Come on in, babe. Ooh, you got Mexican!"

She held up two bags. "Elotes for everyone!"

I didn't have to ask. I could see that by "everyone," she meant Coty, too. He must have texted her his order, because she set the bags down in the parlor and started divvying out plastic utensils, napkins, and sodas for three people from a cardboard holder.

I was steadfastly not annoyed that she'd included him. I forced myself to be cool, and I put on a brave, hungry face.

She handed me a roll of seasoned corn on the cob wrapped in foil and said, "They didn't have Coke products, sorry. Diet Pepsi for you."

"No problem. And thank you," I said, and I meant it from the bottom of my heart—even though I found something else down in those depths, too, now that I looked. It wasn't very pretty. It was suspicion and, yeah, jealousy. I was jealous that I was going to have to share one of my only friends with some guy who wasn't my brother. And jealous—or something very close to jealous—because Ben had been gone long enough that it probably made sense for Kate to start talking to guys again, but I didn't want a front-row seat.

One of these days, Kate will remember that we aren't really sisters-in-law, and she doesn't owe me anything. She doesn't have to be my friend. She has a life of her own to get started, or get back to.

I think I'm just afraid of being lonely again. Maybe that's it. I'm not jealous; I'm scared.

Venita Rost
1932

He's doing it again. I haven't said anything about it, as it seems like it would embarrass him terribly, but it isn't normal, the way he talks to himself. It's weird, that's what it is.

But is it sinister? Of that, I'm not sure.

This feeling, though. I wrote it off for a while. I ignored it. I've been known to be overly suspicious at times and to impulsively assign motives to others that are...shall we say, off the mark.

Regardless, the more time I spend around him, the less certain I am of Mr. Sloan. He's never anything but flawlessly kind and polite—an excellent guest, truly—but I'm beginning to feel like something isn't quite right about him. I feel silly for feeling this way. I certainly haven't said anything to Oscar, and it would break Priscilla's tiny duckling heart if I were to forbid him to visit or stay, so of course I won't.

I have no reason to. I have little apart from a gut feeling that something isn't quite as straightforward, as easy, as pleasant, as...

...I'm not sure what I'm trying to say.

He hasn't done anything or said anything. It might be as simple as increased familiarity, where the small quirks I'd noticed before and found charming...now strike me as peculiar.

For example.

I do need examples, don't I? All right, then I shall offer some.

For one thing, when he thinks no one can see or hear him, Mr. Sloan talks to himself. But we all do, don't we? It's hardly a reason to view someone askance, though it's the things he says—or the things I think I hear, when he says them—that make me wonder if there isn't...more to him.

I don't mean that he's more than a man, that he's a hero or a monster or anything of the sort. Only that there's something unusual, isn't there? About a man who never met a puzzle he could not solve, when all others have tried and failed. It's unusual, to be the one who always succeeds, always answers the questions correctly, and always saves the day in the end.

And the thing is, he knows it.

He's aware of his skill, obviously, but that's not what I mean. I'm trying to write my way toward what I mean, and I'm not doing a very stellar job at all, if I do say so myself.

Let me try again: He never doubts himself. He never wonders if this time, he'll miss a clue or fail to find a stolen treasure. He never considers that a guilty man might run free in the end or an innocent one might hang. He simply arrives, absorbs the information available, and then assembles the pieces as neatly as any set of paper dolls or wood puzzles or anything else that human hands can assemble with ease (or instructions).

Mr. Sloan never needs instructions.

Is it purely due to long habit and considerable experience? It might be, though he's not that much older than Oscar or me. He can't have been doing this much longer than I'd been acting, though I've stepped away from the profession for the time being.

I suppose there are plenty of things I could do without thinking about it, purely from having performed a task so many times before. I could write a clean intertitle with a brush and some paint in ten minutes or less, and everyone, everywhere, would swear it'd been professionally printed at great expense. I could hit a mark without even asking where the tape would go on the floor. I could hem a skirt in fifteen minutes. I could memorize a page of directions in ninety seconds or less, considering how my brain simply seizes on the patterns of previous projects.

But this doesn't feel like that.

When Mr. Sloan talks to himself, he doesn't. By which I mean, I think he's talking to someone else, someone no one else but him can see. And yet, he's usually talking to a mirror.

Well, once I heard him talking to himself and realized it was a window, not a mirror. It was dark outside, though—and bright within, therefore his reflection was as clear and sharp as if he stood in the parlor and gazed into the decorative glass we hung by the fireplace. It's a heavy old antique, but the reflection it offers is clear and lacks any fogged spots or cracks.

He stood at the window and he said, as clear as day, "I know there won't be a next time, but if there should be—if there could be—then I'd ask to try again and be someone with a different life, a different lineage. Different goals and a better sense of morality," he concluded grimly, even bitterly.

I cleared my throat so he wouldn't think I was eavesdropping, then swiftly said, "There you are! Oh, good. Oscar has sent a message from work asking if you'd join us for dinner down on Pioneer Square tonight. He says we can pile into the roadster since it's bright and dry, and we won't get rained on. What do you say?"

As if a switch had flipped, he turned around with a smile and said merrily, "Far be it from me to decline a jaunt in the Studebaker! Of course I'd be flattered and delighted to join you both. When will he be back?"

"The message said four, and it's already three."

Mr. Sloan had spent the night in the guest room again, and he'd been fielding phone calls with Los Angeles for much of the day. Not everyone around here has a phone, but we do, so Oscar said it was all right if he worked out of our house while he was dividing his time along the coast.

At the time, I didn't mind. I've never been afraid to be alone with him, not even once. Until recently, I was never even nervous.

God, I wish I knew what had changed.

Another time, on a different day, he was in the parlor and I was at the top of the stairs. I could see him, just the very edge of him—his hip and shoes, his shoulder, the back of part of his head. He was talking into the mirror and he sounded upset. I might say he even sounded afraid.

What he said was something like: "I've become too comfortable with them, with this. I shouldn't let myself get so close. It's dangerous."

This time, I did not do him the kindness of pretending I hadn't heard. "What's dangerous?"

He jumped as if I'd smacked him, but he composed himself almost instantly. "Travel in this weather, don't you think? Not so much the train, of course, but when the clouds are so low and the visibility so poor...it makes me terribly anxious to drive."

What a clever and peculiar lie, credit where due. I had no reason to think that further pressure would bring it out of him, so I played along. "Oh yes, it's really something else—especially going down the side of the ridge. It's the very worst," I added, swanning into the room as if I owned the place, since I do (in fact) own it. "I mean, it's the very worst of all, when the leaves have just fallen and everything is miserably wet. It's so difficult to stop if you're going downhill into the city, and so difficult to rise when you're coming home uphill."

"The spinning of the wheels, the mud..." He shuddered dramatically, then changed the subject. "I don't suppose Oscar is ready to leave yet, is he?"

"He'll be along in a moment. He felt the need to make a phone call, and I think Priscilla has hidden his preferred shoes again."

"That's quite a...novel new game, she's discovered."

I was still nervous, still suspicious—but I had to laugh. It would have seemed strange if I hadn't. "Oh no, don't tell me she's doing it to you, too? These silly little treasure hunts will drive us all mad, I'm sure of it."

"Madness is relative. And yes, she made off with my new wristwatch, though she was kind enough to return it when I asked her. She'd stashed it behind some books in the library. I would've never found it on my own, not in a thousand years. I didn't even know I was supposed to go looking for it!"

We chattered on like that as I escorted him downstairs. Oscar was finished with his phone call, and now he was tying his shoes. I was relieved in a way that upset me. I wanted to be away from Mr. Sloan. I wanted him to be Oscar's guest, not mine.

It was such a terrible, strange feeling—that he was hiding

something under my own roof while making himself comfortable as if he were part of my own family.

But the two men were leaving for the evening, to attend a fundraiser for some good cause or another. I don't know the particulars because I wasn't listening very closely when Oscar told me about it. He's always doing things like this; he's very participatory.

I am less so, the older I get. I want to stay inside in my own place, enjoying my own things and my own company. Maybe it's due to all the travel and excitement of my youth, when Hollywood still called to me and I still answered it with my whole heart. It hasn't called me in a while, and that used to bother me—but it was only a little fear of being left out. Once I realized that I enjoyed being left out, all of my old angst felt terribly silly.

If I want glamour and companionship, I'll throw my own parties here, in my own space. The house was built with such things in mind, after all, and we've already had half a dozen in the three years it's been standing. Each one better than the last, of course. Each one teaches me something about being a hostess, and what I'll need, and what's unnecessary for your guests to be glad they came.

I bowed out of whatever it is Oscar and Mr. Sloan have planned. I pleaded a headache and the desire to turn in early; I was surely not believed, but my excuse was accepted regardless.

So the men spent the next hour getting ready, primping like schoolgirls.

If I weren't so irrationally peeved at our houseguest—or, or if not peeved, I suppose, but suspicious, or wary, or, or something else I've not put my finger on yet—then I might've found the whole thing amusing.

It was easy to pretend that I did when the fellows saw themselves off, my husband a little pink in the cheeks already from the starter *beverage he'd pulled from the bar before he kissed me goodbye and made for the car. His keys jingled in his hand as he sauntered down the walkway, his dearest friend sauntering merrily at his side.*

I don't know why the sight disturbed me.

I don't know why these small things, these weird little bits of overheard conversation and sensed fibs have put me on edge. It isn't like me. I don't think it's like me, at any rate. Maybe I'm wrong.

But when the men had left and I was in the house with only my daughter—the housekeeper having long gone home—I put on Priscilla's favorite radio program (something with a big band conductor whose voice she finds "dreamy," heaven help me) and excused myself to return upstairs.

I went to the guest room, which had known no visitors apart from Mr. Sloan in the better part of a year.

I'm not ordinarily the snooping kind. I've never snooped in Oscar's things, though I'm familiar with most of them purely by virtue of living with the man and sharing space with him as his wife. But I've always done my best to respect the privacy of others, including Mr. Sloan, and I was anxious about opening that door (closed behind himself, perhaps to deter further thefts orchestrated by Priscilla). My hand practically trembled when I went for the crystal knob, and my palms were damp when I twisted it.

But it opened for me, easy as pie. It was not locked, so Mr. Sloan wasn't that worried about Prissy rooting around in his possessions.

I suppose he trusts us.

The knowledge of his casual faith in his hosts did not deter me. I wanted to see what he'd brought. Maybe I'd even figure out who—or rather, I suppose, "what"—he'd been talking to, considering we had no other guests and I do not believe he was merely talking to himself.

I talk to myself all the time. I know what that sounds like.

When I overhear Mr. Sloan nattering quietly, alone in my home except for the mice in the walls, I hear a man who expects some kind of response. Is that a ridiculous conclusion? Well, so what if it is.

I let myself inside and stood in the middle of the room with my hands on my hips, unsure of what I meant to do next. He'd made his bed, or he'd made some manly effort—which is to say, he'd pulled up the blankets and straightened the pillows. He typically traveled with a trunk and a smaller suitcase. The trunk was on the floor. The suitcase rested on the foot of the bed.

I tried the suitcase first.

Inside, I found only the usual things a man might travel with—clothes, toiletries, a bottle of stomach-settling pills, a pair of reading glasses in a tidy leather case. Nothing at all that might arouse my suspicion. I tidied it behind myself, but not too much. It hadn't been pristine when I opened it. I didn't want to arouse any suspicion on Mr. Sloan's part.

When I tried the trunk, I found it locked.

But I am good at locks. I learned how to manipulate them for one of my little films, years ago.

Or I guess it'd be more accurate to say that the director made me learn what it looks like, when a woman picks a lock; they would've rigged it for me, I'm sure—if I hadn't gotten the hang of the real thing. But I found a man in the city who was willing to teach me for a fee that wasn't too arduous. (He asked for an autograph, a kiss on the cheek, and my handwriting for a sign he would hang outside to advertise his shop. All in all, a very fair trade.)

I found a loose bobby pin in my pocket and a paper clip on the nightstand. I believe that Mr. Sloan had been poring over some legal documents relating to a case the night before; I remember him saying something to that effect. I doubted he'd ever miss the tiny scrap of metal, so I unbent the clip and paired it with my hairpin. Between them, I popped the lock in about twenty seconds.

I lifted the trunk lid and stared down inside.

More clothes—or, no, only a scarf and a sweater, lying atop some other things. I was careful with the scarf and the sweater. They'd both been folded so neatly, I doubted my ability to reproduce the precision creases should I drop or disturb them, so I lifted them and set them aside.

"Now we're talking," I said to myself, then looked around guiltily. I don't know why. There was no one to hear me, no one to walk in and catch me at my snooping. Priscilla's radio program would last another half hour at least, and she'd sooner starve or wet herself than leave when it was running.

The contents were stacked, but only loosely; they lacked the precision of the folded items, so I lifted them out one at a time and set them down in order. It'd be easier to put them back in order that way.

On top of something that looked like a very fancy silk shawl, rested a strange assortment: several soft fabric drawstring pouches, a small box that was perhaps large enough to hold a watch, a couple of rings that looked like gold and had writing inside the bands (but I don't know what language it was, and I could not read it), and a letter in an envelope with a red wax seal.

The letter was the most compelling bit, so I examined that first.

The paper was old and a very good quality. It'd only gone a little brown at the corners, though the ink on the front had faded so badly that I wasn't sure what it'd ever said. Something about Bartholomew Sloan, I could tell that much. Maybe an address, someplace in New York, I think.

The seal was highly intriguing. It was thick and hard, and it held the imprint of an owl holding a snake, as clear as day. Or night. I suppose owls hunt at night. Do snakes come out at night? I have no idea. Was this the official symbol for something or someone? Also no idea. There was a border, somewhat marred by whatever stamp had left it slightly smeared. Laurel wreath, perhaps? Something like that.

I was absolutely seized with the impulse to read its contents.

I was not at all stupid enough to pop the seal and do so. Not without covering my tracks, first.

I slipped the letter into my blouse and darted downstairs to the kitchen, pausing only briefly to check in on Priscilla. She was there in the parlor, listening with rapt attention to some screwball radio play put on by alleged professionals, though I had opinions about their performances.

"Are you all right, darling?"

She nodded and waved me away without even looking at me.

Perfect.

I slipped into the kitchen and turned on the stove. The gas fizzed and the front-right burner sparked to life when I turned the knob. From a nearby drawer, I withdrew a butter knife. I held it with a washcloth over the handle. I held it over the little burner flame until it was hot, then slipped it carefully beneath the envelope's fold, slicing cleanly through the seal without doing the smallest bit of damage.

Delighted with myself, I lifted the fold and pulled out a single sheet of paper, brown around its edges like the sheath that held it.

The burner spit and popped. I jumped, then turned it off. No sense in being careless.

I opened the sheet of paper, and I swear, something fell out of it—some kind of dust? Powder? It sparkled in the light from the kitchen *window over the sink. For a moment I was worried. Was it dangerous? Some kind of weird trap or poison? I felt lightheaded, but was it only my imagination, driven so furiously awry by my sneaking about?*

I don't know, but I know the kitchen felt strange, and I felt strange, and the light looked strange. And that's nonsense, isn't it?

It's not as if our houseguest traveled with arcane and terrible magic—or that's the thought that flickered through my head and then evaporated as swiftly as dandelion fluff when tugged by the wind. The letter was not blank, but I could not read it. The words seemed to swim across the page, the letters slipping from line to line as I struggled to make them line up and speak to me.

After a few seconds I realized the futility of my efforts; I did not recognize the language, or the handwriting, or any of the formulas.

Yes, there were formulas. The numbers were Arabic, at least, and I know those when I see them. Three or four, hard to say for certain—but yes, formulas. Recipes? Maybe they were recipes, or maybe I was standing in my kitchen, feeling dazed and seeking some logical explanation.

Five something of some item. Six measures of something else. Strange symbols that looked like math, but not enough like math to actually be math. And at the bottom, a pair of signatures. One looked like a strange symbol, stretched out and resembling nonsense.

The other was quite clearly Mr. Sloan's. Was this some kind of contract? I'd signed plenty of those over the years. I regretted more of them than I cherished. I had a feeling that Mr. Sloan regretted this one, and deeply.

Something about it was profoundly sinister, and it made me anxious. It made me want to fling the whole thing into the fireplace, though it was cold in the room where Prissy was listening to her radio show, happy as could be, no idea that terrible things were afoot under our very own roof.

But what terrible things?

A man with strange items in his luggage was not automatically a criminal or a fiend.

Why, then? What was it?

I closed the letter and tried not to notice the peculiar sparkle of the dust in the last of the summer sunlight bleeding into the room. I tucked it neatly back into its sheath, closed it, and reheated the knife once more so I could seal it again and replace it without Mr. Sloan noticing my interference.

But when I turned around to head back upstairs, I gasped.

I was not alone.

Though I could hear the radio and its fizzling hum in the parlor, Priscilla was standing in the doorway. "Momma, what's that?"

"This?" I asked stupidly, holding the letter aloft as if it were nothing, certainly not a secret. "It's only a message, not important, don't worry about it."

"What are you doing to it?"

"I'm closing it up and putting it away. Tomorrow, I'll give it to the postman."

"Who's it for?"

"Goodness, you're full of questions," I said crossly. More crossly than I had any right, considering. Since I was in the wrong.

"You said being full of questions is a good thing."

"Generally, yes," I confirmed. "But sometimes, some things are not your business. This is not your business."

She eyed me thoughtfully. I didn't like it. She's much more clever than people tend to think a little girl might be, and I know she was filled to the brim with queries she was now squashing down, purely because I'd stopped her from letting them spill out into the kitchen.

God, she's such a good girl. A worse one would've challenged me outright.

Priscilla nodded slowly, her eyes still quite narrow. "All right. If you say so."

She picked up that expression from her father. It's what he says when he doesn't want to give ground but is prepared to abstain from further confrontation. "Thank you. Yes, I'll take it. Your program isn't over, is it?" I asked suddenly, thinking I couldn't have possibly spent so much time standing in my kitchen, absorbed in a letter I could not read and was not supposed to hold.

"It ended a few minutes ago. You were awful quiet, and I wondered where you were."

"Good heavens," I said out loud, because it was the polite version of what I was thinking, and little pitchers have big ears. "I didn't realize. Well!" I said brightly, as if to change the subject. "Let's get you ready for bed."

"But the sun's still up!" she whined.

"It'll be up until ten, and you know it. At the very least, you should be washed up and wearing pajamas in, oh, let's say the next fifteen minutes."

She glanced at my hand, where I wore a little gold watch that was scarcely any bigger than a bracelet. "What if I make it in five minutes?" she asked, the little opportunist.

Resigned, I said, "If you can be ready for bed in five minutes, I'll read you a story and you can pick which one."

"Even if it's the one with the wolves? I know you don't like that one."

"I'll even read about the wolves, yes."

These details hashed out sufficiently, she darted off to the bathroom, and I exhaled. I ran upstairs to put things back in Mr. Sloan's trunk, exactly the way I'd found them. I do not know if I succeeded, or how well. But I put everything back, and I locked the trunk again (which is harder than unlocking it, should I tell the truth about these things).

Then I read the damn story about the princess and the wolves, and thank the Fates, Priscilla was asleep before I got to the messy bits.

Ronnie

NOW

The next morning I woke up with heartburn and a mouth that tasted like a trash can behind a gas station. I hadn't had that much to drink, had I? No, surely. Hadn't even touched the stuff in the bar cart.

I sat up and rubbed my eyes. My air mattress squeaked and sagged; I needed to inflate it again if I ever wanted the crick in my back to go away.

Coty and Kate had stayed through the afternoon and into the evening. They'd helpfully looked for the vanished cat, and no, they didn't find it. I knew they wouldn't. I don't think it likes people very much. I don't think it'll bother me. I think I feel okay about that one.

I think it's Priscilla's cat, buried somewhere on the grounds—but if I'd said so out loud, they might have thought I was even crazier.

But when they'd finally given up on finding the four-footed

lingerer, I talked them into helping me empty a couple of rooms and load the dumpster, so by the time they left the extra bedroom upstairs wasn't full of trash, and the library was...less full of trash. Likewise the music room, even though we kept some of the sheet music.

By the time we were finished with the manual labor, they were proposing dinner—but I didn't have it in me. I was tired, too tired even to be afraid of my house or anything in it, living or otherwise.

I was also aggravated because I had a strong feeling that they would head off together without me when I recused myself from the suggestion of dinner. Not that it was any of my business. The FOMO wouldn't kill me, and hey, it was probably good for Kate to have some sort of personal distraction. Hell, it was probably *time* for her to have one.

She's going to have one eventually.

I'm not sure why it rubbed me so wrong, except for all the obvious reasons I mentioned before—or admitted to myself, or however that goes when you know you're being an idiot. Or feeling like one.

Except, when I settled in that night, once everybody was gone, I found myself alone with Venita's diary again and something about my reading...vibed with me? I don't have a better way to put it. Something about the way Venita confidently mistrusted Bartholomew Sloan for very vague reasons, it made me think of Coty and how I don't really like him very much—even though he'd given me no reason to think ill of him. He'd been nothing but pleasant and helpful, just like the maligned Mr. Sloan and his locked trunk of secrets.

I wondered if Coty had a locked trunk of secrets.

I already knew he was hiding something, and I couldn't shake the suspicion that it had something to do with his very late uncle—as absurd as that sounds.

Maybe it's worse than absurd; maybe it was just plain stupid of me. It's only a coincidence that I lived in his uncle's old house, right?

Only a coincidence, only it wasn't.

Coty was the nephew of a man who died in this house, a nephew who'd kept one eye on the place and had some peculiarly intimate thoughts about a man who'd died decades before he was born.

I couldn't convince myself that Coty's sudden appearance was a strict coincidence.

I wondered what was in that letter Venita found. I wondered if she ever deciphered it, or if she ever solved whatever mystery the man presented, before they all were dead.

I hoped I'd find out before I ran out of reading material, as most of the journal's last third was illegible, having been dampened too many times and left to congeal into a wad of paper-mache. I'm sure there's some technology somewhere that would let me separate those fragile old pages and read them at long last, but I'm equally sure that it's very expensive and not within my reach. Maybe someday I can talk a museum into taking a crack at it.

Museums do that kind of thing, don't they? They have conservators and the like, and Venita Rost was a prominent star in the early years of Hollywood. Someone, somewhere, might be interested.

Regardless.

The day was youngish (it was already getting late in the morning), and I had the roofer scheduled for noon. I should probably brush my teeth and eat something, even if it meant delivery or takeout, since I still lacked a functioning kitchen.

Getting dressed and presentable took longer than it should have, and I was still dragging, even once I was wearing cleaner clothes and sporting a fresher mouth. I really wanted to go back to bed, but I was hungover and hungry, so I ordered food instead and made myself some more Suisse Mocha coffee because it was hot and sweet and better than nothing.

A burrito the size of a baby arrived via a delivery kid who looked too young to deliver newspapers, but that was none of my business. The burrito was good. It should've been, for what it cost to bring it to me, and I was almost finished with the last of it when the roofing guy showed up ten minutes late.

I wasn't mad. I still had a dab of sour cream on my cheek when he knocked, so I hastily wadded up the last of my waste and stuffed it into the delivery bag, wiped my face, and answered the door.

"Ms. Mitchell?"

"Yeah, that's me."

"I'm Jake Hoff," he introduced himself. "With Quality Northwest Roofing."

"Right. Come on in," I said, then realized how dumb that was. I tried to shut down a yawn and only halfway succeeded. When it'd mostly subsided, I asked, "Or should we start outside?"

He nodded and gestured at the clipboard. "Outside first, but you can stay in here if you like. I've got my ladder, and I'll start climbing around. It'll take me a few minutes, though. You may as well stay comfortable."

I let out a little laugh. "Yeah, it's comfortable enough in here. No heat and no AC, plenty of mold, and all that jazz. But thanks. Just come on back inside when you're ready to give me an estimate."

Almost an hour later he returned with a heavily marked-up clipboard and a face that said he had expensive news. "Ms. Mitchell…" he said as he took a seat. We were in the parlor with my airbed because I'd also pulled the sheets off a couple of the sturdier chairs and dragged them inside. You know, in case of company.

Or for Kate and Coty, anyway. Since I didn't really have any other company at the moment, professional service folks aside.

I sat down kind of beside him, kind of across from him. It was awkward, but he wanted to show me what was on the clipboard, and I wanted to see it. "All right, what's the damage?"

He sighed and pulled out his phone, which meant he'd taken pictures, which also meant expensive. Nobody ever takes pictures of stuff that won't require a shit-ton of cash to repair. "Damage is looking…real goddamn damagey, if you don't mind me saying so."

"I'm prepared for your verdict, Mr. Hoff. Rough as it's bound to be."

"Good, because what you've got overhead is a hot mess. I think the roof is probably fifty years old, at least."

I nodded along. "Wouldn't shock me. This place got some remodeling in the seventies."

"That tracks. It's been patched maybe eight or ten times since then. Some of those patches were better than others, but all of them have quit working by now. One of them"—he pulled up some pictures and turned the phone around—"looks like somebody threw down a tarp and tried to hide it with some shingles, which went…about as well as you'd expect. Have you been up in the attic at all?"

"Yeah, it's a horror show."

"I bet."

He walked me through an assortment of rotted support beams, ruined flashing, loose chimneys, and fascia siding with no more structural integrity than a wet sponge. And when he was finished, the number was almost forty grand.

I let out a low, unhappy whistle.

Mr. Hoff cringed. "I know, and I'm truly sorry. Even a few years ago, it wouldn't have been this bad—but the big patch over your northwest corner broke bad sometime a winter or two back, and everything is just…" He shrugged. I knew what the shrug meant. It's not like I hadn't done my own looking around and shrugging. It meant mold, ruin, and collapse in dozens of spots—some of which would be tricky (pricey) to resolve. "We're gonna have to rebuild a lot of framing."

"No, I understand." I'd budgeted about thirty-five grand for this part of the heavy lifting, but I could scare up another few. A shrinking budget just meant more DIY work down the road, and that was okay. I'd expected that from the start.

Between us, we sorted out the paperwork, made the arrangements for four weeks out, give or take, and I sent the nice man on his way with a deposit check that was positively painful to sign. Then I was alone in my house again, and it was very quiet and felt very dark, even though the sun had come out from behind the clouds a little and the day was warming up.

I checked the app on my phone, and supposedly we were due to hit almost seventy degrees, which was a pleasant surprise. June is often like that, though—and so is October. Every spring and fall, the weather acts like it's deeply confused, trying to make up its mind.

It was barely midafternoon by the time the guy left, and despite the General Foods International coffee and the soda I'd downed with the burrito…I really wanted to go back to bed. My foggy head had never really cleared up, so I hadn't slept that well—and hey, I was alone in my own house. I could take a nap if I damn well wanted to.

After a trip to the bathroom.

I peed, flushed, and listened with a full-body clench as the plumbing rattled and hummed in the walls; but the toilet drained and refilled, nothing spooky appeared in the mirror, and I could have a little lie-down.

Except.

I opened the bathroom door and I knew I wasn't alone.

I heard something, a soft noise, like the faint padding thump of a quiet animal trotting softly through the hall. I peered down one direction, then the other, and I didn't see anything. The sound of tiny footfalls did a muffled tippy-tap to my left, toward the kitchen and the rear of the house.

Not tiny enough to be a rat, not rough enough to be a dog.

I had a feeling I knew what I was tracking, but I didn't want to entertain the thought, not until I had the creature in question in my sights. It would be right around the corner any moment now. No, in the kitchen. No, back toward the room I'd come to think of as "the conservatory" and the rear exit that dead-ended at the side of the hill, and then the trail that went out to the orchard full of happy bees and otherwise unattended blossoms, all of it soggy from a couple of weeks of persistent drizzle and a humidity level that would give Florida a run for its money.

But I stood out in the orchard, heart pounding, squinting against the struggling sun and listening to the bees, and I did not see any sign of yesterday's white cat.

"She isn't ready yet, but she will be soon."

The voice came from behind me, a few yards away, at the back door.

A man stood there, holding the door open with a casual lean. I didn't know him. He was maybe in his sixties, with graying hair that had started out blond, I think. His face was lined and his brows were bushy; he wore jeans and work boots, and a blue T-shirt with a gray plaid flannel sitting over it, unbuttoned. His sleeves were rolled up just shy of his elbows.

"I'm sorry?" I said. It wasn't a useful thing to say, but it was all I had on deck.

"She's still waking up, that's what the, uh…" He gestured toward the orchard, toward me—or whatever I'd been chasing. "That's what the cat means. It always wakes up first."

"You've seen the cat before?" I asked. Why didn't I ask him who he was? What he was doing there? Why the hell he was in my house? Then it dawned on me: "I'm asleep."

"Something like that."

"And you're dead," I guessed.

"Yeah, so's the cat." He grinned, very slightly. It was just the slightest upturn at one corner of his craggy mouth. Then he turned away and ducked back inside, letting the door swing shut behind him.

But I could still see him through the conservatory windows—he was walking slowly, not trying to run away from me or anything, just heading back to wherever he'd come from. I had a feeling it was a spot on the second story, where the floor had a big hole in the middle.

I was utterly, peculiarly without fear. I was barely even confused.

A flicker flashed through my head, and yes, there it was—the second-guessing. Only for an instant, and only because I was thinking of the powder room and the big man in the mirror.

But this man wasn't that big. He was only a bit larger than me, maybe five foot nine. No, this wasn't the mysterious Mr. Sloan. This was the tragic Mr. Crawford.

"Hugh? Can I call you that?"

He didn't answer. I started to follow him.

When I reached the upstairs room with the chunk missing out of the floor...there he was, standing and waiting, looking out the window at the comings and goings of all the big, slow boats.

He said, "I bought this place for the view."

"So...no regrets?" I asked from my spot at the threshold, where the floor would almost certainly hold me.

He shook his head. "My heart would've blown out regardless. Just as well it happened here, though I really did hope to see the place restored."

"Stick around," I told him, feeling drunk more than hungover and sleepy. "I'm just getting started."

He turned to look at me, still leaving one arm leaning on the windowsill. "But the question is, will *she* let you finish?"

Something weird was going on. The hole in the floor… wasn't. It simply wasn't there. The wood was intact across the whole of the floor's expanse, if stained and scratched from years of neglect and abuse. There were different-colored woodstain swatches here and there. A patch of something neutral. Something redder. Something browner. He'd been testing them out when he died, trying an assortment of colors to see what would look best.

Big pieces of masking tape held one end of the window together, though the leaded glass panels were intact across the main stretch.

"I fixed that one," he said when he noticed me noticing. "I stabilized it, anyway."

"What the fuck is happening?" I asked.

"Nothing that hasn't happened before. I came here, I started work, I saw the cat. I fell in love. I died."

"Is that everyone's trajectory?" I wanted to know, but I had a feeling he couldn't tell me. "They show up, they do a little work, and they die?"

"You said it yourself: on a long enough timeline, everyone who ever owned this house is dead."

"You were listening."

He was vanishing, there by the window. The light was pouring through, one stubborn sunbeam stretching down from the clouds and stabbing past the glass, illuminating the dead man like he was made of dust particles, built out of that drifting sparkle.

"We're always listening. Except for Venita, the rest of us can't do much else."

"Who was the man in the powder room? That was Bartholomew Sloan, right?" I started firing questions at him, hoping to get one more word in edgewise before I lost him altogether. "I think he's trying to talk to me. I think I hear him sometimes—but not as clearly as you, as I can…I can see you, and hear…you."

"Yeah, but you're dreaming."

"But you're…" I stopped talking. He was gone.

"Goddammit," I swore. I ran my hands through my hair and reminded myself to grab a bandanna out of my car; the humidity was making me sweaty, and my hair felt really gross. I needed to go back to my crappy apartment and take a real shower. Maybe now was the time at last, yes. I collected my wits, such as they were, and headed downstairs.

Except I was already downstairs.

I was lying on the air mattress, which had deflated sufficiently to let my ass rest on the floor. My head was light, and across my vision I could still see the sparkling dust. I shuddered and climbed to my feet and shook off as much of the…unsettling nap, if that's what it was…that I possibly could.

But I couldn't shake off the memory of the room upstairs, its floor intact, its promise of a new finish laid out in swatches. And I knew that if I headed upstairs to look, I'd find it all gone now, excised via power saw by whatever unfortunate crime scene cleanup tech had been unlucky enough to get the gig.

"This place is messed *up*," I said, rubbing my eyes.

I felt weird, deeply weird. *Dreamsick*, if you've ever heard that word. An author I used to read talked about the sensation of dreamsickness—that sudden waking up that leaves you discombobulated, especially in the wake of an absorbing or upsetting dream.

I did not really believe that Hugh Crawford was a dream.

I needed more caffeine. And a shower. And maybe a nap where I wasn't likely to encounter any dead people or cats or starlets who'd been dead for nearly a hundred years.

I packed up whatever I thought I might need and headed for my other home, where the lease would run out before long and then I'd be fully at the mercy of the Rost Mansion, as I'd come to think of it. No. Maybe the house had a real name once and it'd been lost to history or time or renovators who didn't know their ass from a hole in the ground.

Maybe one of these days, I could just ask Venita.

Bartholomew Sloan
NOW

I remember that day. I remember it every time someone rereads the entry Venita wrote in that battered little diary. (How much longer can that thing survive, anyway? Surely it will fall apart eventually. I don't understand how it hasn't done so already.)

I remember when I returned much later that evening, a little drunk—with Oscar, who was more than a little drunk, if we're to be honest here—and we parted ways for the night. I heard him go to his room and greet Venita, who replied a little stiffly, then warmed up to him as, I suppose, she recalled that he wasn't the man she was mad at. Or suspicious of. Both? But the house is solid enough that I only caught the tones, not the words.

Priscilla had been in bed for hours by then, and she did not awaken when we came home. I passed her bedroom and heard her soft snores through the cracked door.

I was feeling almost elated. It had been a grand night, a

great party thrown by the local newspaper magnate, ostensibly intended to honor our new police commissioner. It was all a bunch of glittering and glad-handing, hobnobbing and ass-kissing, and for whatever reason, Venita hadn't been interested in joining us.

Maybe it was that simple. She didn't want to join us. If I'd been elsewhere, perhaps she would've attended with her husband, rather than allow me to stand in as his fraternal date for the evening.

She'd always enjoyed that sort of thing, even when she wasn't the one hosting it.

Yes, it must have been me.

But I was walking back to my traditional room, there in the Amundson house, and I was feeling positively *marvelous*. I'd just enjoyed an excellent meal and several rounds of expensive hooch, some outstanding music, and merry dancing. I had returned safely to the beautiful home of my close friend; and yes, though I'd already begun to suspect that Venita's feelings toward me were shifting, I was not yet aware enough to be concerned.

I was only tipsy and happy, and it was a joyful relief. I'd gone an entire afternoon and evening without devoting a single, fleeting thought toward my terrible bargain and its eventual cost.

Before I met Oscar and Venita, dread and regret ate up most of my waking moments. I'd buried myself in work to hide my fear and self-loathing, and it'd made me rich. It'd given me opportunities and honor. It'd cost me my soul, but at the time, no one could have known that.

I returned to my room and found it as I'd left it; I'd had no reason to think it would be otherwise, and I wasn't looking closely. I hadn't locked the door. I don't think I even shut it.

I pulled off my jacket and threw it on the dresser, where it did not stay. It slid slowly down, then off to the floor, where I let it lie. I sat down on the bed and set about removing my shoes, one at a time, and I kicked them aside.

One knocked against the trunk I carry with me everywhere, for I did not dare leave it behind or unattended.

(Maybe that's not true—maybe it was never true. I should've put it in storage, or buried it in a basement, or separated myself from that cursed container in any other logical, reasonable way. But I didn't. I kept it close. I held it like a secret. Like guilt, clutched tightly to my chest, lest anyone else should get a glimpse of it.)

I looked at my shoe, its skinny laces splayed obscenely over the leather tongue, and I looked at the trunk, which I only then noticed...wasn't quite where I'd left it. What a strange thing to catch sight of—I thought so even then. I shouldn't have seen it at all. It hadn't moved by more than half an inch. It had not been dragged across the floor but turned ever so slightly. It was no longer perfectly parallel with the foot of the bed.

And my shoe hadn't hit it hard enough to move it. Not by a long shot, as the trunk was quite heavy.

The leftover hum of alcohol evaporated out of my brain in a nauseating burp, leaving only the aftertaste of dread and regret behind. They swarmed me, perhaps annoyed to have been banished even for a few brief hours. I tried to push them aside, but I couldn't—and now they were joined by suspicion, with confusion waiting in the wings.

I left the bed and knelt beside the trunk, examining it with my investigator's eye.

"Something is different," I said quietly, and I could hear the gin in my voice more than I could feel it in my blood, in my bones. In the marrow, even. "What's different here, what happened…?"

I ran my hands along its edges, the seams, the lid and the lock, yes. Were those tiny scratch-marks on the brass fixture that held it shut? Could they be from my own key? Certainly. But I'd not noticed them before, and now I was paranoid. I didn't *think* I'd made those marks? They could've happened at any time, but I was certain they'd occurred very recently.

I retrieved my own keys from the ring in my pocket and, with fingers trembling, inserted the correct one. It caught and clicked and I lifted the lid to see everything as I'd left it earlier that day.

Almost.

It's not as though I'd cataloged every tiny fold in every sheet of paper, or the locations of each loose item to within a hair's breadth of precision, but my nerves were on fire—screaming that something had changed, something was moved, something was different. I reached down into the luggage and pulled out the contents a single piece at a time.

The small box with the crystals that likely do nothing. The bags with the charms I'd picked up in New Orleans, the ones that do…something, but I'm not sure what; I only know that it makes me feel better to carry them, in a way that the cold, sharp edges of the crystals do not. A placebo, perhaps. All the same, I keep them with me—those tiny felt bundles that smell of herbs, incense, and oils. Whatever they do or don't do, they give my belongings a fragrant air. (I cannot carry them in my usual suitcase; if I leave them scattered among my clothes like sachets, people ask questions about my exotic cologne.)

Then I reached the envelope. The sealed one with the red wax and the contents I dare not read again but cannot bear to part with. It was still sealed and appeared unmolested.

But only at first glance.

Something was very slightly different, and I could not put my finger on it, until I realized that the seal had slipped very slightly. A fraction of a fraction of an inch; there was a tiny seam on the bottom where there hadn't been before, I would've bet my life on it. After all, what's my life, in comparison to what I'd signed away already?

And yes, when I pulled out my round magnifier from my breast pocket, I also noted a slight smudge of red, as if a crayon had grazed the paper.

Someone had meddled cleverly.

I don't know why I concealed her with such language—even there, in the privacy of my guest room, where I'd slept so many times before. I knew who'd done it. Venita and Priscilla had been the only two home all evening, and I strongly doubted that the little girl knew the old trick of slipping past a wax seal with a hot blade and a steady hand.

My hands shook, and the rest of me joined them as I snapped the seal, carelessly now, for it did not matter. The damage had been done.

Or had it, really?

What of it, if Venita saw the contract? She couldn't have

read it; she isn't *that* clever, and even if she were, she lacks the education necessary to have understood a single line of what she saw. It might not matter.

My heart was in my throat as I opened the paper sheath and pulled out the single piece of paper, and although its appearance matched my memory perfectly, something had definitely changed. It might sound like an absurd observation, but there was nothing menacing about it anymore.

Was it evil? Yes, most assuredly. As evil as the moment I'd first set eyes upon it. Was it complete and unaltered? Also yes. But I'd been told—or rather, commanded and warned—that its contents were for my eyes and none other. Far be it from me to disregard such instructions; why else would I keep the thing so close?

Because I was a fool, obviously. And as previously admitted.

Now it was as if I held only an ordinary letter, inert and harmless, with contents no more meaningful than the horse race report in the paper's afternoon edition.

The words didn't appear to swim on the page, their evil intent vibrant and electric, the letters sending sparks through my eyes as I ran them along each line again and again, as I'd done before it'd all been sealed away. I read them afresh, and I felt absolutely nothing.

It wasn't that the contract was broken, and it wasn't that I was free. It was that something had changed. Something had been lost. Some intent had been violated, and this was the consequence—for all that I didn't understand it yet.

Oh, how I would come to understand it, and hate it. Oh, how many times since my death have I wanted to shout at

Venita, "Don't you understand? Some of the fault lies with *you*! If you'd minded your own business and left my things alone, I would not have sought council with my wicked benefactor through the parlor mirror!"

I have not shouted that at Venita. Not because it isn't true, but because it isn't fair.

After all, the fault does lie entirely with me. If I had not sought shortcuts and safety nets beyond my ken, if I had not explored the sort of esoterica that could damn a man more easily than lift him up, if I had not offered my eternal soul for a mortal lifetime of wisdom and comfort…then little Priscilla would have never stumbled across the scene. She would have never borne the brunt of my foolishness.

The fault is mine. But if Venita hadn't been nosy, it would never have happened.

I don't care if those two thoughts contradict one another. It does not make either of them less true or correct.

My point is this: I made mistakes. Enormous ones—mistakes so large that they had their own planetary gravity and others were subsequently drawn into their orbit. My orbit. I was the one they came to see, the one who they asked for help as my reputation grew and spread. I was a finder of lost objects, a righter of wrongs, a savior of the lost.

I thought—or I think I thought—that if I could do enough good, I might offset the wickedness I'd so willingly engaged. Surely there must be some tipping point whereby my sins might be overwhelmed by my acts of virtue.

Everyone thinks so, I bet…before they sign such a contract. It's the last bit of self-convincing we require to push ourselves over the line; it's how we justify taking the things we want, through means which are frankly unholy. We tell ourselves, "*My* soul will be redeemed. *My* actions for good will overtake my singular action for evil."

But only the worst of us truly believe it. I know I did.

Ronnie

NOW

Once I shook off the dreamsickness that left me so goddamn groggy, I got some more work done. Mostly I just threw out some more trash and looked for the cat, for all the good that did me. But after a few hours of normal gross-old-house shit, without any spooky-old-house shit, I mean, I was feeling almost normal again. For me.

I was just starting to think about dinner when Kate texted, asking what I would be doing for food that afternoon. It's like we're psychically linked, I swear.

I texted back that I didn't have any bright ideas but I was open to hearing hers. She said she'd be over in an hour, and she had a surprise for me.

I am not the world's biggest fan of surprises, but since it was Kate, I pretended to be excited. By which I mean, I sent her a thumbs-up emoji, sighed, and put the phone away. It would probably be fine. Why was I annoyed? It was only a surprise. I had a feeling the surprise would come with Coty, so that's probably why. And when I turned out to be correct, it took a little work to hide my irritation, but I think I did okay. Sometimes I feel like I spend my whole life suspecting the worst and being miserable about how right I am. Maybe Ben was right. Maybe I'm the problem—or my attitude is, or whatever.

But at this point, I'm not likely to change, so.

I welcomed them both inside like everything was fine, and that's when I realized the surprise had arrived inside two Trader Joe's bags. One was kind of heavy. One wasn't.

Kate handed me the light one, and Coty held up the heavier one. "Guess what!"

I took a shot in the dark. "Booze?"

"Yes!" he said, then set down the bag and pulled out another bottle of whiskey. This one was cheaper than the Maker's, but Jack Daniels is respectable enough that I wasn't offended.

"I can appreciate a guy who was raised right and doesn't show up empty-handed." See? I can be gracious, even when suspicious. I took the bottle, and he whipped out a few plastic cups, then started spreading everything out on the "coffee table."

"What else is in the bag?" I asked. I glanced into it and saw what looked like a laptop.

"Laptop," Kate confirmed.

"This is my surprise? A new laptop? Am I *really* that slow with email?" Mine was back at the apartment. My desktop had died of old age, and I did almost everything digital from my phone, so I didn't feel like a PC was an essential piece of hardware to carry around. These days, there's not that much performance difference between the two, anyway, as long as I'm not filling out forms or trying to type up email.

I guess that's why I'm so slow to reply to emails.

"No, the laptop is Coty's, and you can't have it," she said with a grin.

Merrily, he declared, "I brought it so we could watch the DVDs!"

"The DVDs are the surprise," Kate informed me, and she fished several of them out of the lighter bag. I recognized one that matched something from Hugh's stash down in the basement (which I still had not returned to the library, like the schmuck I am), but the others were new to me. "We went to the library—the big one downtown."

"Oh, really?" Why did that feel like another red flag to me. Why. It should not have. There were closer library branches, but they were smaller.

It wasn't *that* strange, how they'd gone all the way downtown. Maybe they'd just made a quest of it, Holy Grail–style. I already knew that Coty idolized his Sherlockian uncle, and that guy had died right here in that movie star's house, in… well, maybe in the very room in which we were about to watch some hundred-year-old movies that probably didn't run more than half an hour a pop. Those flicks couldn't have been easy to come by.

I don't know, but it felt like a sign that I should look closer.

Jesus, was I losing my mind, just like Venita? Seeing danger in people who meant me no harm and had a perfectly reasonable, friendly interest in my life and home? Was that all it was? The same old pattern playing out yet again? Another matron of the house, suspicious of another guest—from the same family, even?

What's the expression? History doesn't repeat itself, but often it will rhyme. This was a rhyme.

I forced myself to smile it off. I can fake anything for an afternoon.

We ordered food from the Thai place that Kate and I both like, and by the time it arrived, we were all settled in and ready to get retro—though we had to cover a couple of windows first, courtesy of the late-afternoon glare. The sun wouldn't set for another couple of hours at least, not that time of year, and most of the household curtains were too ruined to relocate; so we ended up using a couple of foil emergency blankets I had in the back of my car.

I'm always prepared, remember? Emergencies are where I shine, even when they just involve covering a couple of windows. Those things worked great; it was practically as good as Reynolds Wrap. Before long, the space was as dark as we were going to get it.

Coty held up the Trader Joe's bag and shook it. "In here, there are half a dozen movies, because that's all I could find. The library said they ought to have a few others, but they've gone missing."

I glanced at Kate, but she didn't glance back. I guess she forgot what I'd told her about Hugh Crawford's collection in the basement. She was just looking at Coty, with something that wasn't quite a gleam in her eye…but also, wasn't *not* that.

She stepped forward and reached into the bag with her eyes squinted shut. "We'll do it random-like," she declared.

"Eeny, meeny, miny, *moe*..." She whipped out whichever one had grabbed her fingers' interest. "Looks like we're starting off with *Damsel of Danger*, from 1921."

Coty put the bag down and took *Damsel of Danger*, then popped open the plastic clamshell. He sniffed it like a sommelier. "Ah, yes. A fine vintage. Twelve and a half minutes of some of the cutest little practical effects you've ever seen. Supposedly Ms. Rost did her own stunts and everything."

The danger light in the back of my brain sent out a little ping. Okay, but why did he know that already? I could've asked. I didn't ask. I didn't want to watch him lie. Instead, I asked idly, "Did they even *have* stunt performers back then?"

"For their big stars? I'm sure they had stand-ins," he said with the air of a man who hasn't the faintest idea but is determined to sound like he knows what he's talking about. "Venita Rost was a badass, though. She either didn't want them or was too good to need them."

I'd felt the funniest spark when he'd said her name. The weirdest little thrill, except it wasn't glee, exactly. It was more like an alert. An alarm that no one else could hear.

"Venita Rost," he murmured. "Always a step ahead of the competition."

I almost wanted to tell him to stop doing that, stop saying her name, she might hear you, and we all knew that the white cat was already sniffing around...but I didn't want to sound like a maniac.

Very casually, he asked me, "How are you enjoying her journal?"

I froze like I'd been caught doing something awful. "What?"

"Her diary. You found it here, didn't you? Part of it?" He looked over at Kate with questions in his eyes.

Jesus, she'd told him about that, too. "Um, yeah. It's in pretty bad condition, though. A lot of it isn't readable at all. At some point it got wet. It's kind of a soggy, swollen brick."

"Do you, uh, do you think I could see it?" he asked with just a tad too much embarrassment and eagerness to sound innocent. "Does she mention my uncle? I bet she talks about him a lot."

"She… Yeah, she mentions him. But I don't have it here," I lied through my teeth. "I took it back to my old apartment to let it dry out. It's so damn humid in here, and at least I have a heater I can run over there. I was reading online about how to restore water-damaged books, and apparently you can actually like, iron them once the pages dry out really thoroughly. I mean, they're never the same again; they'll never close right or sit neatly on a shelf, but…" I'd used up all the bullshit half-truth I could scare up out of my cobwebby back-brain, so the thought petered out.

Coty lit up. "Really? Shit, I didn't know you could do stuff like that."

"Well, it takes time. And climate control," I emphasized bullshittily. "I'm serious, it's in *very* rough shape. I'm almost afraid to touch it." I was proud of myself for hardly even lying.

How a man can look both thrilled and disappointed at the same time, I don't know—but somehow, Coty pulled it off. "I understand, I really do. I'm surprised it still exists at all, and glad. I'm *glad* it still exists at all," he clarified.

"You could always send it off to a conservator or something," Kate proposed.

"Sure, if I had nothing but money. And nothing else to do with my time," I said, rolling my eyes rather pointedly at the scenery around us—now complete with foil emergency blanket curtains.

"Fair enough, I guess. But it'll definitely be cool to see it when you've got it all dried out."

"Yeah, I'll throw a little party or something. Put the journal under glass and invite people to gawk at it."

"Now you're just being silly," she said. She disappeared into the next room and returned loudly, for she was dragging a crate behind her.

"What? Where did you…?" I began to ask.

"Under one of the sheets. There's nothing in it, I looked. We can use it for a TV console!" she said brightly.

I sighed. "Sure, that works. I hope your laptop battery is all charged up, Coty. I wouldn't trust this house's electrical system enough to plug it in anywhere."

"Is it that bad?" he asked warily, holding the coiled power cord in one hand.

"That bad and then some. Don't plug anything into any socket in this building unless you're not afraid to fry whatever's on the other end."

"Whew, thanks for the heads-up." He tossed it back into the bag.

I hadn't lied at all this time, but I also didn't want him getting too comfortable—and this was a convenient excuse. Whatever his laptop's battery life amounted to…that would be plenty of hangout time spent with the pair of them.

We settled in, we cued up *Damsel of Danger*, and we hit play.

The DVD had been scored with audio that allegedly—if the clamshell documentation could be believed—had been drawn from vintage sheet music that was likely composed for the movie itself, though film historians could not be certain. This particular flick also included some of Ms. Rost's intertitle cards, written in her own hand.

I recognized it immediately, when the first card hit the screen: *A warm and sunny day beside the ocean*, it read. Then a second one appeared. *But all is not as peaceful as it seems. Danger lurks!*

Venita Rost waded through the low, tumbling waves. She wore a black bathing suit in the style of the time—it went halfway down to her knees and was fitted without being snug. No great surprise, in a time before spandex. Her hair was bobbed short with a touch of curl to it, tousled by the sea breeze.

I exhaled slowly. I absolutely could not take my eyes off her.

She was beautiful, yes—even with the janky frame rate that made every gesture look slightly robotic and just a little too quick for normal motion. She had small, perky boobs and a long waist, and nice legs. It was a normal-looking body, not a supermodern supermodel shape; it was the kind of body you might actually see out in the real world someplace. But the technology of the time—the pancake makeup, the grayscale tones… the artifice of the rest was so crude, all the seams and strings were visible.

The organ music crested and swelled, then warned with a minor key: a shark's fin appeared in the water behind her, trailing along while she strolled obliviously through the sand.

The rest of the footage was similar and escalating. First a

shark, then a mustache-twirling creep chased her on the beach, then a car lost its brakes on a hill and charged toward her, and finally she was trapped in a house that was about to be blown up for...reasons? But she rescued herself every time, with increasingly more elaborate stunts.

The final one involved her leaping out a second-story window into the back of a truck that was conveniently full of hay bales.

When she stuck the landing, rolled off the back of the truck, stood up and dusted herself off...we all started clapping. I don't mind admitting that the Jack Daniels was already cracked open and passed around by this point, so when the credits rolled after that two-story leap, we laughed and sighed at the plotless weirdness of it all.

"Impressive, if not complex," Kate declared. "I give it an 'E' for Effort."

"Movies were new back then. They were still working out the kinks, like, how to tell stories and what stories to tell," I said vaguely, feeling the urge to defend the woman who built my home.

"Whole college courses are taught on the subject of early film. Probably whole degrees, even," Coty said with a slow nod. I was pretty sure he'd pulled that information right out of his ass, but who was I to talk. I didn't really doubt it, anyway.

The second flick, *The House by the Lake*, was allegedly the companion piece (Did they mean a sequel? A prequel?) to a lost film called *The Hollow Face*, which sounded interesting—but according to copy on the clamshell, no prints of that one had survived.

"Tragically common," Coty declared, once again as if this were his personal area of expertise. "I read somewhere that ninety percent of all the old silent movies are lost to history."

"Ninety percent?" Kate's eyes went big. "That's a goddamn tragedy, yeah."

"Is it?" I asked, my voice pitched a little high. "I mean, that last one wasn't very good. If it were lost, would anybody really care?"

He shrugged at us. "Even the smallest, most boring parts of history can be meaningful to someone, somewhere."

Well, he had me there. "Hey, speaking of…" I held up a finger and pulled myself together sufficiently to run downstairs to the basement, where I hastily collected the borrowed flicks Hugh had left behind.

Coty was delighted. Too delighted. "Oh, wow, I'm not familiar with these! Nice find, where'd you get them?"

"The previous owner left them behind. He developed an interest in the house's original owner and did a little digging of his own."

I did not elaborate further. I just added the plastic cases to the pile.

We spun up the next disc and started watching *The House by the Lake*, which had more going for it in the narrative department. It was basically a gothic haunted house story—told in twenty minutes. But there were several other characters of note, an actual storyline to be followed, and when it was over, we declared it "Not bad, actually."

Kate was the one who said, "It's a shame that the other one was lost."

The Hollow Face. I wondered what it was about but didn't ask out loud—lest Coty try to give me some more of his butt-pulled factoids.

We took another drink.

An hour and a half later it was finally getting dark outside—and Coty's laptop was going dark inside. We'd seen all the quiet black-and-white offerings, stashed them in their appropriate boxes, and tossed Coty's back into the bag. He closed up the laptop and hinted like maybe he'd care to hang around a little longer, but I headed him off at the pass.

"That's all I've got in me tonight, folks." I stood up and stretched, and my back cracked with more audible violence than I'd expected. "Jesus. Sorry. Excuse me? I guess? Not sure how I'm supposed to politely acknowledge that kind of noise."

Kate laughed and Coty pretended to. But he was good enough to collect his stuff and receive a few warm, tipsy thanks, and then get the hell out—so he had that going for him. Besides, the booze had made me warmer and friendlier toward him, in the way that booze makes me warmer and friendlier toward everybody. Which sets me apart from exactly nobody else, come on.

By the time he left, I was both glad to see him go, and no longer annoyed that he'd arrived with Kate in the first place.

"You want to stick around?" I asked her, since she was still picking up the little bits of trash we'd left on the floor, as if the whole house wasn't one big garbage can, let's be real here.

She didn't answer me. She asked a question instead. "Why'd you lie to him?"

The abruptness threw me for a loop. "What?"

"You have the diary here in the house; I know you do. I was leaning against it the whole time we were watching those movies." She shrugged a shoulder toward the air mattress and my pillows there. The ruined little book was tucked underneath the whole thing; I'd been sleeping like the princess and the pea, if the pea were a damp and swollen volume of someone else's memories.

"Oh. Yeah, I'm not even sure, really." It was the truth, more or less. So was this: "I guess I just wanted to keep it to myself a little longer. I'm still reading it, and the reading is slow going because it's a total mess. I didn't lie about what state it's in. You've seen it."

"No, no. I knew that part was true. But you showed it to *me*. Why not show it to him? He's the one with the actual family connection to the place. To Venita, kind of."

A fair question, with an obvious answer. I think she wanted to make me say it, but I refused. "Yeah, but *I* have an actual family connection to you, not him. Coty is okay, don't get me wrong. I just don't know him that well—and you know what? It's *my* diary. Because I found it in my house. It's mine and it belongs to me."

"What, were you afraid he was going to steal it?" she asked, looking at me like I'd just grown two heads.

"Steal it? No." That was another fib. Worrying about people stealing my stuff was one of my baseline worries. That part wasn't even personal. "But if he'd asked to borrow it, I would've felt really weird saying yes. Don't make this into a big thing; it's not a big thing."

"Okay, okay, it's not a big thing," she agreed, backing off

the subject and retreating to the kitchen, where I had a big box with a trash bag fastened inside it, because I did not actually have a trash can. I had a dumpster, sure. But I didn't always feel like running every scrap of garbage outside.

"Why'd *you* tell him about it?" I asked, and immediately wished I hadn't.

She took her time answering me, doing the same thing I did—fishing for a good fib that was adjacent enough to the truth. "We talk about the house a lot, and Venita, and his uncle. We don't have much else in common."

I almost pressed for more info. I opened my mouth and got ready to fire off a question, something like, "How often *do* the two of you talk?" But I learned a long time ago that sometimes it's okay to leave things alone and wonder about them, especially when you don't want to hear the answer out loud.

I didn't want to hear her answer out loud.

Bartholomew Sloan

NOW

The *Hollow Face* was one of her better productions, in my opinion. What a pity to hear that it's been lost. Then again, if I recall correctly, it was about a woman who loses a child to cholera and subsequently goes mad, and there's something about an optical illusion—I forget. I doubt Venita would consider its loss a calamity, but I could be wrong. It was a strong performance, for her part.

Perhaps you should see if you can find it. After all, *lost* can mean any number of things, up to and including *filed away in a collector's vault*. In the present day and age, I've come to understand that it's much easier to chase down such things.

Back in my day, if someone had hired me to locate a lost print, I would begin by asking questions around the studio, interrogate their archivists, speak to their scriptwriters, and (if nothing else) attempt to locate whoever wrote it. Even if the footage is lost, something might remain.

Or not.

I wonder what Venita would do, if she were to awaken and find it playing on one of those screens they carry around in their pockets and purses. Would it flatter her? Alarm her? Enrage her?

It might make her smile. It might make her wail, for how its subject matter hits too close to home.

Frankly, there's no telling. For all I know, she's the reason it's lost. She certainly had the clout at one time to make such a thing disappear.

It might be just as well if it's vanished from the earth.

My last winter with the Amundsons was strange before it was terrible.

Did the days drag, or did they speed past like landscape from a train window? Sometimes I remember it one way, sometimes I recall it the other.

There was a snowstorm, you see. We've never had too many of those, out on this part of the west coast, and this was one for the record books. I'd already begun that downward slide from welcomed friend to tolerated houseguest to absolute pariah, though Venita's acting skills kept Oscar from feeling the chill too deeply. I'm not even sure he noticed at all, the way she'd started looking at me. Watching me. Suspecting me of something but having no frame of reference as to what.

How could she have known the truth about the trunk in my room? And how did she come to suspect what little she knew?

The former, I've no idea. The latter, it must have been when she went snooping.

Something shifted for me that day, too. Something other than Venita's trust was lost, when she did her best to read my contract and hide the evidence of her efforts. She replaced the seal without breaking it, so she must've run a hot wire or a thin knife beneath it. It's an old trick. She could've picked it up in a movie script or in a radio program. She might've just been clever enough to come up with it herself.

So she didn't break the seal, but she broke…something. Or fractured it, maybe bruised it badly, if it makes more sense to say it that way.

My abilities began to slip, and so did my luck. The biggest cases did not find me, and I fumbled several smaller ones—only to solve them at the last moment, sparing myself the embarrassment of smug headlines and competition from the Pinkertons. (One or two of their operatives had made it a personal mission to dethrone me as the nation's foremost investigator, not that this mission ever succeeded.)

I did not fail altogether, no. But I began to struggle.

Things that had come easily before now came with difficulty. Conclusions I could've drawn in my sleep were now painstakingly deduced and assembled, and as I came to suspect that my secret and ill-gotten powers had been somehow stripped away, I wondered if they might return, and if so, how long that might take.

I also wondered if they were gone for good—but surely not? I'd signed my name in blood. The contract had been countersigned and sealed. If it was broken, then neither one of us would get what we'd promised the other.

I would return to anonymous mediocrity, and the devil would have to cast his net again to snare some other soul.

Oddly enough, this thought brought me no real relief. If my powers were gone, then my deal was moot. That should've reassured me, shouldn't it? I should've felt nothing but relief to conclude that I was free from my contract, but no. I felt only fear.

Venita's speculation was limited by her experience, I suppose. I know what men demand from women, and how hard it is for women who want to achieve power and success for themselves. Perhaps she feared I was one of them, with tastes that ran toward little girls. I've known of men like that, too.

I'd never given her any reason to suspect anything so awful, but perhaps it was the worst she could imagine.

At any rate, she began holding Priscilla back when the girl wished to hug me hello. She found excuses to leave the house with her when we might otherwise be alone—just the three of us. She made plans that took them both into the city for shopping or shows or meals when Oscar brought me over for a spell.

I think he noticed at some point. He must have. But he never said anything.

I hope that doesn't mean he had any suspicions of his own. The thought would destroy me.

But he had to have known that his wife's sentiments had changed; I know he did—I heard them fighting about me. It was one of those tense, quiet, constrained fights between married couples, when they don't want the guests or children to overhear. But he told me about it later, and he furthermore confessed that they'd had an even bigger confrontation once I was out of the house and had returned to Los Angeles.

"Honestly," he told me, "I wish I knew what was wrong with her. She changed a bit when we were expecting Priscilla, in that way that women sometimes do. She was weepy at times, and hysterical with laughter at others. She began to fret, whereas before she'd never been a worrier. I wrote it off to the baby."

"It would stand to reason," I agreed.

"But this is altogether different. She sees suspicious characters around every corner, and I've caught her talking to herself and even whispering strange things to Priscilla. I swear, she's going to frighten that child to death if she keeps this up."

I didn't really want to know, but I needed to. "What kind of strange things?"

"Warnings, mostly. About all kinds of things," he added with a floppy wave of his hand. "Beware of strangers, animals, unexpected food or beverages, et cetera. Careful who you trust, even among the friends and family you know and love. That sort of thing. It's enough to make me wonder if she's entirely well, if I'm to tell the truth."

"You're not suggesting…"

He shook his head. "No, nothing like that. The doctors don't think we'll ever have another child, and this…isn't like that. It only reminds me of it."

I almost wished I could tell him the truth, the ugly whole of it. But that would've only stretched the power further, and part of the contract was a vow to speak not a word of it to any living being. It might have made me even weaker, when I was already in a vulnerable state, thrown by Venita's trespass and my own lack of security.

I held my tongue, except to offer him my shoulder and my

ear, and he thanked me—even as he insisted that my support was not required.

"She's only feeling some stress, I think. There's a new starlet being compared to her, and you know how she gets about these things." He leaned in closer and lowered his voice, even though she was not home when we had this chat—she was out with Priscilla—so I don't know who he wished to keep from overhearing. "In the bottom of her heart, I do believe that she thinks she could hop right back in front of a camera at any time."

"She could, I'm sure of it."

"Are you now?" he asked with a cocked eyebrow and a faint grin. "My good man, she's closer to forty than thirty anymore, and the new girls are still in their teens—playing the ingenues she might have portrayed twenty years ago."

"Twenty years ago, very few people were playing anything. So far as film goes."

"Yes, obviously, but you know what I mean. Hollywood is a hell of a system, Bart. Youth is the only real commodity apart from money."

"Youth and money, I should think."

"Well, money. But it's the youth and beauty that earns it for the big production companies, and those who walk this world without it won't find themselves on the big screen anytime soon."

"Bah, that's nonsense. Most of the men—"

He snapped his fingers. "The men, yes," he interrupted. "Men are allowed more leeway with these things, just ask my wife. She'll tell you all about it," he concluded on a somewhat dour note. "Frankly, I'm tired of hearing about it, how the boys get to be old men but the women have to stay girls forever."

"Venita is, of course, still terribly beautiful. But she might have a point, though."

"Even if she does, there's little to be done about it. Time marches forward for us all," he said, more mellow, I think. Maybe the whiskey was kicking in. "A face like that, coming along at the dawn of a new art form that traffics in such faces. It was good timing, if nothing else."

I'm not sure why, but I felt the need to defend her a bit. I don't think Oscar meant to be so dismissive, but again, we were drinking. We were tired after a long day. He was irritated with her, still steaming from that big fight, perhaps. I couldn't blame him. I couldn't let him blame her, either.

I said, "She's considerably more than a pretty face, and there's every chance she might've gone on to some other success. Her voice is lovely, her handwriting divine. She might've gone into the art world through some traditional path and made her fortune that way."

"Maybe. Maybe she was just lucky to come along when she did, where she did, how she did. Maybe she's unlucky, in that the profession she embraced would only embrace her while she looked like she'd pass for sixteen in a swimsuit."

"Maybe the luck was all yours, for crossing her path when you did."

He sighed. "Maybe." And he finished his drink, then announced he'd be off to bed.

Ronnie

NOW

Since Kate had also left, I really wanted to turn in and call it a night—but I just couldn't do it. I needed a shower so badly that I could smell myself standing there, stinking, in the parlor I'd turned into my bedroom/living room/all-purpose space. Had I smelled this bad all day? Kate should've said something. Coty'd had the good sense not to.

The truth was, I needed civilization. I needed a kitchen with enough working outlets to scramble some eggs and make some coffee; I needed a very hot shower with very strong soap and some good shampoo to really fix me up good; I needed to do some laundry. All my clothes smelled like the house—mildew, dust, with a faint *eau de long-dead animal*.

I needed a house that did more than host dead people.

I packed up the important things and loaded my car, which (now that I stood on the sidewalk and looked at it) appeared to belong to some otherwise unhoused person. Crammed with boxes, old fast-food wrappers, gas station receipts, and whatever I'd thrown in there thinking I might need it...the poor little Volvo was stuffed so full I could barely see out the back window. I was surprised no one had called the city to tow it.

"I need to do something about that," I said as I unlocked it and climbed in behind the wheel. Sometimes if I say things out loud, I remember them better. Sometimes I don't. Usually, it doesn't matter.

I went back to the Central District apartment that was still mine for a little while and stayed up until after midnight making myself look and feel like a human again—rather than some weirdo who camps out in derelict, abandoned places that aren't safe to breathe in, much less sleep in.

More than once, someone has told me that my internal threat-assessment matrix is hopelessly scrambled, but what can you do. I don't worry very hard about normal things like burglars or funny moles. I worry hard about everything *else*.

I slept in because I wanted to and I could, and then I went to the library.

I'd collected the old DVDs that Hugh Crawford had left behind, since even though they were long overdue (and Hugh wasn't likely to pay any of the late fees at this point)...they were rare items, or so I suspected. Far be it from me to deprive any archivist of these weirdo little black-and-white shorts.

I hit the local West Seattle branch rather than the downtown hub; I just couldn't see going that far out of my way—and besides, the whole system was connected, right? The labels on the DVDs did not specify their branch of origin anyway. For all I knew, Hugh got them out of Fremont or the U-district. Or downtown, like Coty.

I could've just left them in the drop box, but the media department wasn't hard to find, and I had the world's vaguest suspicions running around in my head that Coty knew a little too much about Venita and her house. It would be nice to get a head-pat from a friendly librarian for doing the right thing.

The librarian in question was a small woman with floral tattoos poking out from under the three-quarter sleeves of her lavender cardigan. "Oh goodness, would you look at these," she exclaimed with such wholesome enthusiasm that I was glad I'd come inside. "Wait, these are…wow, somewhat overdue."

"Sorry. I, uh, I'm not the one who checked them out. I bought this old house, and I found these in the basement."

She took a little scanner and blipped the barcode. "No, you're definitely not a man named Hugh."

"That's the fellow I got the house from," I oversimplified.

"Well, thank you for bringing them back! It looks like…" She scanned her monitor's screen with a squint. "Some film students at UW have been asking about a couple of these, trying to track them down through interlibrary loan. Poor kids. Between Hugh and the guy before him, these things have been out of circulation for ages."

"The guy before him left them in a basement and sold the house, too?" I joked weakly.

She shook her head. "Nah. He just checked them out a million times and wouldn't return them to circulation, a couple of years back. Selfish jerk."

"Rude," I agreed.

"Gonna keep an eye out for this Coty guy. *I* wouldn't have let him get away with that."

I swear, the record-scratch in my head was so loud, she must've heard it. There it was. The danger light lit up my skull like a lampshade. "Sorry, come again? Was the guy's last name…" Shit, I suddenly couldn't think of it. It wasn't Sloan, that'd be too easy. I'd only heard it once or twice, and it hadn't stuck.

"Deaver. We ought to put him on a list, like those bars that keep and display the fake IDs they confiscate, right on the wall where everybody can see them. If you're not gonna respect the process and wait your turn, then you don't deserve to participate."

I couldn't agree more and I told her so, then I kept pretty cool on the way back to my car, even though I could feel a bright-pink flush working its way up my chest to my neck and cheeks. By the time I was sitting behind the wheel again, I looked like I was having an allergic reaction, or maybe a hot flash.

Over and over again, I thought about him the night before and how he'd said he wasn't familiar with these movies of Hugh's…when he'd actually had them in his hot little hands for God only knew how long. He probably had all the intertitles memorized. Maybe he copied the discs onto his computer or something. You can do that, right? Or do libraries add DRM or something?

Inside my car, it was kind of warm. The day wasn't warm, but it would maybe hit the low sixties by the afternoon, and the sun was intermittently putting in an appearance.

Still, I sat there and stared through the windshield.

Coty had lied, right to my face, in front of God and Kate and everybody.

What else had he lied about? I didn't know where to begin speculating, which didn't really stop me. My thoughts raced, reexamining every word I'd ever heard him say, as best as I could recall it. He'd never really said or done anything suspicious, had he? If I hadn't accidentally caught him in this single, solitary lie, I would've never had a reason to suspect he was trying to mislead me, now would I?

Then why had I disliked him from the start?

It might be as simple as Kate's interest in the man, whatever the nature of that interest might be. But I didn't think so. That tiny but vivid danger light had been flashing in the back of my brain since shortly after I met him; something had been insisting that he wasn't as straightforward and wholesome as he'd seemed at first blush.

I started the car and rolled down the passenger window to get some fresh air. Then I let the car idle while my gray matter kept churning.

Why had he lied at all?

It would've been easy as pie to get a gander at the DVDs and say, "Oh, wow, I checked these out, too!" since we already knew he'd done all this research on the house and its original owners and occupants, regardless of how brief their residency turned out to be. It wouldn't have been a red flag, in itself. It might've even been awkwardly charming.

Maybe it's simpler than I'm making it, and he just isn't a good liar on his feet.

Coty's long-departed uncle Sloan couldn't have owned the

place for more than a few days, I wouldn't think. He inherited it from Oscar Amundson upon Oscar's death, and Bartholomew Sloan had supposedly died shortly thereafter. Did he recognize his nephew? In the afterlife, did people retain some peculiar, thin thread to their living bloodlines?

I could feel my overthinking juices flowing like mad, trying to rationalize something strange that might only be a coincidence, I reminded myself, as I finally threw the car into gear and left the parking lot to head back home.

Or back to the house. It wasn't really a home yet. It was an uncomfortable place to camp, without so much as a fire. If it were any colder, I couldn't get away with it.

But to paraphrase a Disney earworm, the cold and damp don't bother me much, anyway. Not usually. There's a reason I settled down in the northwest rather than the southwest.

It was maybe one o'clock when I pulled up to the house, and it looked the same as it always does: half-abandoned and thoroughly tragic, maybe even more so now that the sun was out and I could see every rusty nail, every sagging piece of siding, and every chip of peeling paint.

"Hello, House," I announced myself.

I reached into the back seat for the laundry basket full of clean clothes I'd "packed," grabbed my backpack full of toiletries and whatnot, and headed inside, shutting the car door with my ass.

I fished my keys out of my front pocket before I remembered that I hadn't locked the front door. Yeah, I probably should've done that, but there's nothing inside that anyone would want to steal, surely. Might get some lookie-loos. Someone might get inside to take a look around and get hurt. I could get sued. I could lose the house and all the garbage inside it before I ever get to officially take up residence. Really, I should've known better. Honestly, I must be slipping. Perhaps it was a result of lingering aftereffect from those goddamn meds, luring me into a false sense of security. How long do they stay in your system after you stop them, anyway?

Ah, there it was: the old familiar anxiety spiral.

It was almost comforting, like a visit from a friend who annoys the shit out of you but you haven't seen them in a while, so it's okay, maybe it's time to catch up.

I let it churn.

It wasn't bothering anyone but me, and it wasn't even bothering me very much. It's honestly hard to explain, except to say that I don't like panic whirlpools, but I'm accustomed to them. We all have our ruts. Mine are just stupider and more difficult to escape than most people's.

I leaned on the door. It stuck, then skidded open, and I carried the laundry basket and backpack into the parlor before coming back to kick it shut again.

I froze. Something was wrong. Or different.

I smelled something pleasant, like fresh flowers in a clean vase, sitting by a window and warmed by the sun—which I definitely did not have anywhere on the premises.

I closed my eyes and concentrated on the nice smell. Not roses but something close. Gardenias, maybe. It made me think of old-fashioned perfume, and of soft, silver-haired women who hugged me tight as a child and left me smelling like church.

I opened my eyes again and something about the foyer was different.

At first, I couldn't put my finger on it. It wasn't the light creeping in through the filthy windows; it wasn't the shine on the floor or the round table with the centerpiece made with a silk bouquet. No, wait. Yes it was.

The floor inside the front door was shiny, as if it'd been polished, and there was a round table where one might drop one's keys, or leave a hostess gift, or set a glass of champagne at a dinner party—and I've never owned anything like it. I'd only seen such furniture in movies or TV shows, because I'd never lived in a house (and did not frequent such places) with room enough in the entryway to accommodate.

This house in West Seattle, up against the ridge that overlooks the Sound, had a surprising amount of furniture left covered in various rooms. It did *not* have a round entryway table.

Which really begged the question of what it was doing here.

The smooth, shiny ribbon of the floor (no splinters, no water damage, no termite paths, no protruding nail heads) led from the door to the table and then past it, toward the stairs. When I took my eyes off this unusual path, when I looked away, the rest of the floor was as I'd always known it: probably too ruined to restore without a tremendous amount of effort and money.

But it *was* a path. It *did* run from the front door, through the foyer, past the round table I'd never seen before and the fake flowers festooned upon it.

Behind me, the front door was very slightly warped. It needed to be sanded and painted. Eventually, I'd yank the hardware and simmer it in an old Crock-Pot to clean it, then shine it up and reinstall it. One of the panes in the leaded glass peep window was cracked, but I could replace that. There was nothing shiny or new about the door.

Slowly, I pulled my phone out of my pocket and turned on the camera. I snapped a couple of pics, but when I checked them, they showed nothing but the house as I knew it: rundown, dirty, moldering in place. I started walking, the camera still pointed forward, tracking the trail as I walked it, recording nothing of interest. I gave up and put the phone away in my back pocket.

Past the table, the trail wended toward the stairs. It flowed like a creek; I tiptoed like I might get my feet wet, or I might slip on what must be fresh wax.

I could smell the wax. Yes, that's what it was. Just beyond the vintage perfume, I caught a whiff of dusty honey and chemicals and yes. Floor wax. And now I heard music. It was nothing I recognized, and it was somewhere far enough away that I could not catch the tune, nor the words. But it was close enough to be inside the house. Upstairs. In one of the bedrooms, I was willing to bet. If it were coming from the music room it would've been clearer, or that was my reasoning at the time. (If it were coming from the music room, that's where the trail on the floor would have led me.)

I followed the trail to the staircase, where the rotting carpet runner was restored as fully as the gleaming floorboards. A swath of crimson rug with a gold pattern now climbed crisply to the second story, right through the middle of that staircase that otherwise looked like a strong breeze might cause it to collapse. No fraying, no rough edges, no damp, blackened patches destroyed by mold.

I don't know why I followed the trail. I guess I was curious? I guess it made so little sense, that I failed to see it as a threat? There was nothing especially sinister about it; after all, what's not to like about a good before-and-after? My gut said I was seeing the place—at least in fragments—as it'd once appeared when it was new and loved and intact.

Why my gut said this, I don't know. Why I believed my gut, I could not say.

I was terrified beyond words, but the fear wasn't...close. It was somewhere far away, pushed back to the edges of this mirage that was swallowing my home. I could see it, but I couldn't feel it. I only knew it was there, waiting for the illusion to lift before it would sweep back into my brain like a storm.

The music was foggy upstairs, filtered through the floor or drifting down the big hole where Hugh Crawford once rested in peace. It was a simple tune with only a few instruments to lift it up, and the singer was a man, and the beat was happy without being too excited. There was nothing sinister about that, either.

Or the lovely old perfume.

I put one hand on the rail and instinctively pulled away; I knew better than to lean on it, for it was barely more sturdy than cardboard. I put my hand back again. It looked as solid as a baseball bat. It was shiny and smooth, without any splits or soft spots.

I did not put my weight on it. I knew that it shouldn't be able to hold me, and I did not want to push the limits of whatever was happening here.

I stayed on the path in the middle of the steps and at the top, the path was wider—as if it'd pooled up there, and merely spilled down to the main level. There, the carpet runner was tidy and freshly swept. I liked the pattern now that I could see it clearly: oak leaves and acorns, that was the design. A little flashy, a little classic.

The music was louder up there. It came from the master bedroom. I shouldn't have known that, but I did.

That's where the trail led, of course. It trickled away in little eddies, streaming into other rooms but not very far. The carpet runner would be pristine but only in strips and streaks; at the edges it was frayed and brown. Beyond it, the floor was scratched and gouged.

Because it felt like the appropriate time to do so, I called out, "Hello? Is somebody here?"

And I thought about the ghost of the big man in the small half bath downstairs, who'd scared me so badly. I thought of the white cat, the platinum pussycat, was that how it went? The kitty no one ever saw but me.

"Hello?" I tried again.

"In here, darling. I'll be ready in a moment, but it would be... I would be..." I heard a frustrated little grunt. "This would go much faster if I had an extra hand. Could you help me out, dear? It'll only take a moment."

Why did I know her voice? I couldn't have possibly heard it before. There probably weren't even any recordings of it. But it was familiar all the same—the kind of familiar that comes with a name and a face, the toss of bright blond hair and a laugh that sounds like wind chimes.

I followed the sound of it regardless. The trail on the floor widened, it expanded as I drew closer to that master bedroom with the collapsed four-poster bed and nothing else, not even a trash bag.

Whereas before it was only a narrow path, now it was the whole floor, wall to wall in the corridor—and up the walls as I approached: the navy pinstripe wallpaper uncurled and spread out flat, smooth, and clean. The missing gas lamp figures reappeared as if they'd never been removed. They were brass and shaped like parrots, four altogether, offset between the stairs and the master bedroom at the end of the hall. I'd never seen anything like them. They were long gone, and it made my heart hurt.

"Are you coming?"

"Yes," I said back, but not very loudly. I didn't think I needed to be loud for her to hear me.

"Good, because I'm stuck and Oscar isn't home, and I can't find Priscilla. I've been calling and calling, the little minx. She must be up in the attic."

"In the attic?"

I stood in the doorway and stared inside.

A radio the size of a dorm fridge buzzed merrily against the wall. The bed was mahogany and the posts were elaborately carved with Egyptian-revival motifs. I saw lotus flowers and scarabs, reeds and ankhs, and Venita Rost in a lavender silk dress that was just a hair too fitted to call a simple shift. Tiny silver beaded tassels decorated the bottom hem, and a pair of small flutter sleeves graced her shoulders; her hair was straight out of a black-and-white-movie still—cropped in finger waves, so pale that you'd almost call it white. Platinum, even.

Her back was to me, but only for a moment as she leaned

on one of the posts and pried her foot free from a chunky satin heel. She turned around.

"There you are!" she exclaimed brightly. "Would you look at this? I can't quite reach the zipper, and I feel positively ridiculous. I'm trapped in my own clothes, what a stupid predicament. Could you…?" She gestured at her back, and the long silver zipper that ran from her shoulder blades to her butt.

"Sure." What else was I going to say?

I entered the room and crossed a deep-green Persian rug with a pattern that reminded me of tiger stripes, and I barely noticed the emerald-and-indigo wallpaper or the sleek fireplace mantel that was almost the opposite of the elaborate one in the parlor. But I did notice. I noticed the cat, too—silver gray with a hint of gold, and enormous green eyes. It lounged on the foot of the bed, atop a folded blanket. It watched me warily, and with interest.

I almost asked its name, but forgot the question almost immediately because Venita was looking at me. She was all bright curls, big eyes, and that lavender dress that shimmered in the light from the big window on the eastern wall. She was magic, and she smiled at me.

Of course I went to her. What else was I going to do?

I took the small silver tab and pulled it gently, not wanting to stretch or strain the silk. I don't dress up often, and I'm no expert in vintage clothes, but I am not some kind of unwashed heathen, either. I wanted to touch everything. I was afraid to touch anything. The backs of my fingers dragged down her back with the zipper, and she felt cool and solid. She felt human and real.

I will not say that she felt alive.

I cannot say what I mean by that, because I am not sure of it myself.

But she turned to me and she smiled at me, and she said, "Thanks, doll! You're a peach." Then she slipped out of the dress and stood in her bare feet and nothing but a slip lying across the shape of her body, too pale to be living and breathing, too firm to be a figment of my imagination.

"Happy to help."

The brilliant smile dimmed to mere warmth. She cocked her head. "Are you, though?"

"I mean, I'm trying to?" I waved a little helplessly, meaning to indicate the house and everything in it. "I'm trying to put things back together. Is…is that what you mean? Is that what you *want*?"

"Among other things, I suppose. What I want *most* is for my ridiculous little child to turn up. I hate it when she does this, when I wake up and I can't find her. She's around here somewhere, though. You watch, I'll find her. I'll introduce you! You'll absolutely love her," she added with confidence and a little clap.

"I…I don't know where she is. I don't think I can help you with that."

Now she frowned. "You can't? Are you sure?" Before I could answer she walked away from me, padding across that rug on those tiny white feet. She was a small woman, probably about five foot one and a hundred pounds with rocks in her pockets. "Hmm. Well, you only just got here. Maybe we can find her together. Maybe between the two of us, she'll hear us calling, and she'll…maybe she'll answer."

I retreated slowly toward the door again. The clean, warm, new feeling in the room was retracting—the corners were full of cobwebs again, the radio vanished and the music stopped, the fireplace was plastered over, one poster of the bed was lying on the floor.

The floor.

Beneath my feet, it was no longer shiny.

Behind me, out in the hall, I could've sworn I heard something or someone else. I looked over my shoulder and saw something, maybe? Someone, perhaps? A big shape, just an outline—and barely even that. Coming closer in fits and starts. Jerkily drawing near, flickering frames of something dark from a janky projector just before the film strip breaks and burns.

I shouldn't have said anything. I probably didn't need to.

I couldn't help it. I gasped, "Sloan?" But I shouldn't have said his name. I should've clapped my hand over my mouth and held it there until I passed out, because with just that single syllable, barely whispered, with the shade's identity far from confirmed…

Venita *screamed*.

Her scream grew louder and higher until it wasn't a woman's scream anymore, but I don't know what you'd call it. Something almost digital or mechanical, the whine of a failing machine or a steam engine that's ready to blow.

The room went dark for a fraction of a second. It was a reverse lightning flash, the kind that happens when a plane flies overhead, and for scarcely an instant you're caught in its shadow; there's a flicker where reality seems unreal, but it's over before you can even identify it as such.

The room was empty again except for the rotting four-poster bed and Venita, who didn't really look like Venita anymore. She was only a whirlwind, a vivid tornado that gusted forward.

She hit me.

She wailed right through me and past me into the hall, leaving me breathless and confused.

And then the floor was dull and full of splinters, and the carpet runner was made of mildew and old wool of an indeterminate color, and the staircase banister wouldn't have held a kitten with a full belly. Then the steps were crooked and rough, and they creaked as loud as fireworks, and the parrot fixtures were replaced with gaping holes. The hallway was a wind tunnel, so loud, so terrifying, so confusing. I flung myself against the nearest wall and covered my face.

As suddenly as the noise and the whirlwind began, they stopped.

I stood alone at the top of the staircase as the dusty, grim reality of the house swept in from the edges, as I'd known it surely would. I felt as cold and shaky as if I'd slept outside in the rain.

Bartholomew Sloan
NOW

I was only trying to help.
 I was only trying to catch you before she caught you, Ronnie—before she could remember and topple back into her preferred madness. I only wanted to distract her, to lure her away from you before she could cast her net, but I was too late. You'd already found her. She'd already done what she always does and awakened happy, if confused—friendly, if uncertain. It's often as though she knows she's forgetting something but can't figure out what precisely that might be... And some part of her doesn't want her to remember, so she fights it.
 But her desire for her daughter is greater than her fear of remembering, so once that terrible thought-loop has opened, it will close again, the way it always does.
 She always remembers eventually.
 Once in a while it takes her a day or two. She'll roam the place calling Priscilla's name, searching from attic to basement

and all four corners of the compass. But in time, yes. She remembers that the child is dead—and wherever that death took her, it was someplace far from here.

    The poor girl is gone. So much the better, really. What a horror, to be a child trapped in a decaying house, with a madwoman for a mother and her own inadvertent murderer for a fellow resident.

    I know Venita disagrees (or maybe she doesn't, maybe she's only grief-stricken and angry), but I do think it's for the best. Let the girl rest. Or let her have come back around, as souls are said to do sometimes.

    I wonder what became of her, if that was the case. I wonder if she'd find herself in a new place, a new body, a new life…and still remember faintly that there was a house, and a beautiful blond woman, and a gilded mirror in the parlor where she once lost her life. I wonder if she is out there somewhere, and in the very darkest hours of the very earliest mornings, I wonder if she dreams of us.

    Well. That's a nice thought, I suppose.

    Venita can't hurt me anymore, and I can't hurt her, either.

    Not that I wish to.

    I only wish that we could each retire to our respective and respectable deaths, quiet and restful, comfortably buried someplace where we'll never wake again, only to roam and bicker and mourn our mistakes. I don't deserve such an ending, but I cannot help but yearn for it.

I was only trying to help when I came down the hallway, struggling to make myself seen or heard, and achieving limited success at best. I know she heard my voice at least once before, when she briefly considered drinking from the gin on the cart (despite its obvious age and condition), and I know she saw me fairly clearly in the small downstairs bath. She seems to have even determined my identity, which is somewhat impressive, should you ask me. I suppose that a limited number of people have died here, throughout the years—but not all of us remain, and not all of us are even known.

I've seen Hugh Crawford, but we don't talk. I think he'll move on, with time; most of the dead eventually do, and he's barely here at all. Frankly, I was stunned that he was able to reach out to Ronnie for that little conversation while she dreamed.

But good for him, I suppose.

And then there's the house itself. It's haunting her as surely as it haunts Venita and I. Surely, given enough motivation, anything at all can choose to haunt.

Now I sound as daft as Venita. Well, maybe I am. I do not think it's reasonable to expect me to be sane after all this time trapped and silent in this house that I used to love, and shortly came to loathe, and presently tolerate with numb resignation.

But listen to me, look at me. I am pathetic. I am talking my way around what happened, as if doing so can absolve me of my participation in a child's sudden death.

This is what happened, if you must know (and you must, and in case you can hear me on any level, in any form). I wish I'd left behind a journal. I wish I'd written some final missive; even a suicide note would've done the trick. God knows Venita's did.

There I go again. Away from the subject at hand.

Here's the meat of it: I was losing my touch and beginning to panic.

I'd only narrowly solved two simple cases, and the second one purely by a bit of luck and also a bit of money paid to bribe a witness. I did not frame anyone, and I only revealed the truth of a matter, but it was not my preferred way to operate. I hadn't needed to resort to such trickery in years. Not since before I sealed my own fate, since before I made a deal with something I mistook for a someone at first.

And I have no excuses. Even once I understood that the many-named and man-shaped thing I'd found hosting seances for a price could not be—and never had been—a man of any sort, I still signed my own name in exchange for something more useful than my soul (or so I thought at the time).

But there had been stipulations, one of which was my utter and permanent silence with regards to our arrangement. I must never speak a word of it, nor convey through any other action the nature of my debt.

I never spoke of it. I never hinted or gestured or played a telling game of charades. Yes, Venita had found the letter and no doubt tried to read it, but the odds against her success were astronomical. There was not a chance on earth that she could read the contents of a letter written in a language I couldn't have identified if she'd held a gun to my head.

But did that count? Did it matter that she'd even seen the agreement, though it could not have told her anything?

I feared that I already knew the answer. Each new case was a little harder, and luck no longer broke in my direction; clues did not present themselves as if on a platter, and I struggled to correctly assemble the bits and pieces of evidence I was able to locate. It was only a matter of time before my winning spree drew to a dramatic and probably career-ending close. It's the great difficulty of achieving the highest heights: Anything less than perfection pops the bubble, doesn't it? On a staged performance of spinning plates, thirty might pirouette correctly—but if even one should wobble and fall, the magic is shattered and the trick has failed.

My entire adult life, my whole prestigious career, has been such a trick.

So I decided to make an attempt to contact the owner of my soul, on the off chance he might answer some questions or even provide some respite. I'd never attempted such a thing before, and I'd been strictly commanded to try no such thing under any circumstances. Yet even so, the woman who served as the go-between had given me instructions. When I asked her why, she'd only shrugged and sent me away.

I would need a mirror, a candle, my contract, a ceremonial blade, and a night before the new moon. I'd also need the short incantation that'd been spelled out phonetically on the back of the single page, as I didn't recognize even the letters used to inscribe it.

I would've preferred to wait until I was home in California, but I was too anxious to put it off when the new moon was on the horizon—and I was at the Amundsons' again. I should have waited. I knew better; I knew it was dangerous and selfish, and

I knew I was putting the household in harm's way. I was impulsive and impatient. And afraid. But that fear does not exonerate me, not on any count.

I should've been the man in the noose, as I've always said and always known. But when it mattered, no one would listen. Besides, I'm dead anyway, and Venita's the one who killed me. If it hadn't cost Oscar his life, too, I could almost say that justice was served after all.

All too soon, the evening rolled around. I waited until everyone was in bed asleep, or so I thought. It was a quarter until midnight, according to the big grandfather clock in the library. I remember how I held my breath when the quarter-hour chimed out, and I was in my slippers and robe, carrying a lit candle and a secret letter toward the parlor.

Why the parlor? Because it held the biggest mirror in the house, and I'm not sure why, but it felt important. I could've used one of the water closets, or a shaving mirror might have worked for all I knew—except that I had a very strong feeling that I could only try this once, and that I therefore needed to make sure I did it right…to the best of my unconfident abilities.

When the clock was finished with its tune and the only remaining sound was the soft ticking of the mechanism, I exhaled and carried on toward the parlor.

The fire had burned down and the screen was cool to the touch, though the marble mantel was still warm. It was February and that's an awful month in the northwest, one of the worst. Everything is cold, dark, and wet, and it feels like the sun will never return in earnest. Midnight before the new moon felt like the deepest reaches of space, for it was so terribly dark and quiet.

Except for that clock, ticking and ticking. I was so glad when it finally stopped, the weights that drove the mechanism having sunk to the floor. I was thrilled when the damn thing was sold in the estate liquidation held by the city after my death.

(All the items remaining in the house from those days simply could not be sold, and for whatever reason, were never discarded.)

With all the gas lamps turned down for the night my candle was the only light, and it was enough to reveal the room in fits and starts as the flame jerked back and forth in time with my shaking hands. The curtains were closed. The bar cart had been tucked away, and the radio's tubes had gone quiet.

On the wall beside the fireplace, the great gilded mirror was hung. I've always admired the piece; Oscar picked it up in Italy, I want to say. It's a true heirloom, an anniversary gift for Venita. I'm sure they planned to pass it along to Priscilla one day.

I stood before that mirror and could see myself as the phantom I'd doomed myself to become—or that was the maudlin thought that darted through my head at the time. My eyes were sunken and my beard was unkempt. My robe was missing its belt, and I only then realized I was wearing but a single sock under my slippers.

This was by no means my finest moment. If anything, it felt like the lowest point in my life—the absolute rock bottom of despair and self-loathing and fear. And to think, I wasn't even halfway there.

But as I held up my contract in its little envelope with the crumbling remnants of its red wax seal, I wondered if my intentions mattered. If I did not *intend* to speak of my bargain, if I did not *intend* to let anyone (even myself) slip past the seal, if I did not *choose* to transgress any of the agreed-upon boundaries... then surely an exception could be made?

Nonsense, yes, I know.

I cleared my throat, angled my candle to better illuminate the text, and started to read—intermittently glancing at the mirror, trying to determine if this was working. Nine times I was supposed to speak the phrase. Nine seemed excessive to me, but I wasn't the sort to question such precise directions, so when I was finished with the brief lines, I read them all over again. And again. And again.

With each reading, the mirror grew brighter. Or perhaps I should say that something *inside* the mirror did so—for it was not the glass itself, but something beyond it. Something within that interstitial space was waiting, responding, and coming closer.

I could almost see its shape, a terrible twisted knot of a thing without a discernable face or eyes, no teeth or arms. At a distance or a glance, or through the unnatural mists of the mirrored light, it looked rather like a great ball of hands with fingers entwined too tightly to be untangled. It writhed like a rat king made of fingers, or possibly tentacles tied up like a ball of yarn.

I did not want to see it again. *Once* had nearly driven me mad.

But not knowing if our bargain still held would've finished the job. I was becoming obsessive and sloppy, I was not sleeping, I was not eating well, and I was drinking far too much. I could've written off my failures to these things and perhaps been satisfied, if only for a while; I could have lied to myself a little longer.

I am much better at lying to other people, alas.

I was on the seventh round of recitation, and I suppose in my obsession and my sloppiness, I had not detected that I was not alone—or rather, less alone than I thought. The thing in the mirror was nearly with us; I'd almost drawn it close enough to touch. Two more repetitions. Two more passes of the tongue across a stream of unfamiliar sounds.

Two little feet tiptoed down the hall and down the stairs, into the parlor where I was not being half so quiet as I thought.

One little girl in a nightdress, barefoot and wild-haired, with sleepy eyes that were nonetheless bright as stars when I spotted them at last. She was right beside me, staring up at the mirror she could barely reach with her fingertips when she stood as tall as possible. Although she could not see the figure in the glass— and thank heaven for that—her lips were parted in awe.

I did not see her in time to stop her.

I only saw that little hand, fingers as small and white as birthday candles, reaching up for that light with the ghastly blue-gray tint around the edges. It was a terrible, unnatural color—nothing created by any benevolent deity known to man. And when the tiny fingers touched the mirror's frame, in that impossible fraction of a second, the sickly glow concentrated into an arc as pure and awful as a bolt of lightning.

It struck.

It hit the child with a crack louder than thunder, and it sounded like glass breaking but it wasn't. It was Priscilla breaking, flying across the room into the far wall, where she slammed, and stuck briefly in the dent her body left there, then toppled to the floor face down.

My heart was choking me. It leaped up into my throat and grew more swollen as I dashed to the girl's side and rolled her toward me—only to see that her eyes had been burned away into smoking black sockets.

Priscilla was dead and there was no question, no further bargaining to be attempted. Her corpse was as light as a doll's when I pulled her into my arms and held her, shaking her gently, begging her to turn back time and go back upstairs to bed, and sleep until morning when she would awaken to her mother's kiss.

Yes, more nonsense, I know.

I tried to say her name and only squeaked it, only sobbed it when I tried a second time.

Upstairs, I heard commotion in the master bedroom. Her parents were awake—of course they were awake, no one could've slept through the sound of two realities crashing together like that.

I looked at the mirror and saw that it was dark. It was not cracked. It was only dead, like the sweet little girl who'd followed me around like a duckling as long as I'd known her.

I struggled to my feet and carried her to the settee, where I left her covered with a little throw blanket. Then I staggered upright once more and, after a few seconds of contemplation, I ran for the front door. I'm sure I was an absurd sight: a large man in a night-robe and slippers with one sock, his face red from weeping both accomplished and ongoing. But I made it to the door and I turned the screw bolt to unlock it, and then I threw myself outside onto the porch and let the door swing shut behind me.

I'm not sure that I'd consciously put it together yet, what I meant to do. All I really knew of my own motive was that I wanted to get away, as far away as possible, for as long as I could. I could not face Venita or Oscar. I could not face myself. I could not imagine living with what I'd done for even another hour.

This is why I ran for the overlook.

I intended to reach its edge and keep running, right over the cliff and into Puget Sound, or to the rocks below if the tide was out. Either way, I'd be as far away from the situation as possible. Death is supposed to be the great undiscovered country, isn't that what the Bard said?

But when I reached the cliff—a miracle in itself on a night with no moon and only cloud cover where the stars should be—I stood there unmoving, my night-robe blowing around me in the frigid, driving mist. I looked out over the dull, rough expanse of the water I could barely see, illuminated only in slivers of light from the mainland and the south end of the city. The mist had brought its friend the fog, and even those city lights showed me almost nothing.

One more step would have done it.

Back at the house, Oscar yelped, and then, a moment later, Venita screamed.

The scream hit me in the back and dragged itself across my skin. It hit me as ragged and hot as a steak knife, and it cut me to ribbons. The scream did not stop; I don't even remember hearing her pause to breathe.

I stood there with my toes on the brink, my body swaying in the wind, just inches from never hearing her scream again.

When she finally stopped, it could've been fifteen seconds or an hour later, I have no way of knowing, I was no longer present in any meaningful way.

A few seconds later, a new scream: my name.

She demanded to know where I was and what I'd done, then she turned her wrath to Oscar—and that's when I stepped away from the edge, sobbing like a child. I couldn't let Oscar take the brunt of her wrath. He was my truest friend, and I had wronged him in a way I could never make up to him. But I could not wrong him further.

Soaking wet and broken of heart, I trudged back down the hill, to the house.

To Venita.

Ronnie

NOW

Venita left me standing there, alone and confused, vibrating from a lingering hangover that felt not unlike (but not *exactly* like) dreamsickness. I leaned against a doorframe and held myself up by willpower alone, my thoughts swirling, my innate anxiety bubbling over like a pot left on the stove too long. I could hardly catch my breath, a fact that didn't make sense to me—I hadn't exactly run a marathon, but here I was, panting shallowly, listening to a small and raspy squeak in the back of my throat.

"What the fuck just happened?" I asked myself, the room, the ghosts, the house. Anyone who might be listening.

I slid down to the floor slowly, catching myself with my hands and collecting a splinter for my trouble. "Venita," I said her name slowly, tasting each syllable, tripping over every consonant, dragging every vowel.

Good God, what *was* she?

Besides dead. I knew she was dead, a fact that was impossible to reconcile with what had just happened. The beautiful room, the woman, the cat. All of them here, now. With me, for as long as Venita would permit it.

"Everything turns on her, doesn't it? One way or another," I muttered.

Even me.

Thrilling new ghost events aside, I was hungry and antsy and fidgeting. Should I call Kate and tell her all about this? She was the one person likely to halfway believe me. She would halfway believe me…wouldn't she?

Coty might, but I didn't want to tell him anything.

Ben would have, and for a while after he died, I used to talk to him like he was still around. I stopped after a few months. I never felt like he was listening. I never felt any sign of him at all, even though I wanted one desperately—and looked for one constantly.

I suppose we get the ghosts we get, not necessarily the ones we want.

I swung by my apartment to grab my laptop. It was a battered and almost vintage number, but it was okay for internet when I wanted a screen bigger than my phone; so I headed to a little bistro-type place that had sandwiches over at Alki Point. It was a nicer day than the city had seen for the last little while, and the sun was even halfway out—giving the low, light clouds a bright seam of gold around the edges. It wasn't raining and it wasn't that cold, so I sat outside at a small round table with an umbrella like a goddamn European.

There was just enough room on that tiny table for my roast beef sandwich, a soda, and the old laptop, which still had enough juice to pick up the bistro's Wi-Fi.

You might be surprised what you can find online with a little patience and persistence; the public record is considerably more extensive than people tend to think it is, and if you know a guy who's a PI and can do the fancy lookups that would otherwise cost money, well... You can learn a lot, fairly quickly.

I shot an email to my PI friend in Renton asking for just a small favor.

While I waited to hear back, I learned on my own that a certain Coty Deaver was not quite a digital ghost, but you could see it from here. I found two abandoned social media accounts, a one-line reference to him in a *Seattle Times* piece about NIMBYism in the South End, and not much else. I was just starting to get really frustrated when my PI pal became the snoop-VIP with his reply.

> This guy bothering you? Because he sounds like the kind of guy who would bother you, or bother someone else.
> In fact, he has a history of it. First, his name was Andrew Deaver Stack until he got nailed for a DUI in his late teens. Did some community service, new identity, yada yada. I guess you can't blame him for wanting to distance himself from an early mistake, but it doesn't look like he legally changed his name.
> He's made some more recent mistakes, too. I found a

protection order against him, filed by a girlfriend after she dumped him. He let himself into her apartment and tried some big romantic gesture that backfired when she called the cops. The order was extended from three months to six, but I don't know why. He's also passed a bad check or two, but that was a few years back. We all have hard times once in a while, right? Could've even been an honest mistake, for all we know. Probably wasn't.

That's all I could turn up on the fly real quick, but I can do more digging if you like. I still owe you for fixing that blown pipe...or I guess I owe your brother, but you know what I mean.

I sat back and stared at the screen. Then, on a lark, I went back to the auction site that the city uses when it has stray property to unload—like, oh, say, my own house. Other bidders would be a matter of public record, right? Surely? I ran a couple of searches, and even though I'm no PI and I'm not any sort of internet expert, I found him right away. Not as Coty, but yes, there he was: Andrew Stack.

My heart was pounding, and I wasn't sure if that was stupid or not. I was safe. I was in a public place. I wasn't even at home, and Coty was nowhere in the vicinity. Why was my fear reaction kicking in? Why was my mental danger light flashing? It's not like I'd left the dryer running on my way out the door.

Well, for starters, the guy had been trying to weasel into my life, or weasel into my house at least, since before we'd ever met. Now he was using Kate to gain access to my space, and the thought of that infuriated me—almost as much as it worried me.

Kate knew more about him than I did, or she thought she did. God only knew how much of what he told her was true.

I pulled out my phone and texted her: Hey, what are you doing today? And I stared at the screen.

Three little dots said she was composing a reply.

Nothing, you want me to come over? It's lunchtime—I could grab something.

Nah, I'm already eating.

Without me?

Sorry! Feel free to come on over if you want, though. I'll be home in another half hour. Actually I want to talk to you about something. I have some weird information about the house and I want to run it past you.

I sort of fibbed.

Okay, see you in a bit, she concluded.

I packed up my stuff and headed back to the house, so twitchy you'd swear I was on something. I needed to talk to Kate or else I would explode. I was sure of it.

I'd almost forgotten about my findings at the library because Venita was real, and it's not like I could pretend I hadn't seen her, spoken to her, watched her transform her space into what it must've looked like when it all still belonged to her.

"This happened. I am not crazy. That woman is *real*," I reminded myself. "I *touched* her."

Almost like an afterthought, I remembered my earlier rage at Coty, and yes, I'd share that, too. The email from my PI friend had contained a stack of very damning facts, and I would not allow them to go ignored. Coty had bid on the house and lost it to me…but hadn't he said something about the auction? That first time we met? About how he certainly hadn't tried to buy the house? Couldn't afford it?

Maybe it was only implied, I couldn't remember.

Nobody with good intentions goes to this much trouble to hide their background.

So what did he want, then? The house itself?

Over my dead body—or was that his plan all along? Did he want his uncle's stuff? There wasn't any, unless you counted the ancient bottle of gin that still hung around on the dusty little bar cart. And that was only a guess on my part, since Venita's diary talked about him liking it.

Okay. I'd self-soothed enough that my hands weren't shaking anymore, and I couldn't feel my neck flushing up to the roots of my hair. I was not exactly calm, but I'd eaten and had a beverage, and I was no longer inside the house where Venita had shown herself to me. It felt significantly less real when I was sitting outside under a patio umbrella with some food in a plastic basket.

But did I *want* it to feel less real?

The way my brain went back and forth, picking at the smells, the sights, the pretty pathway that spilled through the house like a creek. I couldn't leave it alone. I wanted to keep it front and center, held with pride of place. I wanted to smell her again. I wanted to touch that lavender dress that felt like silk, and run my hands over that skin that was as pale as marble. No, I did not want those sensations to go away. I wanted to enshrine them forever, I wanted to run back home and find Hugh Crawford and tell him, "I get it now. I understand why you held her in your heart, and why you built that little place for her in the basement."

That little shrine. A little spot to focus on what he loved the most. A little corner to feel close, and connected.

Coty, on the other hand. I hated the thought of him. I hated that my aggravation at him had invaded a prettier memory—my first meeting with Venita, face-to-face, in all her inimitable glamor. I could've thought about nothing else for years, and I realized on some level that this glittering ghost could be my new fixation.

She could be the thing that occupies and distracts me, giving the obsessive gears of my brain something to grind other than the calamity of a house I'd bought and dumped my brother's life insurance into.

But no. There he was. Lurking at the edge of this fantasy, haunting it.

Coty was a confirmed and demonstrable liar who I never should've let cross my threshold. He would not be doing so again. I wouldn't have it, no matter how much Kate stomped her feet and called me unreasonable. He was henceforth banned from my presence.

What a day.

I packed up my stuff and left the bistro, then headed back to the house.

Ronnie

NOW

When I opened the front door, I half expected to see that weird, shiny trail threading through the house again, but no. Venita was nowhere to be found, and the house looked utterly normal—by which I mean derelict and dirty, on the verge of falling down.

Home sweet home.

I checked from floor to floor, up and down—seeking some sign of her, some bit of polished brass or freshly washed windows. I checked for bits of intact carpet, a place on the floor with no holes or scrapes; I listened hard for that Victrola down in the music room but heard nothing; I played bloodhound, sniffing around for a hint of gardenia. Even out in the orchard.

I didn't see anyone or anything pleasantly unexpected, not even the cat.

Before long, Kate appeared. She came bearing a big box of

supplies, and it was honestly so thoughtful that I almost wanted to keep Coty's misdeeds to myself rather than upset her.

She'd thought of all the things I hadn't bothered to chase down so far: paper towels, real toothpaste, hand sanitizer, baby wipes, a couple of gallons of bottled water so I could quit surviving on too-sweet instant coffee and sodas from the nearby gas stations. And a bottle of Captain Morgan's, because I am trashy and she knows it.

"Jesus Christ, Kate, this is amazing, thank you!"

"I've just been paying attention," she purred as she threw herself down on my air mattress/couch/sole bit of actual usable furniture. "I was talking to Coty, and he said we should pull together some kind of care package or something. Like, for a housewarming. So consider this a start."

I'd opened my mouth to tell her about Venita, but she had to say Coty's name first, so I closed it. I wish I'd spoken first, or faster.

But here we were, so I said, "Yeah, about him..."

"Oh, come on, let's not do this again. You don't love him, I get it."

"And you *do*?" I asked, half joking—but only half.

She rolled her eyes at me. "I like him pretty well; let's leave it at that. I don't get why you're suddenly so sour on the guy. What's up with that? You seemed to like him at first."

I barked a little laugh that I wish I'd kept to myself. "Let me ask you a question," I tried. "How much do you actually know about him? What's his life story, give me the outline."

"He was born and raised around here, he went to U-dub twice for a couple of different majors and didn't finish either one, and now he works down at the Pacific Science Center, doing something with the exhibits, I forget what exactly."

"That's a rough outline indeed. Either you're leaving out a lot, or *he* did."

"Oh really?" she asked with a raised eyebrow that was more amused than I cared for.

"Yeah, really. Did you know that Coty isn't even his real name? Or not his original name."

The eyebrow dropped. "What? Did you run a background check on him or something? Good God, I knew you were paranoid, but—"

"I have a friend who's a PI, and he owed me a little favor, so I asked him to run a quick lookup. And yeah, you already knew I was paranoid, so don't act shocked. This is *only* my house, all of my money, my whole future, even, and, and…" I wasn't sure how to wrap up, so I went for honesty. "And you. I'm worried about you, getting so close to this stranger so fast. So *yes*, I checked up on your new friend."

"So close to a stranger? We're not fucking on the weekends; he's just a guy I text back and forth with, and fine—we've gotten lunch and drinks a time or two. But we're not engaged, for chrissake. Or is that really the root of this? You don't like the idea of me dating again? Because that's extremely selfish and shitty, and I hope you realize that."

"I'm crazy, not stupid. I'm well aware that you will—and should—move on with your life now that Ben is gone, and I would never be the kind of asshole who tries to stop you. I want you to be happy, for whatever that means to you. I'm just worried—*extra* worried—about this specific man, in this specific situation."

"Mostly because he's the first one," she nailed it, or she thought she did. "Since Ben died, Coty is the first guy I've talked to at all, apart from work friends and internet folks. Give me a break. I deserve a social life."

"His *real* name is Andrew," I informed her.

"I knew that already," she said suddenly and lightly, in exactly the sort of tone that made me think she was lying.

"No you didn't. You had no idea until I told you just now, I can see it on your face."

"Oh, who cares, anyway? Lots of people change their names for lots of reasons; it's not a big deal."

"He changed his because of a DUI a few years back—or that's what my friend assumed when he found it on his record. Did you know he had a DUI?"

She snorted. "I know dozens of people who *should* have gotten a DUI back in the day. There but by the grace of God, am I right?"

I threw up my hands in frustration. "Kate, he's been lying to us all along, the whole time! Everything he said about, about…" I flailed, trying to make a gesture big enough to include the whole house.

She held up her hands and counted on her fingers. "He told us up front that he lived around here, that his uncle died here in the house, and that he knew about Venita Rost—maybe he just didn't know us, or didn't know *you*, well enough to be forthcoming with all that extra information you've dredged up."

"He still doesn't know you well enough, apparently," I said with more of a bite than I intended.

"I told you. We're not that tight." She was mad at me, yes.

But I'd hit some useful nerve, somewhere. I'd seeded a smidge of doubt. "He doesn't owe me his entire backstory."

I kept trying. "Don't you remember? He acted dumb about the old movies from the library, but he'd already checked them out and kept them for ages, long before Hugh Crawford got hold of them. Last night he acted like he was seeing them for the first time, and he's probably seen them dozens of times. Hundreds, even—they're not very long. He held on to them for months, and the library was pissed," I exaggerated.

"He pissed off a librarian? Whoa. Fire up the electric chair."

"All I'm *saying*," I said, and I took a deep breath, trying to wrap up my thoughts before she lost her patience altogether, "is that this guy is draped in red flags, and the more I learn about him, the less I'm inclined to trust him. Or get any closer to him. I don't want him inside this house, ever again."

Kate squinched up her eyes and rubbed at that little spot between her brows. "Fine. Then don't trust him. Don't get any closer to him. Problem solved."

"Not when you're..." I started to say "part of the problem" and stopped myself, because I'm not a complete idiot. "Involved. I'm only trying to protect you."

"I never asked you to do that. I know this is a strange situation for everyone, or it's strange for me and you. But Ben is gone, and I'm allowed to talk to other men. Even other men who aren't your dead brother."

She'd never talked about him like that before. It was inevitable, I know. Maybe someday I'll refer to him as my "dead brother." But it still left me with my mouth hanging open just enough to exhale.

"All right, you've made your point." I tried not to say it coldly. I kind of wanted to say it coldly.

She sighed at me, just hard enough to sting. "I'm not trying to shut you out, you know. I'm just trying to have a life. It'll make me sad if there are parts of it that I can't share with you, but if that's how it is, well, that's how it is."

"Don't be ridiculous. You can tell me anything."

"Apparently not. Not about Coty—or whatever you want to call him."

"Don't say that," I begged. "I tell you everything. I told you about the cat, and the ghosts, and all that stuff. About the house..." I petered out.

"The ghosts," she repeated, and I couldn't tell if she believed me or not.

"Yeah, I texted you earlier because I wanted to tell you that I've seen them now, I've seen them, and—"

She threw up her hands, looking exasperated. "Now you're seeing things, too? Jesus."

"This place is haunted to the gills, and you know it! You've sensed it, you've...you've heard things, too, you were here when the mirror..."

Kate withdrew like I'd smacked her. "Okay, I may have *suspected* something was going on here, but me suspecting spooky shit and you seeing spooky shit are two different things. The mirror was probably just...timing, I don't know. It's been hanging there a hundred years. It was going to fall eventually. But you're seeing ghosts? Not just objects moving around? That's... troubling."

"Yes, Kate. I am literally the first person in history to see a ghost, come on—it's not *that* crazy. I saw Venita Rost. I *talked to her*. She talked to me! She's still here, and she's..."

Kate paused and gave me a look of honest interest. "Yes? Is the silent-film-star ghost with us right now, here in this room?"

"Believe me, you'd know if she was." I was annoyed, but also glad that I'd snagged her attention with another subject. Something less fraught. I didn't want to fight. I wanted to share the most wild thing that had ever happened to me with my best friend, if not my only one. "She's...beautiful, but you knew that already. I can't tell if she knows she's dead. She definitely didn't know her daughter was dead, not at first. But I think she figured it out. She saw Sloan—I think it was him? He made her so angry, I thought she was going to tear the house down. I think she's dangerous. Maybe they both are."

"Okay..." She drew out the second syllable.

I knew I was rambling, but I couldn't stop myself. "It was incredible, I don't know what else to say. I could see her, smell her, touch her. She asked me to zip up her, her dress." I faltered because I could tell that Kate didn't believe me. It was all over her face.

"Sure it was. I mean, I'm sure you *believe* it was, but Ronnie, this place is getting to you. I've been worried about you for a few days now, hiding in a house that's falling down around you, and we both know you stopped taking your meds last year after—"

"Hiding? I've been arranging contractors and clearing out trash and cleaning up, and doing all those grueling, boring things that have to happen before the house can return to its former glory. I know these days everybody watches HGTV for a week and thinks they can restore a mansion in a month, and I'm here to tell you, that's bullshit."

Cautiously, choosing her words like she was talking to a fragile psycho, she said, "I know that's bullshit, and that's not what I'm saying. I'm talking about *you*. You're alone a lot. And you're alone *here* a lot. Here, where there was a weird little shrine to this woman in the basement, and where you watched all her old movies—"

"All the ones we could find. You watched them with me, don't act like you think I made those up, too."

"Right," she continued, still talking carefully, like I might grab a rifle and climb a tower if startled. I hated it. It made me irrationally angry, and I fought to lock it down. "But there's also mold—black, and every other color of the rainbow, I'm sure. Why don't you go back to your apartment for a few days? You could clear your head. Breathe some air that isn't full of spores and the faint odor of a dead guy who was left indoors too long."

"I just went back there last night and it's no worse than this house, I assure you. I'd rather be here."

"Yeah, that's what worries me. You're way too keen on being isolated in this place."

I snorted. "I thought you liked it. I thought you were thinking about asking for one of the upstairs rooms."

"I was. I am. When things are…not the way they are right now," she said, her eyes wandering from cobwebbed corner to rotting carpet runner. "But really, nobody should be living here, and you know it. Do you want to come home with me for a night or two? Maybe you shouldn't be alone right now."

"No!" I said too sharply. I knew it as soon as the syllable flew out of my mouth. "No," I repeated in a more ordinary voice. "This is *my* house, and I'm not afraid of it. I'm not afraid of Venita, or Sloan, or phantom cats or weird noises or black mold."

"But you're afraid of everything! That's your whole deal! You talked real big about ghosts being basically feral cats, but now you're losing your shit and talking crazy. A woman who's been dead for a hundred years is no danger to you; rationally, you must know this."

"Obviously I know this!" I lied. I knew in my bones that Venita wasn't harmless, but I couldn't convince myself that she wanted to hurt *me*. She'd asked for my assistance and talked to me like a friend. When an enemy had appeared in the hallway behind me—or struggled to do so—she'd chased him off. She didn't have to do that. She *chose* to do it.

"Look, babe, I'm worried about you," she said firmly. "You sound like a woman who's teetering on the edge of a cliff, thinking about jumping off."

"I'm not teetering anywhere, on anything. And I'm sure as shit not jumping. Just leave me alone if you're going to get all judgy—bitching at me about meds and seeing things. I don't need that right now; I have enough problems, thanks."

"Fine," she said lightly, as if I'd made my point and she was going to let it lie. She picked up her purse and slung it across her chest. "You're welcome for the fresh supplies."

"Thank you. If I didn't say so already."

She paused, eyeing me from head to toe, deciding something. I don't know what. Then she concluded, "All right. I'll leave you alone, and you can hang out and talk to all the dead people floating around this place, if that's what you want."

"It's what I want. For now."

She sighed again; this time it hit me softer, like a sad little shove. "Please be careful. Please take care of yourself. Please call me, or text me, or whatever, if you need someone. You can't live like this forever."

"I will. And I'm not planning to live like this forever."

"I know."

Of course she knew—or that's what I was thinking when I listened to her car start up and pull away from the ridge. She knew I'd call her eventually. I didn't really have anybody else, except for the dead, and I wasn't sure they counted.

Venita Rost

1932

I've been sitting with this little book open for the last hour, staring down at the blank page, fiddling with my pencil so long I've chewed the end down to a nub. I can't think of what to say. I can't think. Sometimes I think I can no longer feel, either, but then the rage and the horror and the misery come flooding back. It's a wave—not the gentle wave of the tide slipping out to sea, but the wave of a storm washing onto the shore, something fast and hard and utterly invincible. It knocks me to the ground, where I fold up like a love letter and cry and can't find my feet to pull them back up underneath myself. My knees don't work, my ankles don't work. My hands don't work, when I try to hold the small things she last touched, last held or played with. I cannot stop shaking, even when I'm far too tired to do anything else. I can't sleep.

I need to sleep.

Who cares about sleep. I'll sleep when I'm dead, like Priscilla. Like Bartholomew Sloan, if I ever get my fingers around his throat.

Then, I suspect, my hands will work. Then they will turn into threads of chain, tightening and tightening. I want to watch the blood fill his face, turning his cheeks the color of her bedroom curtains. I want to watch his eyes bulge and his veins turn purple. I want to watch the light of his soul leave his body.

I don't know how he did it, exactly. I don't know the mechanism by which he felled my daughter, that innocent duckling who loved him so and would've trusted him with her life. My God, she did trust him with her life, didn't she? Such misplaced affection. Such misplaced confidence.

I saw her body, before they could take her away and hide her, dress her up like a toy, bury her, I suppose. We'll close the casket. I don't want to see the mortician's efforts at reconstructing her eyes. He showed me some glass ones, the kind they use in dolls.

Well, he said they're not that kind. They're false eyes, for people who've lost theirs—and she surely did lose hers. They were burned right out of the sockets, leaving nothing behind but charred black holes seared deep into her skull.

When I held her there on the floor, screaming because I couldn't do anything else, everything else was broken...when I held her there, I looked down into her face, at her perfect skin without a blemish or a scar, and now with those holes blasted right into her brain. I had the most absurd thought: I thought that her skull was now hollow, and if I were to take a marble and drop it into one of her eye holes, it might roll around like I'd sent it loose in a fishbowl.

The thought only made me scream louder, harder. I didn't even know I could make those noises.

I didn't know human beings could.

But a scream was the only word I had, so I used it. Over and over again, a phone call dialing, no one picking up. A scream, a demand, a refusal. And the hollowed-out eyes of my child, utterly dead, lying in my arms as limp as a feather pillow.

Her hollowed-out eyes. They're all I can think about, and thinking about them brings me nothing but agony. Her pretty brown eyes, as warm and golden as fresh-steeped tea in the morning, in my mother's little old teacup.

My child is silent and cold and waiting for her grave. We'll lower her down tomorrow, at the cemetery here on the peninsula. I have no idea how I'll get through it. I'm thinking I might not go. Funerals are for the living, aren't they? Surely they can't force an unwilling living person to attend? Priscilla does not care. Priscilla is beyond caring, wherever she's gone.

Wherever she was sent. Let's keep that part straight.

I've thrown Sloan and all his remaining belongings outside into the rain that's halfway to snow, but won't quite freeze enough to stick, or be anything less than miserable. It's fitting weather. It feels like what's swirling between my ears, if a little less murderous.

Oscar and I have fought incessantly since our daughter was somehow killed by our frequent houseguest. Did he always have ill intent? Or "untoward" intent, as my mother would've put it, or maybe she was talking about something different, something worse.

I don't think he was the sort to touch a child, not in a bad way. Of course, I once believed that he held true affection for her, and I was confident he would never harm her, and I was wrong.

He refuses to explain himself, even as he keeps begging for an opportunity to explain himself. Oscar understands, or he tries to understand—given the limited information we've gleaned from the killer himself.

"It was an inexplicable accident." That's the firmest statement Mr. Sloan has provided. A cold, nasty little statement that says nothing, denies blame, and refuses accountability.

I hate him. I hate him like I've never hated anyone else before in my life.

Maybe I've never hated anyone else—not really. Maybe this is true hate, the kind we should hope we don't find more than once or twice in our lives. But oh, how I hate Bartholomew Sloan. And oh, how I hate my husband when he rises to that man's defense—feeble though his efforts might prove. I don't know what Sloan told him. I don't know what makes Oscar so willing to side with the man who murdered our little girl. He keeps citing "lack of any true evidence" as if that were proof of anything; he reminds me that we don't know how she died, or what happened to her eyes, her hollowed-out eyes, her hollow little face.

"Who could've done such a thing on purpose?" he asked me, exasperated by my unhappiness and anger.

"Who could've done it by accident?" I fired back. "Who could have done it at all? No one but that man, with all his secrets, and his papers in strange languages, and whatever occult nonsense he's gotten himself into. Dangerous, deadly nonsense. Why didn't it kill him rather than her? He's the one who's been playing with fire all this time!"

I swear, I had the worst sensation that Oscar would've dearly liked to hit me, or at the very least shake me by the shoulders. He didn't do either of those things. He threw up his hands. "You don't know that! He's admitted to esoteric interests, that's no secret. But he doesn't know what killed her, or why!"

"That's not true. You know it's not true. He was the only one *present. The only one who saw her die, and then he ran away like the coward he truly is."*

"He came back. He's only gone now because you threw him out."

"What else was I to do? Summon the police? Tell them that my child had been killed by a wicked man who dabbled with devil worship?"

He slapped his hands over his face and groaned. We were both pink-faced and salty from crying, both of us brined in our respective sorrows. "That is what you did, as if you don't remember. I almost had to bribe them, to keep them from carrying you off to a nice quiet hospital for some private convalescing. You can't accuse the man of witchcraft just because our daughter died in his presence. You sound like a madwoman—and for the moment, people will make allowances. Our child is dead, and we are in mourning, and, and—"

"And it's his fault! Why would you defend him?"

"Why would you see him dragged to the gallows? He swears on his life that he never laid a finger on her. Not a single finger, nor anything else! She could've been, I don't know how it happened, or what happened to her to cause such awful damage. The mortician said it looked like she'd been struck by lightning."

"In the parlor? Straight through the windows, without breaking any glass? You're a bigger fool than the mortician if you can't see through that pathetic excuse for an explanation."

"Fine. We're all fools. Everyone but you."

"That's right! Everyone but me is a fool! I'm the only one who can see him for what he is. I know what he did. I might never prove it, and I might never see justice served for what became of Priscilla—but I'll be damned if I'll ever let that man back in my home. I'll be furthermore damned if I'll stand here and listen to you make excuses for him!"

"For Christ's sake, Venita! This was some kind of inexplicable accident, maybe the wiring in the walls. Electrical burns. Lightning. God Himself only knows, but not you. Not me. Not even Bartholomew, I don't think. You," he said with a pointed finger a little too close to my face. "You think you're seeing the truth, but you're not. You're seeing what you want to believe."

I was aghast. How could he be so wrong? How could he misunderstand so completely? "You think I want to see that a man I treated as a brother, a man I welcomed into my home and trusted with my child... You think I want to believe that I was wrong? Careless? A terrible mother who should have known better in the first place?"

"I think you want to see a reason—any reason—for what happened. You spent too long in Hollywood, and you think every ending needs to be tied up in a bow, some credits to roll, and everyone needs to understand what just happened. But we're not in Hollywood anymore, this isn't a script, and sometimes bad things happen for no reason at all, to the people who least deserve it."

"He was there. In the room. By his own admission, to you and me and the coppers, too. How can you pretend he had nothing to do with it? How can you betray me like this?"

"Betray you?" He looked very much like he wanted to throw something out the window. Me, I'm sure. "Betray you by taking a good man at his word? We have no evidence at all to suggest that he harmed her!"

"His refusal to tell us what happened, that doesn't strike you as suspicious?"

"He has told us!"

"He's told us nothing!" Just the same nonsense, a piece of fiction.

He got up late at night to make himself a drink of that disgusting piss-water gin. Behind him, he heard a terrible noise and then...and then. He turned around and saw Priscilla on the floor. She'd followed him, he thinks. He doesn't know what maimed her, what killed her. He doesn't know what could even be capable of doing so in such a violent and awful manner.

Nothing. That's what he told us.

Why it was good enough for the authorities, I wish I knew—why they didn't just take him away, I'll never understand.

Oh, rationally I know why they let him go. They claimed a lack of evidence, but we all know it's because he's one of them: an authority figure, an investigator, a famous solver of puzzles the likes of which they all aspired to be.

A man.

It could even be that simple. I've seen men walk away from terrible things by virtue of what rides around in their pants. It's like carrying a magic wand, I swear.

But usually even a man, even a powerful one, might meet some kind of punishment for murdering an innocent child! Surely, though it might be naive of me to think so.

No, not naive. Clear-eyed. All too aware of the way the world works and who it works for. Naive is a word powerful people use to shut you up. They don't like you suggesting that the world could be less awful, because the world isn't awful at all for them. They like the world exactly how it is.

But what does it even matter. What does anything matter. Priscilla will likely never know any justice, and neither will I. Not unless I make it for myself.

Maybe I'll do that.

How will I do that? And what will it cost? What do I have to offer? What am I willing to part with?

Anything, yes. Anything.

Ronnie

NOW

"A hollow face," I murmured, letting the diary fall to my chest.

It wasn't late—not really. Barely eight o'clock, and still light enough that my camping lamp and a few candles were plenty of light. I liked the candles. They made the place smell nice, or at least less *green*. Less mold and mildew, more... whatever synthetic oils or perfumes went into the cheap-ass drugstore candles. Now the parlor command center (as I'd come to think of it) smelled like mold and mildew and lavender and rosemary, and I think one of the others was an "ocean" scent that mostly just smelled like laundry detergent, not that it was unpleasant.

My phone buzzed. It was a text message from Kate.

I picked it up and let my face unlock the screen. She wanted to know if I was okay. If I needed anything.

Man, she's really no good at all when it comes to being

mad at somebody or doling out the silent treatment. It's sweet. It's also a little annoying, because now we're in the negotiating phase of whatever kind of fight this is, where she tries to convince me that it's fine to be tight with both Coty and me.

But it isn't fine. It won't be fine. I won't be getting over it. He won't be coming back to my house.

I didn't answer the text. I didn't leave her on "read," either, I'm not a monster. I just wanted some time to think about my response. And I *would* make one. It would probably not involve an apology, not when my wounded pride said that I needed to hear one before I delivered one.

I took a deep breath of the soupy, scented air and reclined on my air mattress, adjusting pillows as I went. I only had a couple, but I was improvising—using a backpack stuffed with my dirty laundry for a neck bolster. The situation was...not bleak, exactly, but not especially domestic. Yet.

Those things didn't matter, and they wouldn't matter for a while. I'd roughed it harder in my misspent youth; camping in a parlor was no big deal. Not when I had reading material, snacks, and booze. My immediate comfort did not matter, and my long-term comfort was months or years away. Why get fancy with it.

Fleetingly, I thought of Hugh Crawford and his shrine downstairs, with the tiny hibachi grill for his candles—and his DVDs, his notes. His damp-spoiled diary that belonged to a dead woman in a place of honor, the only thing that mattered. I lifted the book up off my chest and looked at the pretty handwriting where it could still be read.

I wondered if a UV light would help illuminate some of

the rougher patches, and then I wondered if Kate wasn't right, and how I'd go about finding a conservator. But the thought of parting with the little volume made me want to die; I realized that I was clutching it again, pressing my fingers into the sodden, swollen cover.

I relaxed, or I tried to.

I glanced at the dusty bar cart, its sheet hanging off one corner.

No, I didn't sample the dregs. I wasn't even curious enough to try. I wasn't that desperate. I had weed and diet soda to sustain me.

I popped a lone edible. It wouldn't do much, and I knew that. But it'd take the edge off my strange, very stressful day and make me mellow. It would make me forgetful, in the way that the psychiatric meds made me unbothered. Maybe I'd forget that I wasn't alone in the house, or maybe I'd remember that I'm not supposed to care, because ghosts are like stray cats and there's no harm in their presence.

I know, I know.

But there was no one around to harm except for myself, and I did not value my well-being that strongly. I liked the warm, fuzzy apathy of the cannabis, and I relied on it more than I should, but I'd stopped worrying about that for now. If it made me forget I'd left a candle burning at bedtime, and a phantom cat knocked it over, and the place burned down around me…it wouldn't be ideal, but also? Not the end of the world.

I was not suicidal.

I do feel like it's worth making a distinction here. I wasn't looking to kill myself, either by design or contrived neglect;

I just wasn't bothered by the idea of not being alive anymore. If anything, from a certain angle it felt like a benign convenience.

But that's not the kind of thing you can say out loud. People tend not to get it when someone shrugs at life vs. death, and it scares them. It makes them want to "help" in a thousand ways that aren't helpful at all. So I keep thoughts like that to myself, for the sake of everyone's sanity, happiness, and liberty. I mean, I'm not an idiot.

I leaned back on my pillow conglomerate and put my phone aside.

It chimed again. Just Kate, I was pretty sure, but I leaned over and sneaked a peak at the screen anyway. My phone didn't recognize the sender—but I did when I read Hey, this is Coty, and I got your number from Kate. She said you were getting worked up about me, something about me? I didn't mean to mislead you about anything, and if I did, I'm sorry.

I picked up the phone again, unlocked my screen, and poised my thumbs for rebuttal. But the thumbs hovered. What could I even say? *I know you're a lying piece of shit. Stay away from Kate, you toxic hipster wannabe.*

Nothing felt right, so I set the phone beside me again and pulled up Venita's diary.

I was running out of readable pages, if I was honest. What remained was in fragments, difficult to scan, because her handwriting might have been terrific, but water damage had really done a number on the back third of the little book. I think maybe it sat in a puddle for a bit. The pages that were loose enough to turn were mostly illegible. The rest had merged into a single brick of mildewing paper, clinging to the rotted remnants of a spine that was on the verge of falling off.

"I get it," I said out loud. To Venita, in case she was listening. "I get why you thought Bart Sloan had something to do with it. It was the only logical conclusion, given the facts at hand. Nothing else makes any sense."

Once again, my phone chimed. It was a loud and foreign sound in the almost power-free parlor without even so much as a log burning in the fireplace. I only glanced down briefly, for the split second it took me to see that it was Coty again.

> We can talk if you want. We should probably talk. Can I come over?

Surely he would interpret silence as a no. But what if he didn't? I didn't want to respond, but I didn't want any surprise visitors, either. I reached for my phone and my thumbs hovered again, trying to figure out what to say. It needed to be fully, 100 percent complete and firm and understandable. No wiggle room for "misunderstandings" later on.

Should I resort to profanity? "Fuck off and die, creep." Or maybe, "Stay the hell away from me, and my house, and my friend, you goddamn weirdo." Probably a simple "no" would suffice.

> No.

I hit send and then immediately blocked his number. I picked up the diary again and picked at it, painstakingly pulling the ruined pages apart with my fingernails.

Here and there, I caught fragments. I dedicated myself to extracting every last word possible from the personal little tome.

When I held it up to my face, all the better to squint at it, all the better to bring myself closer to her, I imagined that I could even smell her, that old-fashioned perfume I'd gotten such a strong whiff of when the house had lit the path to her room. I wanted that to happen again. I needed to see for myself that I wasn't completely insane, though how exactly I'd accomplish this feat, I didn't really know. I already knew that I couldn't record it. If I pulled out my phone and set it to video, would it work better than merely trying to catch a series of photos? I doubted it. I very badly wanted to believe it was possible, though—to capture that strange trail of light that brought the house back to life, or sent some piece of it back in time, maybe, or brought a piece of me back, I don't know.

I surprised myself by peeling two pages apart without tearing anything and found a full paragraph still clear enough to parse.

...live like this anymore, in this peculiar purgatory, this unsettled agony that rises and falls in waves like the tide. My child is in the ground, cold, eyeless, hollow. I have dreams about it. Nightmares, even—where she's been put in the ground too soon, and she beats her little fists against the lid of her casket until her fingers are bloody and her knuckles are bruised, and her perfect little fingernails as pretty as porcelain. Her fingernails peeling back, popping free, exposing the nail bed. She pounds her mangled hands on that lid, lined with satin, more comfortable than any bed I ever slept in when I was her age.

Then I wake up screaming, and Oscar comes running in, and I throw something at him from pure rage and horror and fear and rage. I'm just so angry, all the time. It's so unfair, and my husband still seeks to clear his friend's name—though the police have...

That was all I could make out.

"Sounds like you kicked Oscar out of the bedroom. Good for you," I said, even though it sounded corny. "And to hell with him, choosing his friend instead of his wife. He's supposed to be *your* partner, not Sloan's."

I thought about the bottle of Captain Morgan in the box of loot Kate had so thoughtfully brought me before she left in a huff. The box was almost out of reach, but not quite—not when I set the diary to my right, and stretched, and leaned, and caused a ridiculous squeaking ruckus from the air mattress. I got two fingertips on the bottle's neck, then hauled it into bed with me.

I didn't need a glass. It was just me, nobody else's germs to be afraid of. No one to watch me and be judgy.

I had a feeling that Venita wouldn't be judgy.

I glanced again at her bar cart and the dust-covered bottles thereupon. Nah, this was a party house at one time. Even rich people drink straight from the source when nobody's looking, I bet.

I cracked the top and took a swig. It burned in my mouth, but not too badly—with the brown-sugar sweet fire left behind as an aftertaste in the back of my throat. I took another swallow, then recapped the bottle for the moment. Not because I didn't want more, but because sometimes I'm clumsy, especially after an edible.

Oh yeah, that's right. I'd had the edible. I'd already forgotten, so the little berry-flavored gummy square was doing its job. "Well done, gummy." I held up the bottle in a little toast, but I didn't unscrew the cap again. Yet.

I wasn't out to get shitfaced, and a mere edible on top of some rum probably wouldn't do that, anyway. Not unless I sucked down half the bottle, which wasn't out of the realm of possibility—sometimes with weed, I forget I've had enough, and I keep sipping—but that wasn't my goal. My goal was to make myself soft enough, sleepy enough, calm enough, for the household residents to reach out again. Hugh came to me while I was dreaming. Maybe Venita would, too. Did I need to make myself harmless and weak for them to seek me out? I didn't think so, but maybe it wouldn't hurt.

No. It's too much easier to lie to myself, after mind-altering substances.

The truth, I mean the utterly garbage-shitty truth, was that my goal was to quit being angry about Coty/Andrew trying to muscle his way into my home or my life. I didn't care if it left me a semiconscious vegetable with a smile on its face; I wanted to shake off the worry that I might be wrong about him, that he might be an okay dude and I was overreacting because of Kate.

Kate was usually pretty good at seeing through bullshit. She has a good social nose, if you understand what I mean. Or she usually does, but this guy seems to have flown under her radar.

I just couldn't let go of the fact that he'd lied in so many ways, large and small, to hide the fact that he'd tried to buy my house out from under me, and he'd given us a fake name, and, and, and.

I fished around in my messenger bag until I found another gummy. I unwrapped it but didn't eat it. I just liked knowing it was there.

I drew the diary back into my lap and tried to rearrange my "pillows" again for better sitting-up purposes. Then I started picking at the pages, one fragile corner at a time, trying to peel the sheets apart with all the delicacy of a surgeon. With patience and caution, I retrieved a few more fragments.

> *...charge him with anything, and on the one hand I understand, evidence is nonexistent and the facts of the case are absurd, but they are facts nonetheless. I don't know how he did it, and I may never know why, but I know...*
>
> *...clothes and toys and the like. I can't throw them away like so much garbage, and I can barely stand to go into her bedroom. I can't leave it like a shrine. Maybe I should nail the door shut and...*

And then one very telling, if brief bit of prose.

> *...aligned against me, against a childless mother. The pair of them so evil in their sad looks, their pitying gazes. They think I've lost my mind, but I have lost a child, and that's not the same thing. I am in mourning. I am vengeful. I am not interested in surviving any longer without her. I think I have an idea. I think I will write a letter to Mr. Sloan.*

A letter? I wondered what had become of it. I hadn't seen any such thing anywhere in the house, and I guessed that wasn't so strange. It had probably disintegrated into dust by now.

"Sloan's nephew tried to buy this house," I said out loud, in case she was listening. "He never knew the man you hate so much, but he admires him in a way that's honestly downright weird, if you ask me."

When I finished talking, I stopped to listen. Did I hear something? Anything in reply? When the answer was a resounding beat of silence, I thought I must be losing my goddamn mind. But was that the worst thing, really? I kept trying.

"The detective guy's a real piece of work, so I wonder if the apple didn't fall far from the...tree, well, that doesn't work. Coty isn't his son or anything. Andrew, I mean. That's his real name. He wants the house, I think because his uncle died here. That's pretty damn morbid. Right?"

At the very edge of my hearing, I thought I heard someone murmur in assent. But I wouldn't swear to it.

I wondered what Venita's letter had said. Did she predict that her husband might kill her? "What happened to your letter? Did you tell him to rot in hell? I bet you did," I added, more to myself. "You strike me as the kind of woman who wasn't afraid to tear somebody a new one."

Another swallow or two of rum. One more. Kate texted again. I didn't read it. I flicked off the volume switch and turned the phone face down onto the floor beside the diary, and I settled against my pillows. Oh yes. The edible was definitely kicking in.

Well, maybe my imagination kicked in, too. I let the journal sink back to the sleeping bag I'd unzipped and was using as a blanket. I leaned my head back and closed my eyes; I told myself it was to listen for ghosts. I chewed on the second edible like that, eyes shut and lounging on a sleeping bag. It beat staying awake.

Bartholomew Sloan
NOW

She fell asleep on that inflatable mattress, as uncomfortable as it seems to be. Every night she tosses and turns, wrestling with her sleeping bag like she's fighting it for money. I can't help but feel like she'd be more comfortable directly on the floor, but I suppose she has her reasons. Perhaps there are termites or ants. She doesn't strike me as the kind to be afraid of random spiders. She's too eager to crawl around in these rotting, disused rooms, digging around in old furniture and cabinets without so much as a pair of work gloves, as often as not.

Sometimes I watch her sleep. Not for long, and not like a criminal. I watch her because I've had nothing else to watch except for the aforementioned insects in quite some time. Unless you count Venita. And most of the time, she either does not see me, or she prefers to ignore me because she knows she cannot escape me.

The day before, when she charged me in the hallway...that's the most interaction we've had in decades.

She did not catch me. Or rather...she did? Perhaps? But she passed through me like a flashlight beam aimed through a windowpane. For all my fear, and all my anger, we can't seem to touch one another. It's a blessing, surely. Or a curse? Both? One of each? I don't know.

She can touch things and manipulate them, and she can appear to people at will. I struggle to make myself seen at all, much less heard. It feels like a half-forgotten dream, now. I strain to recall the sensation of gooseflesh, or hunger, or drunkenness. I would very much like some gin. There are many things I miss, but that bar cart covered in dust...it's a bit of a beacon for me. Maybe because it killed me. Maybe because I was just too damn fond of gin.

But I digress. The point I was reaching for is this: I still have my vision and hearing, if no other senses to speak of. Those two work fine. I can hear, I can see, and I am mobile.

So when I heard the noise at the back entrance—the one by the small orchard, in the glass-covered room at the rear of the hill, the one Ronnie thinks of as "the conservatory"—I had nothing better to do than go and investigate.

Ronnie had been asleep for at least a couple of hours—no, likely longer than that. It was not completely dark outside, but it was overcast and raining, the Pacific Northwest's perpetual, seasonal twilight that sometimes feels like midnight on the dark side of the ridge.

At first I wondered if it might not be Venita, sending her white cat around the premises for a little investigation of her own. She was awake now, after all. She would be restless, and grieving, and then she would rage. She is nothing if not predictable.

But no. These little noises were coming from outside, where the storm door's screen had rotted away decades ago, though the frame remained.

I heard it swinging and catching on something soft. Someone pushing it back open or holding it that way while they fiddled with the main door's hardware. It was the original hardware from the thirties, as far as I know—and it wouldn't be difficult to force. Someone was scraping with small tools.

Lockpicks. I knew the sound.

I approached without ducking or hiding, since there was little point. I slipped into the conservatory and through the wall beside the rear door. There wasn't any light back there, but I saw a shape all the same: a dark and hunkered one, fumbling with the picks.

Such crude but useful tools, those picks. Scarcely evolved in a century. But they get the job done, in the hands of someone who knows how to use them.

This fellow was crouched over them, muttering and swearing, and that's when I knew who it was: my fool of a nephew, a terrible young man with intentions that are every bit as bad as mine used to be—when I bargained with darkness for the prospect of light. It was stupid of me then, and it was stupid of this fellow now.

I didn't know exactly what he intended. If there was a way for him to absorb my curse into himself, seeking his own modern form of light or success or power—who can say—I don't know what it might be, or how he might accomplish it.

I thought, maybe he knows something I don't.

It was within the realm of possibility. Wasn't everything? Anything?

"Stop it," I told him, as if he could hear me. "Stop this immediately. You leave that woman alone."

He shivered and pulled his jacket tighter around his shoulders, dropping the tools as he did so. They clattered to the ground and scattered, and he swore some more as he collected them. It made a bit of a racket, but I didn't imagine that Ronnie could hear it. Or even if she could, it wouldn't be enough to rouse her.

My nephew's hands were so unsteady that I wondered if he'd been drinking, too—or if he were under the influence of some other substance. It wasn't *that* cold, was it?

"It isn't *that* cold," he said under his breath, and I jumped.

Could he hear me on some level, of which he was largely unaware?

"This weather just sucks," he concluded.

I couldn't argue. It was spitting rain and there was plenty of wind, and yes, it was cool enough that he could see his own breath. But sometimes my presence will chill an area, too. So that might've been my doing.

I backed away, returning to the house's interior. I know he didn't knock. I would've heard it, as I've been awake all this time, even when I'd rather not be. Men who don't knock, men who seek a quieter entry point with tools of such nefarious trade…they aren't men with good intentions.

I tried to keep calm. Panic never serves anyone except the wicked.

I watched my nephew for another few minutes, all the while keeping one ear out for Ronnie. I heard only snoring, interrupted occasionally with a hiccup or a snort, or the squeak of the inflatable mattress.

I prayed for her. Is that ridiculous? It might be. But I had no defenses at my disposal, and here was an innocent woman trying to do right by this place I've called home for a century—whether or not it was against my will. I prayed to God, to Mary, to Buddha, to every saint and spirit and angel I could name.

Or maybe I was only wishing as hard as I could.

Maybe Ronnie would wake up. Maybe she'd summon the police. Phones are so much more sophisticated now—an entire universe in the palm of the hand. What I would've given for such a tool in my day. I would have never needed to hock my soul to a maniac.

Another minute or two passed while I ran back and forth between them. My kin at the back door, struggling with tools so simple that I could use them even now, if I had hands with strength enough to lift them. The new lady of the manor asleep in the parlor, rather drunk.

Surely Coty was bound to fail. "Give up and go home," I begged. I watched him through the cracked window in the upper half of the door. He'd cut himself on one of the tools and was bleeding enough to unsettle him, but not enough to cause serious harm. He was hurt, not injured; he only needed a bandage and an ointment, nothing more.

I went back to check on Ronnie in the parlor. She was still out cold, but breathing steadily and low. Snoring in fits and starts.

Did she have any weapons handy?

I looked around the room. Being unable to lift things or rummage through bags, my ability to assess this was limited. The mere fact that I'd *seen* no weapons did not mean that no weapons were present.

I suddenly wondered if my nephew was armed. He was carrying a bag, and I couldn't tell what was in it. It could've been literally anything.

"With any luck, he's as ill-suited to weaponry as he is to lockpicking," I mumbled and began to dart back to the conservatory—but there was a muffled crash and then a tinkling of broken glass. Coty had given up and broken one of the little leaded panes in the door, I just knew it.

I was right. He'd used a stray rock or brick to punch out the bottom right panel.

I watched in horror as he reached through the hole and felt around for the knob. He found it, winced at a piece of glass poking through his sleeve, and flicked at the dead bolt latch until it gave way. The splinters that gave way with it suggested it might've been faster and less bloody to simply body the door and force it inward, but he was trying to be quiet. Broken glass notwithstanding.

The door slid open, scraping across the shards on the dirty floor.

My nephew winced again, this time at the sound of it. He was bad at being quiet. He was also bad at breaking and entering. I fervently hoped he was bad at everything else, too. If he weren't catching this woman by surprise, if she weren't dead asleep and drunk to boot, I would've easily put the pair of them on even footing. If anything, I suspected she could take him without much trouble.

But these were not those circumstances.

He was inside, alert and awake. She was still asleep. And drunk.

Perhaps he would leave her alone. Perhaps what he was looking for was something he could take without bothering her. As he began exploring, he rummaged through the first drawers he found—in the kitchen and butler's pantry. They stuck and squealed when he tugged them, and he paused to listen after every small noise.

Ronnie did not stir.

He must have known she was home. He must have seen her car parked out front. He knew she was inside somewhere, and he was breaking in regardless, and I was beginning to panic.

I ran back to Ronnie. No change.

She was sprawled out surrounded by her accoutrements and a bit of take-out food garbage, drooling slightly, breathing deeply. "Ronnie!" I shouted as loud as I was able. "Ronnie, wake up! You have to wake up! You're in danger! Please, you heard me once—please hear me again!"

Nothing.

Wait.

I heard my nephew now skulking around in the library, but that wasn't what'd caught my attention. It was something more like the tinkling of a bell, coming from upstairs. It wasn't that—not exactly. It was the sound of sparkling music, muffled and distant. It was the sound of Venita, wondering what the hell was going on in her house.

For an instant, I froze with a knee-jerk terror.

Then I saw an opportunity. I saw the cat.

It wandered into view at the top of the stairs, peering down at me between the banister rails and regarding me with its usual mix of apathy and idle curiosity.

"Fine. If you won't wake up for me, I'll find someone louder," I vowed, and I darted back to the stairs, where I nearly collided with my nephew.

He started, not because he saw me, but because he must've sensed some shift in the air when I went past him. That happens sometimes. Never when I need it to. On second thought, he stood there distracted long enough that I tried it again. We were blood relations, of a sort. It might matter?

I made myself as large as I could, standing up and spreading out like a great brown bear's efforts at intimidation. I rushed him, shouting, "Get out of here!"

He shuddered.

He looked warily around the room. And he shook off whatever unpleasant sensation I'd managed to cause. He was standing at the edge of the foyer, with the great staircase behind him. His eyes swung back and forth between the steps and the entrance to the parlor.

"Take the stairs!" I hollered. Let Venita deal with him.

But no, I was not so fortunate. He turned on his heel and began creeping toward the parlor, where Ronnie slumbered on.

Up the stairs I went, as fast as I could propel myself. Venita's room was at the end of the hallway on the left. Oscar's room. Their room, I don't know. It's been only hers for a hundred years, I'm not sure why my mind went straight to Oscar, considering I've tried so hard not to think about him for so long.

He flickered through my thoughts. I shook him away.

And I went to my immortal enemy, the woman whose wrath I would never escape—*could* never escape. Did not deserve to escape.

Just this once, let me use the fallout from my crimes for something good.

"Venita!" I called. I flung myself into her quarters—or I tried. I got as far as the doorway and could proceed no farther.

She was faced away from me, hands on her hips, looking down at an assortment of dresses laid out on her bed. The room looked the same as it had when we'd been alive—a huge bed with tall posts, luxurious curtains and expensive imported rugs. A lamp was lit in the corner, but the light was not real. None of it was. I knew this, but I could not look away. It was so beautiful, the simple domesticity of it. Or the opulent domesticity, as the case may be.

I've spent a hundred years watching mold grow, books rot, insects infest, and plaster grow soggy with damp. My world has been some shade of gray, with hints of green and brown and black, for decades.

The vivid, lovely memory of this vivid, lovely woman seemed too much, too bright, too loud. I said her name again. "Venita? Can you hear me? Venita, someone has broken into the house."

She turned to me and her eyes were hot red coals. She opened her mouth—to rage at me, no doubt—but I cut her off before she could get started. "Venita, listen! Just this once, my God! Someone has broken into the house, and I can't reach him. You seem to like that woman downstairs. Would you see her harmed? Killed?"

She lunged.

I held out my hands as if I could stop her. She blew through me, then stopped and turned around to do it again—the old dance of frustration. Was it part of my curse? To never be touched by another soul, even the ones who'd prefer to annihilate me?

I left my hands up, palms forward. "Listen to me, Venita. Just this one time. Please, it's important."

Was she even sane enough to respond with anything like logic or curiosity or interest? Did she actually have any fond feelings for her house's most recent owner? I did not know, but I knew she loved the house itself. She loved it in a possessive way, an anchoring way that kept her here as surely as her grief and anger.

I was nearly surprised when she hesitated. I was all but convinced that she was too far gone to address in any meaningfully human manner but yes, she hesitated, and she looked at me. Right at me, not through me. Not past me.

Before the moment could pass, I repeated myself. "My idiot nephew has broken into the house. He's looking for something, and I'm afraid he's going to hurt Ronnie. You know Ronnie? The woman who's been sleeping in the parlor?"

She frowned thoughtfully. "She is saving the house."

"Yes."

"She won't tear it down."

"No."

Venita stayed thoughtful. "Where would we *go*?" she asked, as calmly and innocently as when we both lived and breathed.

"I don't know. But I don't want to find out. Hate me all you like, and I know you *will*," I emphasized. "But *help her*. Help the woman downstairs. Get that young man out of this house before he burns the place down around us." I didn't think he had any such intentions, but I had her attention when it came to the house, and I intended to leverage it as best I could.

She nodded. "Andrew."

"Y-yes? That's his true name. How did you know that?"

Now she shrugged. "Sometimes I listen." With that, she vanished—perfectly and completely, even taking the bright and beautiful room with her. When she was gone, nothing remained but the ruins of the poster bed on the floor, some old tools, and some trash that had piled up in the corners like snowdrifts along with the cobwebs.

Ronnie

NOW

I woke up hard, with a gasp and a groan. It felt like dying in reverse.

The back of my brain was complaining that something was wrong, and I couldn't argue with it—I was still lying on my half-flat air mattress. I'd been there for hours, and it wasn't even all the way dark yet. I'd had too much to drink. My head was ringing. Where was the diary? I felt around for it, and my hand landed on top of it—I felt its shape beneath the rapidly deflating air mattress that must've had a leak someplace.

I sat up, and my ass nearly settled on the floor despite the mattress. I'd hook up the pump again later, grab some duct tape, and see if I couldn't patch it together again. I didn't need it to last forever, but another few weeks would be great.

Something was pinging in the back of my head: a stupid little whisper that said I was forgetting something. Or missing something? They're similar feelings, a low-level confusion that says I need to pay attention to my surroundings.

What woke me up?

It was raining again, the downpour ramping up as I sat there. There would be wet spots on the ceiling in the morning and the world would smell like mildew. I wondered if I'd rolled up my car windows all the way. I wondered how much black mold I was breathing in every hour. I wondered if I'd heard rats in the parlor and if they'd gotten into my bedding. I imagined insects and fungi growing in the walls, waiting to poison the first person to smash the old plaster and horsehair with a sledge for remodeling. I imagined a pool of water collecting on the roof, or spilling down a badly pointed fireplace and into the walls where it would sizzle and spark on the old cloth wiring.

Hmm.

I took a mental step back.

I recognized this. I was riding an anxiety spiral, the kind that can slide into a full-blown panic attack with the slightest push. I recognize these spirals—I can see them a mile away when one's building up to a good freak-out—and sometimes I can logic my way out of them or ahead of them.

I can outrun one if I'm wearing good critical thinking shoes.

Usually when a spiral spools up, depending on its flavor I might be able to reverse-engineer what prompted it, if the cause isn't already obvious. Yes, fear comes in different flavors. Scents? I don't know. There isn't a word for it, I guess. It comes in different categories, different shapes. This one fell into the "immediate physical danger" category, which didn't narrow it down much. It could've meant anything from smelling smoke to feeling an earthquake.

I let my brain taste it, sucking on it like a cough drop.

Had it been a ghost?

"Inspector? Are you there? Are you listening?" I tried, but no one answered. Not the detective, then. "Not the rain, either," I muttered. But I did hear another unexpected sound: a loud creak from something much heavier than a rat.

The creak cut off abruptly.

Too late.

I'd already heard it, and now I knew what had dragged me out of my dehydrated, uncomfortable sleep. Someone was in the house, *that's* what woke me up—some back-brain alarm system, a web of neuroses knit so tightly and embedded so deeply that it even works when I'm out cold and frankly rather drunk... which is the only time I ever sleep deeply enough to require a subconscious trip wire.

Someone was inside the house, trying to be quiet.

Someone would have seen my car out front, and through the windows anyone could tell that I still had a lamp burning on an upturned milk crate like the hopeless Gen X loser I truly am. *Someone* damn well knew that somebody else was home, and *somebody* had come inside anyway. Without knocking. My alarm system would shoot a dart of adrenaline into my heart at the sound of a knock on the door, even if I were in a coma. A handful of sounds will do that. A phone ringing. A baby crying.

A floorboard creaking.

"Shit," I whispered to myself. I commanded my brain to get into gear. "*Think.*"

I had nothing at all of value, not anywhere on the property. A hundred years of Seattle winters had seen to that. Could it be some dumbass urban explorer, wanting to see inside the decrepit old estate? Possible, but most of those guys won't enter an occupied building. Garden variety trespassers? Sure, but why?

"It *has* to be Coty."

Kate would've just beat on the door until I surrendered and let her in.

Well, I'd been saying it, hadn't I? That he wanted something from the house, or from me, or from his long-dead uncle. Sometimes I hate being right. Maybe if I could keep myself from catastrophizing over every minor detail and assuming the worst about everyone, I'd be happy about being right. But that was a fantasy, and this was the reality: I was alone in the house, and I had an intruder.

Now I almost wanted to be right. I *wanted* it to be Coty, but that was a silly knee-jerk response to what was happening—the kind that made me feel like I might have some control over this situation.

I wanted it to be him because I didn't like him, and I wanted Kate to dislike him. If he broke into my house, if he let himself inside while he thought I was asleep—then that was a crossed line that he couldn't uncross, and Kate couldn't write it off to a misunderstanding.

Besides...

(And now my brain was really spinning up, really going into danger-management mode.)

Besides, I told myself, my heart beating so loudly that I wondered if he could hear it. Besides, Coty wasn't that much bigger than me, maybe thirty pounds heavier—and he's hardly an athlete. I mean, neither am I; but I've done enough manual labor that I'm a lot stronger than I look. He's younger than me, though. Younger in just the right way, with just the right gap, where he'd have an advantage.

How much of one? Hard to say.

Even if he was unarmed, Coty might have an advantage. The difference between thirty and forty-five is the difference between a five-minute mile and a fifteen-minute mile. Could I outrun him if I had to? Probably not.

Maybe I could work the element of surprise. With age comes cunning, so I might have an advantage after all. Then again, he'd been slick enough to hide an awful lot about himself. He could be smarter than I thought.

Another creaking board, this one closer. He was skulking around at the rear of the house, working his way forward. He must've come in through the back entrance in the conservatory.

I reached for my phone, beside the brick of a ruined old diary under the sinking vinyl of the mattress. I fished it out while trying not to wiggle around too much. The mattress let out a low, big-balloon squeak when it moved against the floor. I pushed the journal farther under the mass of bedding. I wasn't sure why, except that it was something that Coty/Andrew might try to take from me, and he might not look for it there.

I rose to my feet while clutching the phone. I flicked the switch to silence it.

Should I call 911? Should I call Kate?

No, not Kate. Kate would come rushing over to check on me, and...

And that might mean she'd believe me, because she'd catch him in the act of trying to burgle the house. But…it might also put her in danger, so that plan was a nonstarter. I threw it out the window.

Creak.

He was near the staircase.

I aimed the phone at my face. It unlocked. I dialed 911 but didn't start the call. I wanted to see first. I didn't want to be one of those fools who cries wolf and then gets told she's a fragile little woman living alone so maybe she should get a dog, or a security system, or a man.

I craned my neck. Changed my mind. Retreated to the wall beside the inflatable mattress because from there, I could see the giant mirror on the floor next to the fireplace. From that mirror, at just the right angle, I could see the foyer, the staircase, and the entrance to the kitchen and dining area.

There he was. Creeping out from behind the staircase. I watched him in the mirror.

Yes, it was him. Of *course* it was him.

He stood at the bottom of the steps, looking around like he was trying to decide where to poke around next. Whatever he was looking for, he had no idea where it might be.

Should I confront him? Should I dial, report a crime in progress, and then…hide? Flee? Fuck. All these perfectly decent options, and I had no idea which one to pick.

He picked one for me when he caught my eye in the mirror. His face went briefly tight with shock.

I took what was left of my chance to surprise him. I kept my cool. I said, "Whatcha doing there, Andrew?" and I hoped

I sounded cooler than I felt. I did not feel cool. I felt feverish and faintly hungover, with full fight-or-flight waiting in the wings.

"I... Hello. No one answered when I knocked," he lied. I know he lied. I saw an idea flicker across his face. He caught it like a butterfly. "I thought I saw smoke. I wanted to warn you."

"You just happened to be, what? Driving by? And you saw smoke? Coming from where?" I took a deep breath and strolled out from around the corner. We stood face-to-face, separated by maybe twenty feet across the big foyer and the staircase landing. "Because *I* don't smell any."

"The...the back of the...on the side of the..."

I looked him up and down. I tried to do it without being super obvious. I didn't see any weapons, but he had a messenger bag thrown over his chest; he reached inside it, pulling out a large knife.

It was the better part of a foot long and peculiarly ornate; it looked like an antique, or an accessory for a costume, or a ceremonial object. The knife was bright silver with deep oxidization lines showing off engravings I couldn't see clearly at this distance. A large red gem was mounted on the butt of the handle.

My stomach was hot, like I'd swallowed a shot of Fireball and it was just sloshing around in there. It took some work to keep my voice flat. I could hear a faint quiver in my words, but he probably couldn't when I said, "There wasn't really any smoke, was there."

He shifted, or relaxed, or...it's hard to describe. It was like he'd been clenching a muscle, and he finally felt free to release it. "You think you're so goddamn smart." He almost looked like a different person when he spit the words in my direction. He looked sharper, meaner. More desperate.

Whatever I'd been expecting when I blocked his number, this wasn't it. I'd expected whining and begging via Kate, or notes left on my front door, or ridiculous little gifts of alcohol. Not...*this*.

I asked him, "What are you doing here? What do you want that's so important you'd break in to find it? Answer fast, and make it good." I held up my phone, with the unsent 911 call still bright on the screen.

"Don't do that," he said sharply, an undercurrent of darkness to the order. "I'm not here to hurt you."

"Then what's with the weaponry?"

He paused and looked at the knife like he'd forgotten he was holding it. "This isn't a weapon. I need it for my ritual." He tucked it back into his bag. "I just want to *borrow* something. And then I'll leave, I swear."

I didn't believe him. "What else do you have in the bag?"

"Okay, as a gesture of goodwill, I'll show you, but don't be grossed out."

It was such a funny, incongruous thing to say. I met it head-on. "My dude, I cleaned half a dead raccoon out of a rusty vent the other day. You'll need something pretty spectacular to gross me out."

I should've just pressed the send button on the call and let the 911 operator hear what was happening. I'm not sure why I didn't.

My anxiety and curiosity and the reality of the situation were mixing around in my head like pool balls. I could almost hear them, cracking against each other again and again. Wait. Was it just in my head, or was it something I was hearing inside my house? Jesus, I couldn't even tell anymore.

Coty reached back into the bag and pulled out some kind of container. It looked heavy, and it was about the size of a coffee can. "I, uh, I brought Uncle Bart."

"Those are his *ashes*? Where the hell did you get them?"

"I stole them. It wasn't hard."

My mind was reeling. He'd stolen a dead guy, right out of his grave. His cranny in a wall? What do they call those, when it's a mausoleum but only for urns? Now my brain was spinning out in a new direction, seeking some path that did not terminate squarely in a meltdown.

It was a struggle to sound firm and tough, but I did my best. I said, "You...you went grave robbing. And you brought the spoils here. To my house. Take that can and get the hell out," I said, raising the phone again. "I don't know what weird-ass nonsense you have planned, but—"

"It's taken me *years* to pull this together!" he interrupted angrily.

I lifted my phone to unlock it and held it forward like a talisman, like I was holding a cross and he was Dracula. It was stupid and I knew it, but I didn't know what else to do. The phone's screen had gone dark, but when I tilted it back and forth, it opened again.

It took all of two seconds to bring 911 back into play.

Unfortunately, it took *less* than two seconds for my intruder to locate a small handgun from its resting place at the bottom of the bag next to the knife.

"Please don't," he said. He was calm now. I didn't like it. Aggrieved begging is whiny man-child stuff, and I can play that shit like a fiddle. Calm meant he had a backup plan.

"Put that away," I commanded, in case I was wrong. My thumb hovered over the icon that would send the emergency call.

"No," he told me bluntly.

For the moment, we were still talking. While we were talking, no one was shooting, but I was running out of time and I could feel his patience slipping away. I did my best to keep the conversation rolling. "Coty, this shitty old house is all I have to lose—and it ain't much." I was lying about the house. I hope it heard me and knew that I loved it, despite the fabrication. "Get the fuck out, before I do what I should've done immediately and call the cops."

"Wouldn't do you any good. Not in time." Coty shook his head. "Emergency dispatch doesn't know where we are—they don't have some magical cell phone locator. And besides, you're not seriously counting on the Seattle PD to solve a crime, are you?"

Okay, he had me there.

I opened my mouth to…I don't know. Maybe try to establish a cop-distrusting rapport? Coty looked like the kind of guy who once had an ACAB patch pinned to a denim jacket, and I could work with that. Maybe?

Yes, I was fully out of ideas and flailing desperately. The situation had spun out of control and now I was just scrambling, trying to reassemble the pieces into something I could use to defend myself.

If a 911 call wouldn't do it, and me ordering him to leave

the premises didn't do anything, and he was armed and inside my house, then I should do something. Shouldn't I?

Should I force this moment to a head, even knowing what that might mean?

I started to argue with him. "Coty, I…" But that's as far as I got when I saw that Coty and I were not alone.

A shape shimmered behind him, and unlike the first time I'd seen it in the powder room, what felt like a hundred years ago… this time, it gave me the weirdest surge of hope. It was roughly human and quite large, and it was screaming for our attention—not that either one of us could hear it.

Behold, an ace that'd been hiding up my sleeve. Or in my powder room.

I seized on a name, looked past Coty, and said, "Bartholomew Sloan? Is that you?"

Coty's head whipped around. He took a step back and sideways and gasped. "What? What is…? What? You're just trying to…"

Then he saw it. I might've been full of shit most of the time, but not this time. This time, a familiar shadow struggled to hold itself together, but it was sputtering out into vapor again even as Coty and I stood there, twenty feet apart.

A gun in his hand. A phone in my hand.

I was almost as in awe of the sight as my intruder, who couldn't peel his eyes away.

I whispered, "I told you so. He's here. They're all here," I added, not sure if it was true but praying for more spectral backup.

"Is that you, Uncle Bart?" he asked the quivering, fading

shade, in a tone that suggested he might be speaking with some kind of blessed archangel and not the lingering dust of some familial phantom. "I brought...you, I brought your ashes."

The shadow flared again, sharper and stronger this time. The detective's ghost was beautiful in its way: transparent and full of motion. A man made of smoke and sparkling moonlight. No. Steam. Steam and stars. For an instant I could see a face, round and bearded, its fluffy facial hair a dark shade of ginger. The face looked horrified, and unless I was misreading this shifting mist of a figure...it looked afraid.

I did not like the idea that a dead man had anything to be afraid of. It made me want to run away screaming, leaving the front door hanging open behind me; and I could've done that at any time. But I'd chosen not to, and I was choosing not to, right now.

I stood my ground, shaky though it was. I asked, "What do you intend to do with his ashes?"

He set the urn on the ground to free up one hand, then used it to fish some papers out of his bag. "I figured out what he did, how he did it. It took a long time of looking and asking around, but I did it. I looked. I asked. And I found out that I can take his...his..." He flapped the pages around, as if I could read them from where I was standing. "His blessing? His powers?"

A word rang between my ears, and I don't think it was spoken aloud. I think Uncle Bart said it just for me. "*Curse.*"

I repeated it. "It was a curse."

"Oh, shut up." He stuffed the old, brittle-looking notes back into the bag. "Just tell me exactly where he died, and I can reverse-engineer his bargain. I can take the reward for myself, that's what the old guy told me. Why does Uncle Bart get to be the only successful member of the family? For fucking *generations?*"

I held out my hands. "Look, I get it, believe me. I'm not exactly thriving over here, now am I?"

"You had the money to buy this place, right out from under me."

"I didn't even know about you! And I guess Kate told you how I got the money, so between us, I'd prefer to have my brother back—not that I expect you to understand."

He returned his attention to the dead man who worked to hold himself together in the foyer. Without looking at me, and with a coldness I felt in my bones, he said, "I don't have to understand. I don't even have to care."

I directed my attention to the specter that still held itself partly intact, through pure fury, if his face could be believed. "Stay with me, Bart Sloan," I begged. I didn't want to be alone with this dangerous fool. I wondered where Venita was. I wondered where Hugh Crawford was. I wondered what they were thinking, and if there was any chance they could help me.

"Uncle Bart," Coty said warmly. "Tell me, where did you die? Where *exactly*? The old man said I needed to know that much, if nothing else."

I was curious about the old man in question, but not that curious. He'd obviously found someone who understood bad magic, just like his long-dead uncle had—a hundred years earlier. Some things never change. Some people will always hold that sort of knowledge, for good or for ill, and Coty had found one of them.

The phantom of Inspector Sloan flared and waned, with more waning than flaring. He was running out of energy. He rallied, stretched, and held his shape for a second or two at a time. Then, like a balloon, the specter popped and was gone.

Once again, the house was silent.

Ronnie

NOW

Both me and Coty jumped.

"Where did he go?" Coty asked, sounding desperate. "Where did he... How did he..." Then he remembered that he had a gun pointed in my general direction. "Where did he go?" he demanded, the muzzle aimed at my midsection.

"How the hell should I know?"

"It's *your* house!"

"He's *your* uncle!" I fired back. "You know more about him than I do!"

He spun around, checking the room for any sign of the spirit and finding none. "Maybe he'll come back. Maybe he can tell me where he died. Do *you* know where it happened?"

I flung up my hands. "What? No! All I heard was that he killed himself after he inherited the place. Where do *you* think he did it?"

"He was found sitting somewhere. The family thought he

just had a heart attack from the stress of it all, because there were no signs of violence." Now he looked around the room, and toward various doors and corridors—seeking some likely spot.

"How about... How about this?" I held out my hands to appease him, to ask him, to lie to him. "You can do whatever weird shit you've got in mind, and I won't interfere. So just put down the gun. I'm serious, you don't need it—just as long as you get out when you're finished and you don't come back."

His attention sharpened and returned to me. He lifted the gun again. "First, give me Venita's diary."

I recoiled at the thought. It was mine. No, it was hers. Well, it definitely wasn't *his*. "It's barely legible. It's worthless."

"*You've* been reading it."

"Well, I've been trying," I said. I was going to add some details about the soft, damp, loaf-like state of the thing, but something stopped me. I felt a strange, tiny change in pressure—somewhere in the back of my ears. From the corner of my eye, I thought I saw a flash of white running across the staircase landing.

My heart did a little gasping flutter.

He followed my eyes, checking to see what had distracted me this time.

I kept my breathing level and returned my gaze to him while his eyes darted around the room. Maybe he was only looking for his uncle—but his frown of confusion said he could feel it, too, the house's change in...not temperature, but atmospheric pressure maybe.

My ears wanted to pop. Maybe his did, too.

As he paid less and less attention to me, his handgun sagged slightly at the end of his arm.

Now, as established: I've always been a worrier. I worry about intruders, natural disasters, diseases, and wild animals. I worry about getting old, being broke, living out of my car, losing Kate, wasps and yellowjackets, food poisoning, car wrecks, and drowning.

But I have never been especially worried about guns.

I grew up around guns. Military family, remember? I was taught healthy respect, not fear, in the face of a firearm.

My dad took me on my first shooting lesson when I was in kindergarten—not in a right-winger, prepper kind of way… more like "This is a gun, and we have some of these in the house, and here's why you should never pick one up or play with it." He braced me from behind when I pulled the trigger but let me feel the kickback—like I'd been head-butted by a mule.

It was maybe ten years later that he told me Jimmy Hoffa's rule, the one that gets litigated to death by armchair warriors all over the internet. But if it's good enough for a teamster, it's good enough for me: *Run away from a guy with a knife; charge a guy with a gun.*

"Hey, Coty." His eyes snapped back to mine. "You want the diary? Okay, just take the diary and get out, all right? I don't want any trouble, and I've read as much as I could."

"You'll give it to me?"

I turned my back to him, like I trusted him to behave himself while I fished around for the journal. I shoved my sleeping bag and dirty clothes off to the side of the air mattress and lifted the edge. What else did I have under there? I peeked down low. Not much.

That small book was my only leverage and only weapon, and it was a fragile little tome that had already survived so much.

I whipped the book out and held it up. "Found it."

He all but salivated. "Give it to me."

I took a step toward him. He took three toward me.

We weren't more than fifteen feet apart when I silently apologized to Venita, and the book, and anyone else who might care about it. Then, rather than reach forward to hand it over, I chucked it at his face.

He winced, flinched, and fell back. He yelped, then yelped again louder when I crashed into his torso and shoved him back into the foyer toward the stairs.

He didn't drop the gun. He swung it up, trying to hit me with it. For a moment we were tangled and we toppled, me on top of him, him swinging up, trying to clock me upside the head since there was too much commotion to aim.

I knelt on his chest and grabbed his armed hand, then smashed it up and down on the floor—but he brought up his other hand, the one that was holding the messenger bag with the old knife and a candle.

It had enough heft to throw me off-balance when it caught me in the neck.

He shoved me away—and he rolled to the right to escape me, hitting his hand on the floor in the process.

The gun went off, and a light fixture shattered in the library. It was loud enough that I clutched my head as if I'd been hit—which gave Coty a chance to collect himself and scramble toward me, the gun clacking on the ground as he righted himself and was standing once again.

I hunted frantically for the nearest cover.

Where was the nearest cover? I wasted a precious second or two deciding that it was the library. I staggered that way and tried to shut the heavy wood pocket doors but he was too fast.

He got off another shot and I heard wood splintering, and I felt splinters slashing across my cheek. His aim wasn't great, but he was no Stormtrooper, either. He kept coming, and I kept trying to hide around one of the doors, half-open, and when he was forcing his way into the room, shoving against me, trying to reach around and grab me. He didn't want to kill me. He needed me. He thought I knew where his uncle had died, and I didn't, and I'd told him, but he didn't believe me.

It should've comforted me. It didn't.

Then.

In an instant I did not understand, the air went out of the room. The noise shifted. Not quieter, not louder. Someone was playing with the settings on a cosmic radio, adjusting the bass, treble, or midrange. Something changed.

Coty stopped. He went quiet. He retreated into the foyer as if he were hypnotized, and I heard him say, "Oh my God," but he wasn't talking to me. I knew it without even seeing him bright-faced and glassy-eyed, moving dreamily through my house, through someone else's memory of another time.

My ears popped.

I let go of the pocket door, and it stayed stuck where it was, yanked partly off its track. I let go of the door and left it behind, peeking into the foyer.

There, I saw the cat. A platinum-silver beast, small and smug, with big green eyes. Sitting on the stairs. I swear to God, it winked one slow blink at me. Then it only stared.

"Coty?" I called. I didn't see him until I stepped all the way into the foyer. He was at the foot of the steps.

I looked for the cat again, but now it wasn't there.

A keen white light flooded the stairway. Coty froze like he'd been pushed onto a stage, squinting and shielding his face. "I can see you," he breathed. "You're real, you're here. You're *beautiful*."

Ronnie
NOW

Venita stood at the top of the landing, having caught my burglar in her spell so completely that she might as well have thrown a net over him and fired a tranquilizer dart into his ass.

I quit cowering and stood up straight, but I couldn't stop the shaking so easily.

I heard her voice, as light as silver charms on a bracelet. "My goodness, has no one offered you a drink yet? I hope you haven't been here long—oh, how rude of me. How rude of *us*," she amended the sentiment, though apart from Hugh and Bart, I didn't know who she meant—and I didn't see either one of them.

Maybe she meant me. Maybe this meant it was *our* house now.

She wore a cream satin dress and a pair of spangled silver shoes with the tiniest buckles sparkling in the glow like diamonds. One small, delicate foot at a time, she slowly descended, holding him fixed in her gaze.

Her voice so light. Her face so flushed and smiling. Her eyes like fishhooks, lodged in Coty's brain.

She was dangerous. Truly dangerous, and I was sharing a house with her. I was making a home with her inside it, and as perilous as that sounded, all I could do was look at her. Jesus, just look at her. She was a paper doll cut from a silver screen, moving through the world of the living with a soft-focus glow, Vaseline on the camera lens.

I shook my head. Couldn't let her bewitch me, too. Could I? Would it matter? She and I were on the same team, weren't we? *Surely* we were on the same side.

Every stair, every step, Venita dragged 1932 behind her like the train on a wedding veil. Everything her wake touched lit up and returned to its original state. The carpet runner, the polished wood, the light fixture above her head—which was no longer a terrible seventies model. It was a crystal piece, long gone and forgotten by everyone alive.

She descended from on high, a goddess of some lost time, some lost magic.

Coty had put one foot on the bottom stair only to forget everything except for Venita. Now he retreated, slowly, making room for her to join him. "Venita Rost," he said, choked and baffled and delighted. "Ma'am. Ms. Rost. Mrs. Amundson?"

"Oh, silly. You're a guest in my house, and I'll stand for no such formality. I'm Venita," she told him, extending a hand for him to kiss it.

The gun fell out of his hand and hit the floor. I flinched, but it didn't go off. It only clattered heavily and rested like a stone. He took Venita's hand and kissed it, never breaking eye contact.

Never blinking. Maybe he couldn't. Maybe he'd forgotten literally everything except for her. He wouldn't have been the first.

"I'm Andrew Stack, but everyone calls me Coty."

"Coty!" she exclaimed and clapped her hands together. "I like it. Very Hollywood cowboy, isn't it? And I'm to understand that you're Mr. Sloan's nephew, is that right?" She caught my eye and gave me a nod. Then she said to him, still weaving her little spell, "Come on, sweetheart. This way. Won't you join us? I believe I can help you achieve your goals. Let's find out, shall we?"

Now Coty remembered that I existed. He tore his attention away from her for long enough to flash me a puzzled look—then the look changed to one of concern, as whatever brain cells went uncolonized by Venita recalled that he'd held me at gunpoint a few minutes ago.

Venita didn't let him dwell on it. She slapped him gently on the back and beamed a smile his way. He wobbled under the glittering weight of it, and—freshly enchanted—began to follow her through the foyer.

"She should come, too," he said, meaning me.

"I will," I said. Even though I shouldn't have. I should've taken the opportunity to run, to go get help, summon the police in case they might make themselves useful. But I didn't. I refused. This was *my* house, not his.

He'd already forgotten about me again. I could tell by the sleepy earnestness in his voice when he asked her, "Could you… could you tell me about my uncle? I have something I need to do in his memory."

He toddled after her, a duckling, a thrall. He stepped on

a piece of paper. It stuck to his shoe, then came loose again. I glanced at it as I followed them; I think it'd fallen out of the diary—which now rested on the floor against the wall. Open-faced, several pages shaken loose.

"Of course!" Venita assured him happily, but the words had a false, tinny note to them. "Oh, let's see. He used to come over to stay with us, several times a month, in the winter. When he was working cases in the city, he preferred to stay here rather than a hotel, you understand."

"Sure." He fell into her wake, which spread and sprawled.

She was no nature goddess, spreading flowers and butterflies everywhere she went, but a glamour engine, a being of a specific place and time and light—and she carried it all with her. She used it to paint the terrible old canvas of my wretched fixer-upper; everywhere she went, the house was new and beautiful and warm, and it was a happy, welcoming place. As welcoming as this ethereal woman who'd been dead for nearly a century.

Coty was adjusting his messenger bag, feeling it to see if the contents remained and how easy they'd be to retrieve. Then he wasn't *completely* lost to her charms. That might be useful to know.

Venita chattered on. "He always came to our parties, too—even if he was on the East Coast, he'd find his way back to us. No one could refuse an invitation, could you imagine?" she asked him earnestly.

"No, ma'am."

"There you go again, with your 'ma'am.' You are the most *darling* creature I believe I've ever met. Here, why don't you have a seat?" She strolled into the parlor, where my makeshift bedroom/campsite was nowhere to be seen—not now. Now there was a large, comfortable chair facing the fireplace, where a small fire burned unobtrusively. The bar cart was full and shiny, and there were no sheets over anything, no dusting of ceiling plaster on every surface.

A long velvet couch with a low back and curved armrests was parked where my mattress ought to be. Venita flung herself upon it dramatically, taking up two-thirds and motioning for me to come for the rest.

I was still in the foyer, but I nodded back—pausing only to pick up that scrap of folded paper that had stuck to Coty's shoe. It wasn't a sheet from the journal; the paper was different. It must've been jammed in there somewhere all along, and I simply hadn't read far enough to find it.

Coty took the overstuffed "easy chair." This one was no longer a ruin of rusted springs and moth-eaten fabric, but smooth burgundy canvas with a winged back and wide, square arms that would conveniently hold a book or a beverage. I wondered how he was doing that, and if the old structure of the decrepit chair was still enough to hold him, despite the illusion… or if there was no illusion at all, only temporary transformation.

"Your uncle loved that chair," Venita purred wistfully, suggestively. Almost directly into his ear. "I have so many fond memories of him sitting there, sipping his favorite gin in front of the fire. The radio humming or the phonograph spinning… He would tell us such stories about his adventures and cases."

"He liked gin. I heard he did."

"That's right. I've never cared for it, myself—but anything for a houseguest, isn't that how it goes? I wouldn't want to be a poor hostess. Oh!" she said, and suddenly popped up from her lounging position. "I'm doing it right now, aren't I? Hold on, darling. Let me get you... Yes, I'll make you a drink."

She sauntered to the cart and made a show of whipping out that bottle of gin from the cart. She held it up to the light of the fireplace and swirled the contents around.

It struck me, only for an instant, how the bottle was unique in the room because it did not appear brand new. It rested in her hand the same as it'd been when I first bought the house, with a yellowed label and perhaps a quarter of its original contents.

I didn't know what that meant. Not yet.

I watched her in stunned silence. What the hell was she doing?

She winked at me. "Would *you* like something, dear? I understand you're not a gin drinker, either, but I have a little bit of everything..." She held up a cut-crystal glass and waggled it enticingly.

"None for me, thanks. I've had enough to drink already today, and I'm not as young as I used to be."

"Bah. Excuses, excuses," she said with a grin. Then she picked up another glass and began serving herself. "Very well, I'll have...the Canadian rum. I've always liked rum; it's so warm and spicy, without feeling too medicinal. Too much aftertaste of molasses and vanilla for that. It's more like a dessert than a drink, if you catch my meaning. Gin always smells like turpentine to me." She chose a glass and poured a couple of fingers anyway.

While she nattered on, I opened the little sheet of paper, and I began to read. It was a fast read. It was written by a woman with famously pristine handwriting, even when she was only writing to herself.

My eyes widened. It was a suicide note, written by Venita herself. Her legendary handwriting made it easy to read quickly, top to bottom, all the way down to the last line, where she swore she'd see Bart Sloan in hell.

She handed Coty the drink and smiled brightly enough to give him a tan. "Here you go, doll. Bottoms up!"

Coty took the glass from Venita, returned her dainty toast, and swallowed half the contents in one gulp.

Ronnie

NOW

Coty licked his lips. "This gin is still fantastic! And you're telling me," he said to Venita, "that my uncle drank from this very bottle?"

"That very bottle, indeed. Now, why don't you just sit there, put your feet up, and relax a bit. Enjoy the fire," she urged, crouching prettily beside the seat so she could look up adoringly into his face.

The room smelled like the wood fire that crackled in the marble fireplace, and the brown-sugar smell of old rum, and the piney stink of gin. It was warmly lit, and the shadows were long, and the flames were bright, and Coty was remembering his messenger bag and what was inside it.

"I need to do a thing," he announced.

He sounded pretty clear, so maybe whatever poison Venita had used on Bartholomew Sloan had lost its potency over the years. Surely he wouldn't just drop dead. I didn't really *want* him to drop dead. Did I?

"Coty," I said with a small note of warning.

Venita shushed me with one lazy wave of her hand. "Oh, it's fine. *He's* fine. He wants to be close to his uncle, isn't that right? I don't know about you, but I can't think of a better way to make that happen!"

"Yes, but…" I held up the note, unfolded.

"Oh, *that*." She tossed her hair. "You weren't supposed to see that yet, but I'm glad you know. You might as well know, anyway. Nothing I can change about it now, even if I wanted to."

"Coty—listen, man. We should probably…get you to a hospital or something," I proposed weakly. I didn't want him to die in my house, at least. What if he stayed? What if I was stuck with him, too?

Venita was watching me think, waiting to see which way I was going to land. Would I opt to assist Coty, or would I follow her lead and potentially let him die? Calmly, coolly, and none too warmly, she told me, "Choose your next moves carefully, darling. Neither one of us wants anything to happen to *you*."

Coty finally asked, "What's that? Where'd the journal go?"

"Don't worry about that, baby—I'm right here. Now, what's this thing you have to do?"

"Thing?" Now he sounded muddy.

"You mentioned a thing you came here to do. Something about your uncle? You had some questions?"

He lifted his glass and looked at the firelight glittering in the crystal and what was left of the old liquor sloshing around in the bottom. He sniffed it; he held it up one last time, and brought it to his lips.

Venita and I locked eyes. I had made my decision. I did not offer any further warnings.

He took another drink.

Satisfied that I wouldn't interfere, Venita returned her attention to Coty—who was visibly going foggy. "Did it have something to do with his ashes?"

That shook a memory loose. "Yes! His ashes, I have them here." He pulled the urn out of the bag, and it sank into his lap. "He's heavy. Or this is…strong. This gin is really strong."

"Yes, it is." She nodded.

"I need to find out, before I use the ashes…" He was fully slurring now.

"Find out what, darling?"

"Where he died. I know it was. It was in here. Right? In the house?"

She nodded again, and her smile shifted by the tiniest fraction—but it went from charming to slightly sinister in an instant. "I can help you with that, yes. In fact, you're much closer than you think. He died right here, in this parlor. Sitting in this very chair." She tapped her fingernail on the end of its arm in time with the last few words.

His eyes went wide. "This chair? This is where he had a hearrrrt…a hurrrr…hurt attack…"

"Heart attack? Oh no," she said, now shaking her head, those perfect platinum curls bouncing back and forth, not more than a foot from Coty's face. "That's not how he died at all."

"H…hooow?"

She looked at me, and I looked at her, and then I looked

at Coty. I took this as permission to fill him in, so I did. "She poisoned him. She poisoned the gin, dude."

He frowned at me and sniffed the glass again, squinted at it, and blinked hard like he couldn't see it very well. "But... ashesss..."

"Nonsense, all of it. You have the ashes, you have his seat, and you have his gin. My dear, that's all you need. That's how he did it, you know. He took the bargain from someone who didn't want it anymore, a man who wanted to die with his soul intact."

"Did it work?" I asked.

She shrugged. "Who knows? But that's what this is, baby, isn't it? You came here to take something that belonged to your uncle."

"He's dead."

"So what? So am I. And you'll be dead soon, too, I expect. I don't remember how long it took for Mr. Sloan." She drummed her fingers while she considered it, searching her memories for that long-ago triumph in the wake of personal tragedy. "It was long enough for him to read the letter, and long enough for him to be shocked about it. A few minutes," she said again. "No longer than that."

He was starting to believe her and starting to panic.

He tried to stand and fell back down—but caught himself and used the chair to pull himself back up.

Venita got out of his way and stared at him dispassionately. "Go ahead. Take what's his, in the time you have left. Maybe it'll make a difference. Oh, Mr. Sloan," she called his name into the ether, and it almost sounded friendly. It was, at least, an invitation. "Mr. Sloan, if you ever expect to leave this place, I think this might be your best chance."

Coty had figured out that he was on a timer. His motor skills were failing.

He fumbled with his bag, and the knife fell out, then he picked it up again. He reached for the urn and knocked it over; the lid popped open, and ashes spilled on the seat. Visibly swaying, he took the knife and tried to nick a finger but nearly punched a hole through the webbing between his thumb and index digit.

Blood squirted, then ran and dripped to the seat, which was looking less like a comfy leather wingback and more like a sheet-covered wreck of vintage furniture.

That's why I noticed that Venita was walking away, back into the foyer. She was taking the scenery with her.

Without even looking back at me, she told me, "It took me forever to figure out how he'd done it, how he'd murdered Priscilla. Magic is always a double-edged sword, in folk tales and kids' stories, but he brought it into my house. He was selfish and careless, and he deserved what I gave him for it." She leaned against the stair rail column with more insouciance than I've ever seen in a single human being. "I didn't care about living anymore. I decided that dying would simply be…more productive."

"No, I…I get it."

She nodded and gave me the sad half of a smile. "I thought you might."

The air around Coty was shimmering and congealing into a man's shape. It hovered close around the seat and seemed drawn to the ashes and the blood. Not eagerly, not even deliberately, it disappeared into the bloody mess on the rotted cushion with its protruding springs. It sprang tentacles of smoke and light and swirled, a small vortex spinning a ghost into threads and pulling them tight, pulling them down.

For a moment—a few seconds, no longer—I saw Bartholomew Sloan's face so clearly that I almost gasped, except that I was beyond gasping by then. He and I exchanged a look. Mine was surprised. His was…serene.

It was the very last I saw of him.

Coty was spellbound or possibly dying. I was torn between calling for help and waiting him out to see what happened. Part of me didn't honestly think he'd die; he'd probably just wake up sick as a dog in a day or two, and wish he was dead.

Part of me felt like a murderer all over again.

"See, that's just ridiculous," Venita griped.

"Wait, you can read my—"

"Not like a newspaper, no. But I can pick up the gist. You've never murdered anybody—and I've only ever murdered one person. Maybe two or three," she self-corrected with a glance into the parlor, which no longer had a fire burning. It had a mantel with a crack and a flue that hadn't opened in decades. "Either way, shouldn't you call the police?"

"No police!" Coty shouted.

He came stumbling out of the parlor, looking a little brighter now—he was rallying, and I had the sudden thought that I should probably pick up his gun. Where was it? He'd dropped it when he was making moony eyes at Venita.

He saw it before I did. We didn't even have time for a

standoff—he spotted it on the floor and threw himself at it, on top of it. It was a belly flop, but it worked.

He scrambled woozily to his feet with the weapon in hand, and without thinking twice, he fired at me. One, two, three times. Four bullets gone in total, including the one that had taken out the seventies light fixture. No, five bullets—he'd winged the pocket door.

It was only a 9mm, or maybe a Luger; I hadn't gotten a good look. It'd hold fifteen shots, so even with him flailing around, he might get lucky.

Now. Where the fuck was my phone?

I couldn't remember, and I wasn't holding it. I must've set it down on the couch—I mean my mattress. Or maybe I'd dropped it in the library.

Paralyzed by my options and unsettled by the gunshots, I wasn't sure which way to duck until I saw Hugh Crawford standing on the second story landing. "Up here," he urged, waving me toward him.

I looked for Venita but she was gone. My phone was gone. My opponent was groggy and firing wildly.

I was standing there like a bump on a log, as my brother would've put it.

I chose Hugh.

I zigged toward Coty and zagged around him, because you don't run in a straight line when someone is trying to hit you with a bullet. It's like running away from an alligator, if there's any truth to that lore. Back and forth is harder to hit than straight ahead. Don't make it easy for him.

Three more bullets chased me.

One sank into the wall across the foyer, one hit the banister, and one wound up somewhere in the kitchen. Two more went wild, and I don't know what they hit. Then a pause. He was either running out of ammo, or he'd stopped to reload.

I pivoted with a skid and looked for Hugh, who was now halfway down the hall, standing in front of the room where he'd died. I heard Venita say, right in my ear (though I saw no sign of her), "Don't hold the party up for me! Go on, I'll be there in two shakes."

I didn't have any better ideas, so I did what she told me and dashed toward Hugh, who held open the door. Or he stood like he did, though I didn't know if he was as solid as the lady of the manor. "Hurry. She'll be back, but it'll take her a minute to do that again."

Behind me, two more shots.

Inside the room with the enormous windows overlooking the water, I would be more or less trapped. But there weren't any emergency exits anywhere in the house, and shit, push come to shove, maybe I could climb down through the big-ass hole where Hugh had died. If I absolutely had to.

I think that was my reasoning, but it all happened so fast. Some of it must've been instinct.

I threw myself past Hugh and yanked the door shut. The knob was broken, and I couldn't lock it; I scanned the room for anything that might work to hold it there, and saw nothing but Hugh's old construction detritus—none of which was heavy enough to be useful.

Another shot, this one racing down the hall to break a window at the far end.

How many was this? I was losing count. Ten? Eleven? Fifteen?

I didn't want to brace my back against the door, because he'd probably try shooting through it. I mean, that's what *I* would do.

Carefully, awkwardly, I circled the hole in the floor and started looking for something that would work as a weapon in a pinch. Outside, I heard Coty crash against the hallway wall. He wasn't well and he wasn't sharp, but he didn't have to be.

He only had to get close enough that he couldn't miss.

But if I could get *beside* the door with my back to the wall, and if I could surprise him with an attack when he came inside…I didn't need a Rube Goldberg plan; I only needed to get a step or two ahead of him, and he wasn't on top of his game either mentally or physically. Something that simple might work.

He slammed his body into the door, and I didn't know if he did it accidentally or purposefully. It flew open and he almost fell on his face right behind it—but caught himself on the frame with one hand.

"Goddammit!" was all he had left to say.

He was bleeding badly; he must have cut himself worse than I'd thought with that ceremonial dagger. He was angry, too. Really angry—the kind of angry he wasn't a good enough actor to fake. He was now fully murderous.

"Jesus Christ, Coty!" I swore at the top of my lungs. "Just take your magic and go! You got what you wanted, didn't you? Get the fuck out and leave me alone!"

"Can't do that. *You* know." He sounded clearer, but nowhere near 100 percent. "No one gets to know. It's part of the deal."

All I could do now was stall. "All along, you figured you'd kill me once you got your way?"

"Why do you think I was, I was, I was…" He lost the thread for a second, then found it again. "Sneaking in? I *didn't* want you to know." The last three words ran together. "Easier if you don't know. Safer."

Where was Hugh? He'd been there ten seconds ago! And where was Venita?

Through clenched teeth, I said, "Venita, the party's starting without you…"

Like an answer to a prayer, the air in the room changed. It smelled like violets and jasmine and baby powder, and there was no hole in the floor, no construction garbage lying against the wall beneath the big, beautiful windows.

Instead, I stood inside a wood-paneled billiard room, complete with a radio and phonograph pair; they looked much like the ones in the parlor—I guess it was like having two televisions back in the day. On the wall to my right there was a large painting of Mount Rainier, and to my immediate left, the long wall of windows.

Where the floor should have a hole, it had instead an enormous pool table with green felt and brightly striped balls that had scattered and rolled. A rack of pool cues was mounted beside the door next to Coty, who was struggling to stand and shoot.

He was fighting to keep from falling under a spell again, either Venita's or the poison he'd so happily chugged. Now he knew it was a trick. Now he wouldn't go so easily.

But Venita was no ordinary shade. She sashayed into the room behind him.

"Look at you, holding up so well! Your uncle was already unconscious by now. If I were you," she said pointedly. She pointed an eyebrow, and pointed a pout, and then she pointed a finger, "I would leave this house with the greatest of haste and seek out a doctor. You don't have long. It doesn't take much."

"It's been sitting in the bottle for a hundred years," he accurately and bitterly noted. "I'll walk it off."

"Maybe," she granted. "But you're almost out of bullets, and you can barely see straight. So settle down, would you? There's no point in doing any more damage to my beautiful home."

"You're a bitch. You're *both* bitches," he spit. Literally, spittle drooled out from the corner of his mouth.

"Yes, yes," she said, and she sounded bored.

She flipped her hand up in that little move I was coming to recognize, that dismissive wave that says she doesn't care and it doesn't matter. She walked saucily around the billiard table to stand at my side, as if I was plotting anything useful.

I wasn't. I was standing there with my tit in my hand, unsure of what the hell to do.

It was so disorienting. I knew what the room looked like, smelled like—and it did not look or smell like *this*. It was not beautiful and grand, and no matter how hard I tried to project a mental image of what it looked like without Venita, I couldn't do it. The two pictures had too little in common.

She leaned against the wall between me and the row of windows and pulled a small silver case out from some magical pocket that didn't appear anywhere on her dress. "Fancy a smoke, doll?"

"I...don't. But you know that."

"What about you?" she asked Coty with a batting of the eyelashes.

As if she'd said some secret phrase, he roared and charged us—following her path around the billiard table, gun waving, eyes red and runny, hands shaking like a paint mixer.

I shrieked. Venita vanished.

The room returned to its normal state just as Coty slammed into me, not even trying to shoot me anymore, just trying to kill me with his bare hands—as if any of this was my fault or my idea.

And this was *my* house again, in all its sudden, god-awful glory.

It was *mine*. My falling-down, moldy, dead-animal-infested, termite-eaten wreck of a house deserved some goddamn respect.

And so did *I*.

I got my hands behind myself, braced on the windowsill, rested my back against the ledge, and wrestled my knees toward my belly. It only took a twist of my ankles to bring my feet up, too. Right against his chest.

I didn't exactly kick him.

I shoved him as hard as I could, straining to hold myself upright and send all the momentum forward—lest I rocket backward through the glass and onto the front lawn.

The moment slowed. Time stretched. It might've been Venita.

I watched him soar backward. He had a couple seconds of hangtime, a moment of cartoon physics where he didn't look down and didn't understand his predicament, and therefore, he didn't fall.

But eventually, he fell.

Not onto a billiard table, but through a tarp that covered a hole in the floor that once swallowed someone else. He landed in the library below with the kind of swooshing thud that contains a crunch, and I almost couldn't bring myself to look.

I looked anyway.

Ronnie

NOW

By the end of the summer the place was starting to come together. Sort of. I had a new roof and new plumbing, and a new water heater. The electrical work had taken longer than anyone expected, and turned up a truly astonishing number of dead bugs and rats in the walls, but what can you do.

I told the electrician I'd think about getting a cat.

We had evidence of termites past, but no active colonies on the property, which is nothing short of a miracle—unless it's something to do with Venita. She hasn't said one way or another.

I explained to her that things would be getting loud and that I was sorry for the inconvenience but it really *was* necessary work that would keep the house standing for another hundred years. She accepted this not happily, but with resignation. Then a bit of enthusiasm, asking if she could make some suggestions with regards to the decor.

She's actually pretty easy to talk to. She can be a good listener.

Kate rolled up with two bags of takeout from Dick's Burgers and two sodas that were each big enough to drown a rabbit. "What's on the docket today?" she asked when I opened the door and helped myself to one of the bags and beverages she offered.

"Drywall guys," I told her.

"So the mold remediation is done?"

"As of yesterday afternoon, yep." Now it was just a matter of putting the walls back together. I didn't have the money to replace every bit of plaster and horsehair, so new-fangled drywall would have to suffice. I had plans for vintage-style wallpaper, anyway. No one would ever know the difference except for the ghosts, and Venita was content as long as she felt like she had some input.

Sometimes, late at night, I'd hear Hugh poking around, checking the work. He fancied himself a construction guy, and once in a while he'd do the construction-guy thing of pointing out flaws or things he would've done differently. I always just thanked him and reminded him that he wasn't the one who'd left me a bunch of money, so we were doing this on my budget, not his.

"Then what's next, what did you tell me?" Kate said as she came inside and dropped her own food bag onto the giant tiger maple table I'd set up in the dining room. I'd found it at a salvage shop and it was on my list of things to eventually restore, but it was fine as is for the time being. "The floors?"

"The floors," I confirmed. "That will take some time. Some of them can stay, most of them have to go; the parts that are staying need stripping, patching, and sanding. The new stuff will match it fairly well, but it'll be an ordeal."

"Wanna crash at my place?"

"Hmm. Maybe for the worst of it, if that's okay." I'd long since lost the lease on my little apartment, which was fine, I didn't want it or need it anymore.

"Always. All you have to do is save me a room when the place is finished."

"You finally made up your mind?" I asked.

"About living here? Yes. About which room? No. Are you enjoying the old master suite better than the parlor?"

"Yes, but that's more to do with the mattress than the location." I'd sprung for a cheap memory foam off Amazon. It was only a couple hundred bucks, and I could throw it down over anything, and I'd never feel it. Better yet, nothing could ever pop it—like the stupid little wood screw that'd worked its way under the air mattress, causing the slow leak and a weird mark on my shoulder.

But not the memory foam. That thing is Princess and the Pea–proof.

Upstairs, several guys and a couple of women were throwing up sheets of drywall while Mexican pop music played through the halls. They'd knock off for the day in another few hours, but they'd already had lunch.

"Did you bring—" I started to ask.

"All the ketchup," she finished for me. "When are you going to get real appliances installed? I thought that was happening when the electric stuff was done."

"The electrical stuff only got finished a week ago, and the city hasn't sent an inspector out to sign off on it yet. After that. I already have all my measurements, and hey, I might keep the stove."

"You're daft. That thing is a rusty hunk that would be rejected at any reputable scrap yard," she told me.

"Maybe I'll put it up on NextDoor." It was easier than telling her I was looking forward to the prospect of restoring it despite its absurd decrepitude, just like the table. Just like the house. My whole life is a work in progress, but she gets that, now.

"I'm just saying, one of these days you'll have a roommate who would prefer some modern conveniences."

We spread out the napkins and condiments, stabbed our sodas with straws, and started chowing down on the best greasy walk-up and take-out burgers in the county. It was a peaceful scene, with the background music coming from upstairs, the windows open to catch the late-summer weather…and a small white cat licking its paw on the yard outside.

Kate saw it through the window and cocked her head toward it.

I nodded. "That one belongs to the neighbors. It has a spot on the back of one ear, see?"

"Aw, I wanna see the ghost kitty," she sulked.

"Maybe once you move in. I think it takes her some time to get comfortable with people."

"She got comfortable with you pretty quick."

"Fair," I agreed. "But that situation was forced by, I mean. You know."

Coty broke his neck when he fell.

My story for the cops was as close to the truth as possible, and it'd worked. The guy had broken into my house while I was asleep. He was obsessed with his dead uncle and he'd brought all kinds of weird stuff, but then he drank the gin on the cart and became disoriented. He became violent. He chased me around the house, cornered me in that upstairs room, and slipped right through the floor—and through the ceiling of the library, where he'd landed at a bad angle, and, well…

That was it.

It was too weird not to be true—and besides, I had plenty of evidence. He'd left the pile of bloody ashes, the empty urn, the mostly empty gun, and the almost empty bottle of gin. I asked a cop if they wanted to take it and test it, and he just laughed at me. "It was cheap booze that was over a hundred years old. It would've given him brain damage as a best-case scenario. That idiot dug his own grave," he concluded.

And that was pretty much the end of the authorities and their involvement in the matter.

"Any sign of…?" Kate asked, adding a little "cough, cough."

"The uncle? No. But I think whatever Coty tried to pull off…he successfully…you know. Pulled it off."

"You think he's a ghost now? Or something else?"

I sighed. "Sometimes I feel like he's here, just barely. Somewhere I can't reach him or see him or…it's hard to explain. But I think he took Bart Sloan's place in whatever deal had held the inspector stuck to this place."

"You haven't seen the inspector, either?"

"Not a hint of him. I hope he's..."

"Yeah?" she pressed.

I wasn't sure how to finish the thought, but I tried. "At peace?"

"Didn't he kill that little girl?" she asked. I'd told her a lot about the diary, though she still hadn't read it.

I paused before answering. I didn't sense the lady of the manor anywhere. "Somehow, yes—but I suspect it was an accident."

"Why give him the benefit of a doubt?"

"Because he tried to help me," I said simply. "Venita said he came to tell her when Coty got inside. He asked her to help me, because she was stronger and could communicate the danger better."

I hadn't meant to say his name. These days, it was harder to say "Coty" than it was to say "Ben."

"Okay," she agreed thoughtfully. "Does that mean he's stuck here, watching us?"

"No idea. But I saw and heard Sloan within a couple days of being here, and I've only gotten the vaguest impression of Coty in the last few months."

"Maybe one of these days we can do an exorcism. Do you think that'd work?"

"An exorcism?" I gasped. "And risk evicting Venita, too? This is her house as much as mine. And she was here first."

Kate waved an extra-long fry around, then stabbed it into the puddle of ketchup we'd created between us, courtesy of fifteen or twenty packets. "If you say so. I'll take either one of you for a landlord if it means getting out of South Park. I do have one question, though, about that night. Can I ask it?"

"Go for it."

We'd kind of had an informal deal, where we had avoided the subject in general—but if it came up, we'd essentially offer a trigger warning by asking first. Neither one of us had really come to terms with it or really knew how to talk about it, but maybe it'd been time enough.

She nodded and sucked on her straw for another couple of seconds. "Okay. Why did you run upstairs? Why didn't you try to get out of the house? He had a gun. He still had bullets when he fell. Isn't going *up* instead of *out*, like, a classic blunder?"

I considered my answer, buying time by slurping on my own straw for a few beats. "For one thing, I was scared and hungover and confused. For another, Hugh was at the top of the stairs, and he told me to come on up."

"For a third thing…?"

"For a third thing, I didn't have a candelabra and a slinky nightgown."

She barked a laugh and chucked a fry at my face. "I thought the slinky nighty and the candelabra is what you wear to go down to the basement. You need big hair and a storm if you're going to run away from a house. That's what the old book covers say!"

"Well, according to the lady of the manor, Bartholomew Sloan ran away from the house in a rainstorm. Does that count?" I flinched away from the fry and smiled around my straw, sucking up the last dregs of Dr Pepper.

I didn't tell her the real reason, the one that had dawned on me after the fact: I'd already run away from one house, and it'd changed my life for the far, far worse. It'd cost me my brother, and I'd gotten this place as a sorry trade. I ran away from my brother. I will never run away from the house he'd bought me with his life insurance policy. I've learned my lesson. When it comes to things you care about, you don't high-tail it. You stay and *fight*.

Venita says I'm not a murderer like her, and I've decided to believe her.

I've also decided to start taking my goddamn medicine.

ACKNOWLEDGMENTS

As always, this book was a group effort—and I owe great thanks to my agent, Stacia Decker; my editor, Rachel Gilmer; and all the fine publicity folks at Sourcebooks for all their hard work on my behalf. Thanks also to the nice folks at Black Dog Salvage, who were so very helpful to me a handful of years back when I was doing research about salvage and restoration, and thanks to my husband, who got me a little Victorian bungalow to fuss over.

Last but never least, I send warm waves of appreciation to a certain ladies group that day-drinks in the outer reaches of the galaxy. You know who you are, and you know why I love you.

ABOUT THE AUTHOR

Cherie Priest is the Philip K. Dick–, Hugo-, and Nebula-nominated author of more than two dozen science fiction, fantasy, mystery, and horror novels and novellas, including *Boneshaker*, which won the PNBA Award and the Locus Award for Best Science Fiction Novel, and the critically acclaimed *I Am Princess X*, which was a YALSA Quick Pick for Reluctant Young Adult Readers. Her books have been translated into nine languages in eleven countries.

Born in Tampa, Florida, she currently lives in Seattle, Washington, with a menagerie of exceedingly photogenic animals.